The Woolly Ha

Poppy Dolan lives in Berkshire with her husband, where she is a keen baker and crafter as well as a prolific author of many laugh-out-loud romantic comedies, including the bestselling *The Bad Boyfriends Bootcamp*. You can get in touch with Poppy on Twitter @poppydwriter and on Facebook at PoppyDolanBooks. She doesn't bite. Unless you are a dark chocolate digestive.

Also by Poppy Dolan

POPPY DOLAN

The Woolly Hat Knitting Club

CANELO

First published in the the United Kingdom in 2017 by Canelo

This edition published in the United Kingdom in 2020 by Canelo

Canelo Digital Publishing Limited
31 Helen Road
Oxford OX2 0DF
United Kingdom

A CIP catalogue record for this book is available from the British Library.

Print ISBN 978 1 80032 040 6
Ebook ISBN 978 1 911591 26 9

Look for more great books at www.canelo.co

Printed and bound in Great Britain by Clays Ltd, Elcograf S.p.A.

In memory of my wonderful grandmother Christine: clever, kind, industrious (and so, of course, a brilliant knitter).

And for ES and VN, some of the best women of all time. Both have supplied support and advice with the same patience and good grace with which they accept wonky knitted gifts.

Chapter 1

Weird. Definitely weird. There are lots of 'weird' things about my brother that are actually pretty normal for him – he likes to put Marmite on Pop-Tarts, he's never seen *Game of Thrones* and, the thing that baffles people most, he is a knitting obsessive with his own yarn shop. But not replying to three texts and two emails in a row from me is super weird for JP. With not even seven minutes before my next meeting, I'm scratching the back of one leg with my new leopard-print loafers and firing off a quick text.

Hey. You're scaring me. OK?

Other siblings might talk more on the phone rather than just batting messages back and forth like ping-pong balls, but it works for me and JP. My full-on, frantic job means that spare time is usually only found in lifts or canteen queues or during a particularly dull budget forecast. And experience has only too painfully taught me that if you get JP on the phone and onto the wrong subject, your ear could be throbbing forty minutes later and you still wouldn't have worked out why a customer buying sock yarn for a blanket pattern was quite so hilarious.

Nothing hits my inbox in reply. No *JP is typing* reassuringly whispering to me at the top of the screen. Weird. Really weird.

'We're up, Dee. Unless you're too busy sexting your boyfriend?' Ben Cooper appears at my office doorway. He has just as much experience in management consultancy as me – we graduated in the same year, his birthday is only a few months behind mine, for goodness' sake (I've worked it out from the mandatory office cake celebrations) – but somehow he puts on the air of a total industry leader who begrudgingly gives me the time of day. And I never invited him to use my nickname – when it comes to work, I am Delilah. Only friends, family and non-nobheads get to call me Dee, thanks.

I'm working very hard not to roll my eyes. I catch the eyes of my assistant, Clive, who nods just a tiny nod to let me know that he's just as irked. Clive is such a lifesaver in so many ways – not just helping with the mountains of projects we tackle but making sure I don't forget family birthdays or overdue dentist trips. He's a legend.

As I know Ben's just itching to put me in an annoyed, harried mood before a big client meeting; I let out a long, calming breath. At the same level of seniority, we're always looking to get one over on each other. Like the time he 'offered' to shadow me on the Shenwood project, as a 'unique learning experience', even though everyone knew there was nothing for him to learn there except new ways to wind me up. Not that I let that stop me working it like an absolute boss. And maybe I sent him to the wrong meeting room a few times along the way. Maybe.

Which reminds me. A quick swipe of the screen. But still no reply from JP.

So I plaster on my work smile – not too big as to be fake and cheesy, not too small as to seem nervous or meek. And just smug enough to show Ben he is having no effect on me whatsoever. Ha!

'Born ready, Cooper. Born ready. Can't wait to catch up with Guy from TechBank. Did you know we play squash together? He said he won't sleep at night until he finally wins a game.'

Ben's sour expression tells me that my artfully placed throwaway comment has hit the mark – he doesn't know how much overtime I've been putting into bonding with this huge new client. My mates, family and JP certainly know – they won't stop grilling me for putting work first and everything else second – but I know that if I can make this client mine it will give me the most massive boost up the corporate ladder. And, not that I'm competitive at all, Ben can just scrabble around for a bottom rung in my dust.

–

With the meeting under way, posh coffees and pastries laid out by the brilliant Clive in our slick Canary Wharf office, I can feel myself leading more and more of the discussion points, and it feels good. There is a problem at TechBank's Brussels branch – no worries I already have a flight booked for Monday morning. Staff in the investment teams in head office are unhappy that consultants have been coming in and telling them what to do – I've already engaged a party-planning firm to throw a top-of-the-line Vegas theme night at the end of the month. You can always distract the investment bankers with a good gamble... My boss Devon nods sagely as I talk the client through my action plan, as if he's personally helped me devise the whole thing. Well, he personally held the door open for me this morning and that's about as useful as he gets. I can't hate Devon if I want to be Devon, I remind my inner grump, challenging the positive mantra of the business book on my bedside table.

Just as I'm expanding on how we'll implement the next round of employment cuts, my phone vibrates on the glass table, sending a grumble of noise into the meeting. If it was my work phone I would ignore it, never wanting to show a client they are anything other than my every waking thought, but it's my personal iPhone – and a cold twist in my stomach makes me turn it over and unlock the screen.

JP
Can't move. Arms. Not. Worry here. Come.

The breath catches in my throat as I grab at my things with clammy hands. 'I'm so sorry, personal emergency, my brother... I have to go. Sorry!' I call over my shoulder as I leg it for the door, Devon's weary head shake and Ben's wide eyes are the last things I see as the doors slam behind me.

Chapter 2

Fifty-seven sweaty minutes later, and so much poorer for paying the first cab driver I could find £100 to get me to Liverpool Street station faster than is strictly legal, I leap out of the train in Fenwild, a little village outside our home town. All my calls to JP have gone straight through to voicemail; his chirpy recording, telling people to, '*Go on, leave me a message – I'm a millennial, I never check them!*' hasn't broken through the cold clutching feeling around my heart. Not again, not again... I'm tempted to call Mum but seeing as she and Dad are on the other side of the world, visiting Uncle Dave in Australia, and I'd only be passing on the panic in the wrong time zone, I shelve that idea. Better get to JP first and assess just how bad it is. But I do bash out a quick IM to Clive: *Cover for me?!?!*

Pelting down the gravel track behind the tiny station, I take the short cut through the copse, which in five minutes will spit me out at the bottom of the high street. Sorry, new loafers, you've got to take the hit right now. If mud is good for facials it can't be all that bad for shoes.

The chilly air is really rasping in my lungs as I turn on to the small row of shops. Just a few more to go and there it is – the Blackthorn Family Haberdashery. With that kind of name you'd think the shop was set up in the time of Victorian lace cuffs and brown paper bags, but in fact JP opened four years ago and seeing as I gave him the investment capital and we're fifty-fifty owners, he insisted it should have our family name.

Wheezing a little at the side door, I don't bother knocking. I just fish out the spare key from underneath the hedgehog boot scraper and barge the wonky wooden door open.

'Julian! Julian! Where are you?'

A deep groan comes from the living room. Oh God, please, not again…

But there's no crumpled figure on the sofa, no detritus of beer cans and old newspapers. JP is sitting up, dead straight, on a dining chair. Two wrists in plaster laid awkwardly on the little table in front of him.

'When you call me Julian, I know I'm in trouble.'

He winces. 'Christ, what are you doing away from work? Has Canary Wharf sunk?'

I gulp some breath back into my system, my heart rate coming down from hummingbird to anxious 31-year-old. 'You… texted me to come. You said you couldn't move and you were worried! What the hell have you done to yourself?'

I flop down on the brown cord sofa, feeling it flatten under me.

JP tries to move some of his sandy hair out of his eyes with a head tilt. It doesn't work and he huffs. 'Actually, I was trying to tell you not to come. And the arms… you're only going to laugh.'

'After sprinting out of work and catching my best coat in the train doors, all the while thinking… thinking the worst, I could do with a laugh. Spill it.'

He looks down at the off-white plaster keeping his forearms and thumbs locked in place. 'I fell off a ladder.

6

While trying to put up some bunting. Broke my sodding wrists.'

I bite my lip. 'Blimey, JP. How long will you be in casts for?'

JP stands up and stretches his back, wriggling his shoulders. 'Six weeks. Hopefully. They weren't bad breaks, just… embarrassing.' He manages a shrug but yelps straight after. 'When you said you were thinking the worst, you didn't think…?'

It's my turn to shrug now. 'You get a message like this, and you tell me you wouldn't go into a major tailspin?' I hold up my phone screen.

'Ah. Well, I guess that's no workable thumbs and some pretty mental painkillers for you. Sorry. But I am fine, now, Dee. You don't need to worry about another… you know. That's the old me. Not the real me.' He smiles his impish smile, the same one that used to ask for my last penny sweet, and I can feel my heart finally wriggle free of that death grip that followed me all the way from the office to his front door.

After a brief, awkward hug around his stiff arms, I dig out my work phone from my handbag.

'Well, that lasted all of two minutes. A new record for you.' JP walks awkwardly into the small kitchen, his arms held in front gingerly like a nervous zombie. 'Still, two minutes of Dee time these days is a rarity, so I count myself lucky. How long do I get if I break both legs as well?'

My eyes scan over the 30-ish emails that have come in during the last hour. Nothing too catastrophic… Until I see:

Balls. I bet Ben is worming his way in right now, probably
making innocent-sounding comments about how I have
so much to juggle and how it must be really stressful.
The implication being, it's all too much for me and he's
a safer pair of hands. Show me one man who's ever
been described as 'juggling' at work. I swallow down the
ball of anger squashed against my windpipe. Actions, not
emotions. That's the way. As soon as I get home tonight,
I'll jump back on it and totally smooth this over. It's one
tiny blip in my faultless record.

'... so that's neither, then? Or do you want to crack the
whisky out?' I tune back in to my little brother's voice.

'Sorry, sorry. Tea, if you have it. Wait, can you even
make tea?'

In the doorway, JP surveys the taps, kettle and cupboard
doors of his galley kitchen. The Formica is peeling off the
green kitchen doors but that's the least of his problems
right now. Without easily flexible thumbs it's going take
him as long to wrangle a cup of tea as it would just to wait
for a bus down the road to Cheeky's Greasy Spoon.

'Come to think of it, no. Er... would you?'

I leap into gear, and run some hot water to wash up
a few plates while I'm at it. 'What's the plan, JP? If you
can't make tea, how are you going to cook for yourself?
Take the bins out? Open the shop? Oh my God!' I spin
round to face him, suds dripping off his baggy Marigold
gloves. 'You can't knit!'

8

'I know,' he grumbles into the crew neck of his grey T-shirt. 'That was literally my first thought as I lay on the pavement. Well, after "Shitting hell, this hurts." I haven't gone six weeks without knitting in years!'

I stack a chintzy plate on the drainer and start brainstorming helpful suggestions as I tackle a few egg cups with concreted-on yolk dribbles.

–

As an older sister, I've been helping JP his whole life. I used a plastic dinosaur to tease him into taking his first steps and from then I don't think I've ever stopped. It's not that he's a useless man in the way that he's lazy or thinks domestic tasks are beneath him or – God forbid – women's work. More that he's just always been the dreamy one, the one who forgets you need to pay for parking, and I'm the practical one, the one who finds the parking fine notice tucked down the back of the sofa just in time, before the figure doubles. Maybe being the oldest put me in this position, but I can't deny my naturally bossy side really quite enjoys it.

It's probably why I threw myself into helping JP apply to the big law firms when he graduated and I coached him in interview technique and CV buffing. I even went with him to a networking drinks event, just to get him started. I was so happy when he got his coveted, kick-ass job and started working all the hours. He worked hard and he played hard, taking up squash and urban golf with his new work buddies. He got a fancy one-bed in Islington, not all that far from where I live in Crouch End. It was all going perfectly.

Except it wasn't. Three years into his career, I had a call from his HR manager on a random Tuesday. They hadn't heard from JP since the Saturday (he'd been working through the weekend with his colleagues, as usual) and they were concerned – he wasn't picking up his mobile or checking emails immediately, as was his norm. In that moment I felt my heart shrink to a third of its size and rattle around my chest. Just like today, I rushed over to his place and used my spare key. But unlike today, there was nothing funny about what I found.

JP was lying on his sofa, staring at the ceiling, not moving. The flat was like an upturned bin – kebab wrappers and beer cans and old newspapers crumpled into balls. And JP just didn't move. I kept talking to him, shaking him, I even threw a glass of stale beer in his face to try and shock him into action. But he was broken. He had broken down. So I called my parents, started cleaning up the place and then just sat and held his clammy hand until they got there.

After a lot of talking and listening back at Mum and Dad's, JP eventually confessed that he hated being a lawyer. A colleague had said, 'See you tomorrow,' as they'd left the office that Saturday night and something in him had snapped. He hated working Sundays. He hated working all the time. He felt so alone. All four of us cried when he said that. Him, because it was the truth he'd been afraid to admit, and us because it was the truth we'd completely failed to see. I vowed to myself right there and then, forcing down burning tea just to stop the tears, that I'd never let him be alone again.

As part of his therapy, JP tried art classes, then some sculpture. Using his hands made his head shut up, he said. No evil inner critic could tell him he was a failure when he was being active, making something. He helped Dad wallpaper a room, he scoured their garage for unfinished

DIY projects. When every last plug was changed in the house, he re-insulated the loft. And then he kicked over a stack of Gran's old knitting magazines at the back of one of the eaves.

He now admits his first thought was how much a vintage knitting pattern might fetch on eBay, but as he flicked through them, laughing at the mohair and Fair Isle balaclavas, he began to think that maybe knitting would be a lot more comfortable than painting another Artex ceiling or mending bike punctures. He could make something for Mum, for her birthday. That navy, lumpy scarf still hangs with pride of place in her hall, on the coat stand. He'd never felt a real affinity with corporate law, but the needles quite literally clicked for JP.

–

'I'm a bit worried about the shop…' JP looks through the frosted glass, into the shopfront that backs on to his living room. 'I think I could work the till, sort of. And knock down any yarns from the top shelves for customers with a big stick. But if someone comes in with a buttonhole query or they're scared of cabling on a purl row… How can I help them if I can't demonstrate?' He lets out a puff of breath and slumps back against the wall.

Stacking the last mug in the drainer, I hang the gloves over the tap and fold my arms. 'Well, you have your great tutorial videos, on the website. People love those – you get amazing click-through, right?' As I invested in the shop, JP has always been really good at sending me updates, not just on the sales numbers but also how the online shop and his blog perform. I have to say, I wasn't quite sure who'd want to see video clips of a hulking pair of male hands showing you the best way to knit, but they really do. *About a (Knitting) Boy* is a great blog – I just wish he'd let me get him into some ads so it could bring him in a bit more cash.

He colours a little at the tops of his ears. 'Yeah. The crafting community is pretty supportive. But if you don't post every week, you lose your appeal. And fulfilling online orders for the shop is going to be tricky for a while. Not sure I could work a roll of Sellotape without breaking something else.' His forehead creases with worry.

'You could always ask—'

'Julian! Julian!' A voice squawks from the back door.

'Auntie Mags. Just what the doctor ordered!' I laugh with full-on relief and rush out to meet my godmother.

–

'Auntie' Mags has been in our lives since Mum cracked in a supermarket one day: me (three years old then) and JP (just one) had pushed her to her limit, sleep deprived and exhausted and not really enjoying being cried at and puked on and poked round the clock. When she came back to the trolley with her arms full of nappies to find me cramming raspberries up JP's nose and laughing maniacally, she just lost it. She sat down on a pallet of granulated sugar and sobbed. Auntie Mags was inspecting the dried apricots nearby but swiftly marched over.

'This won't do!'

Mum had assumed she'd be getting another 'well-meaning' lecture on how they used to beat children in the good old days, but instead Mags whipped out a tissue, cleaned us both up, took Mum by the hand and led us all to the Sainsbury's cafe. She bought us tea cakes and told my mum to 'get it all out, love. I don't mind tears – I'm a fan of *Dynasty*.' And so Mum did. And Aunt Mags has been Mum's agony aunt ever since.

She's actually only 10 years older than Mum, and still a sprightly 60-something now, but she always had that air of being ready for old age. Maybe it's because she's always been the carer for her mum, and didn't have kids of her own. But the one thing I do know is that she is the lighthouse in any storm – whether it was being dumped or being spotty or being bullied, she was always there to talk to as we grew up. 'Julian!' Mags's eyes start to fill with tears as she takes in the clumsy casts. 'Darling boy!' She covers him in lipstick kisses, blocking any chance he has of actually explaining this predicament.

'He fell off a ladder but he's fine now,' I chime in, over her shoulder. 'But I think we really need your help.'

With Maggie on her second cup of tea and fully filled in on the what's and how's and what's again, we have a battle plan. She can't stay with JP full time as she needs to be home to care for her mum between nurse shifts (we used to call her Extra Granny when we were little, though now Doris's Alzheimer's is so bad she doesn't remember us at all, the poor love), but she can do some time in the shop and pack up Internet orders here and there, and I can come and stay to be around at night and first thing in the morning. I'll just have to commute into work. It's not ideal with the hours I work and the infrequency of the Fenwild trains, but when Mags pointed out that JP won't be able to easily dress himself or butter a piece of toast, I realized it was the only thing to do. JP said something about an occupational therapist visiting him but he couldn't remember what he'd done with the appointment letter, seeing as he'd been so addled by mega painkillers. Finding that was my first task.

It gave me a slight headache to recognize I couldn't just nip back to work and dive right into the emails pinging in at a rate of knots. But my brother is my brother, and I can kick ass at work at any other time. Besides, Clive can combat any business headache: he is a super-organized pocket rocket and he'll sift out anything urgent. We've worked so closely together for the last 18 months or so that he totally gets the way I work and think. I email him with my computer password and instructions to text me with anything that will explode without my attention. And, in caps, DO NOT LET BEN GET WIND OF THIS. I can smooth things over with Devon for missing a day or two of work, but if Ben got the chance to stir things up while I was away… I'd just rather he didn't spot anything was amiss in the first place. If I'm really honest, I'd rather he spontaneously combusts at work tomorrow morning, just a pool of soya latte and breakfast bap left on his ergonomic chair, but we can't have everything we want.

I'm fishing around in the cupboard under the sink as JP rests up on the sofa, next to Mags.

'What are you after?' he yells.

'Bags. I'm going to pick up some overnight bits from Mum and Dad's, then do your shopping. And I'm going to call them while I'm out, let them know what's going on and try to keep a lid on the hysteria from Mum.'

'Sorry.'

'I can handle Mum, it's not a biggie.' I lean on the kitchen door frame.

'No,' his eyes wrinkle, 'sorry for making such a dog's dinner for you to sort out. Yet again. I will pay you back, one of these days.'

Maggie chips in, slapping JP briskly on the thigh. 'Silly sausage! She's your sister, and she loves you. Besides, our Dee can do anything. Everything, in fact!'

Chapter 3

Doing everything includes steering a shopping trolley with my elbows, it seems. And I'm actually doing a pretty good job: pushing the trolley with my forearms, dashing out emails with my thumbs, every now and then throwing in a fajita kit or tin of beans. Easy.

My email to Guy at TechBank is not grovelling, not squirming, but clear and calm about why I had to leave the meeting – a family emergency that's now tied up. From 8.00 tomorrow morning, I'll be back on the ball or on the money or on point or just on top of anything they like. Within reason. And Devon will have no call to roll his eyes at me. I've got this. He knows no one works like I do.

I'm making a grab for a tin of chickpeas – JP makes a mean hummus; well, he can dictate instruction for me to make it – when I hear a familiar, smokey voice. 'Delilah Blackthorn. Is it really you?'

I spin around and there is Becky Bairns, one of my best mates from secondary school. I haven't seen her since… A flush of shame creeps up my neck. I haven't seen her since our A level leavers' party. I've always meant to keep in touch but the mad pace at uni and now at work means the only socializing I seem to do is with the guy who brings me a tuna mayo baguette at my desk. (He's called

Neal and likes Motocross.) She looks older and thinner. But actually not in a good way.

'Becky! Oh my God, how *are* you? This is so weird, I don't live round here anymore, just had to come back because JP's not well. How are you? Sorry, I said that.'

She looks down into her basket. There are digestive biscuits, wet wipes and a pack of size one nappies knocking about in there. She takes a big gulp and I realize her eyes are ringed with a red raw line and she's madly blinking back tears, despite her lopsided smile. 'Oh, I've been better.'

It's like time has looped back on itself and Mum and Mags are meeting by the spilt sugar all over again, except there are no toddlers to wrangle at our feet. I pay for my shopping and get us into the local Costa within three minutes. Becky keeps looking at the door and won't take off her coat. 'I can't stay, I've got to get back—'

'You've got at least five minutes spare to get whatever it is off your chest and bolt this hot chocolate. You look like you could do with the sugar.' I push the cream-topped mug in her direction with my best headmistress look.

She takes a sip and closes her eyes. 'I've had a baby, Dee. A boy. Chester.'

I can't help but clap my hands, like a happy seal. 'Congrats! You clever thing. Wow, you look good on it. So, is he at home with his dad? Is this your time off?! If so, that bloke of yours has got to get you a spa membership because the supermarket is hardly "me time".'

Becky shakes her head, wincing as she does so, like there are loose items in there bashing about. 'He's in the hospital. He came too early. Much too early. So he's in the special prem baby unit and I... I... I haven't even held him properly.' Tears slip down her face, leaving irregular splashes on her blue T-shirt. 'Two weeks old and I haven't held my baby. They tell you about how important skin-to-skin contact is, when you're pregnant. But he just has plastic gloves and plastic boxes and wires, you know? How's he supposed to know we're here if he can't feel us?'

Her eyes search mine. I really wish I did know. I really wish I knew what to say.

Becky suddenly sits up straight, as if waking from a daydream. 'I'm sorry. I didn't mean to pour that out on you. It might all be fine, we don't know. We're waiting. That's what gets you, you see, the waiting. The not knowing. They're doing tests to see what effect being born so early might have, what could...' Her voice cracks and she busies herself with her whipped cream while she takes a breath. 'Steve told me to take an hour's break from the hospital, go out and see if I could find something I fancied eating. Thought I'd get some nappies, too. That's the kind of thing a mum does. And I need to look online for some smaller clothes. Everything we had ready for him is just miles too big. He needs to be warm in there.'

'Of course.' I squeeze her hand. 'That sounds like a good plan. You're doing a great job.'

She laughs with one tired shrug of her shoulders. 'I don't know about that. God, listen to me,' she drags her hands down over her face, 'I haven't asked anything about you. I bump into JP sometimes but, you know blokes, he never has any updates. He just says "she's working".'

I pick up my green tea. 'Well, he's not wrong. I'm working a lot, doing well at the firm. It's kind of round the clock, so... not much else to report!'

She frowns. 'No one you're seeing then, in London?'

'Nope. No.'

'Oh.' The frown lines drop from her forehead and she leans forward. 'Do you want my brother's number?'

I can't help but squeal with laughter. Talk about breaking the tension. 'Don't you dare! I can do without reliving that, thanks.'

Becky clutches her hands in front of her chest and says in a moony, slurring voice, 'Dave, you're just so cool and I would be the best girlfriend ever and we could go travelling like in *The Beach* except I can't actually swim but I have a sleeping bag and everything!'

'Thunderbird has got a lot to answer for, OK? And you promised you'd take that to the grave! There were a lot of emotions swirling around that night, we'd just got our results and I was freaking out about leaving home. For a minute I thought hooking up with your brother was the answer. He did not agree, though, did he?'

She slumps back into her chair and wipes her eyes. 'Oh, wow, I needed that. The perfect distraction! And actually, he's married now, so back off. Don't go seducing him with your three-tog sleeping bag.'

I clink my mug against hers. 'Here's to that. But we should meet up again. I'm going to be around for the next six weeks, here and there. I could meet you when you're taking a break, if you fancy it. And if my drunken idiotic antics are helpful, don't forget we have that whole school trip to Wales to relive, and the sixth form Halloween party.'

'Where you were sick in Mrs Arnold's witch's cauldron! Ha, yes! Oh God, yes, I need this right now. Let me give you my number.'

I open up the contacts on my phone and pass it over.

She lets out a long breath. 'Someone up there has been listening to me, because bumping into you was just what I needed. Now,' she swallows heavily, 'I'd better get back to the hospital and some premmie clothes shopping. Sadly, there's no category on ASOS for it – it was the first place I checked.' She's working up a smile but her eyes are nowhere near as convincing.

As I walk back to the car park with Becky, suddenly two broken wrists, some online orders and a backlog of emails doesn't seem like much of a problem at all.

–

'Shit, no! I knew she was pregnant but I hadn't heard… Shit, what can we do?' JP is sucking up soup through a straw, between sentences. He's getting major crow's feet from the concern across his face, but if anything it makes him look younger to me – like that little brother who didn't want to pay for his football stickers in the post office, because the woman behind the till had a bit of a scary moustache.

'I'm not sure there is much. Becky hasn't even held him yet. Maybe there's a charity we could donate to? And she said she was having trouble finding small enough clothes, so we could look for some—'

'Argh!' JP barks.

'Why?'

'Normally, I could knit a small baby hat in two hours or something. If I didn't have these bloody things,' he nodded at his casts, 'he could have a whole ensemble by the end of the week. And a blanket.'

'I'm sure she'll still be glad of something in six weeks.'

But I know JP isn't listening, his eyes have drifted off to the slightly cobwebby ceiling. Must find his Hoover soon.

'Would you boot up my laptop, sis? You are going to have to be my typing bitch for a second.'

I shoot him a warning look. 'Typing helper, then. But quick, while it's in my head. And then I need you to brush my hair for a quick vlog.'

—

Now, the power of the vlogger I know all about. We consulted with a beauty brand last year and after extensive insight work advised them that to launch a new lipstick with built-in nutricrystals, or whatever the science nonsense was, they didn't need one mega celeb to wear it. They needed twenty passionate beauty vloggers to love it, genuinely. If you're part of a community, you want to connect with people with those same interests. Logical. So I get why craft-loving types would take to YouTube too.

It's just the craft itself I don't get, if I'm totally honest. It's so... well, slow. If I do something, I want it done. I want an idea, an action, a result. And preferably all within twenty minutes. I see why knitting and stitching and crochet and all the rest is therapeutic and calming to JP. He needs those moments to pause, to quieten, to take a breath. But I'm the opposite. Like a shark, though a friendly one I should say, I have to move forwards or I just go kaput. When JP has tried to teach me a basic craft skill over long, cold holidays, I've always pretty quickly grasped what's going on and given it a good effort, but when I look up and expect to see a finished throw with amazing patterns and textures, I see eight millimetres of holey knitting. And then I'm a bit done and fish out my *Die Hard* box set instead. And when John McClane is on his way home in a fully filthy vest, more than ready for a cup of tea and a sit-down, I can always dig out my work emails.

It actually feels like a treat to be back in the office after an evening of tending to JP. We're close but even close siblings don't need to be that involved in each other's toilet habits. Roll on six weeks' time, when he is back to normal operation. Still, I've got my personal phone right by my keyboard, just in case.

I'm scrutinizing a workflow sheet, looking for any oversights or loopholes when Devon's perma-tanned face looms over my screen. He doesn't say anything but the arch of his eyebrows might as well shout, What the hell is going on?

'Hi, Devon, can I—?'

'Our meeting was scheduled to start at 8.30. It's now 8.45. I passed up my morning Spin class to be here. So where were you? Or is my time no longer valuable, Blackthorn?'

I quickly click on my calendar tab but it's empty until 9.15. I have not a clue about this meeting I've supposedly missed. But thinking on my feet is one of my best and most useful skills. 'I'm sorry, that appears to have slipped out of my diary. Why don't we catch up at lunch? I know there's a Spin class in the corporate gym at one p.m.'

The eyebrows slip down to a neutral level. 'Fine. You're on. Come ready with those takeaways and action points from the Dunreddy account.'

I nod with confidence. I have no idea who Dunreddy are.

As Devon strides away down the plush carpet, Clive pushes through the double doors and dumps his coat into his chair. 'Morning, boss. Tea?'

I'm already back on to the workflow and my mind is starting a new To Do list at the same time. 'God, yes. You're a star. And can you google the nearest sportswear shop, call them and reserve something suitable for Spin, a size ten – I'll pick up at noon. Also pull the Dunreddy file quick as you can, ta.'

Clive is muttering the list back to himself, so he doesn't forget anything. Not that he ever does. 'Okey-doke.'

'And did anything come through from Clara yesterday, arranging a morning meeting with me on Devon's behalf?'

Clive blinks. 'I heard her ask Ben last thing in the evening if you'd be back in by tomorrow morning. He said he was pinging you an email there and then about it. Did it not come through?'

I close down my document with a heavier click than necessary. 'No. No, it didn't.'

Thank God for my lunchtime Spin, because I suddenly have a lot of aggression to burn off.

–

'I want that drill down.' Devon's voice is almost too low and gravelly to be heard over the techno beat and the whizzing of twelve sets of bike wheels. 'I'm talking low-hanging fruit. I'm talking meaningful growth. I'm talking the next Uber.'

I can barely hear Devon, but can he even hear himself? I mean, I love the language of real business – negoti-ating, analysis, management all come with their own set of terms. It's almost an academic study. But 'business speak' is something else. If I hear one more investor who's put a million in a tech start-up that they don't really understand use the description, 'It's the Uber of...' I will book myself an Uber to the dark side of the moon and never come back. But seeing as Clive could only dig up the file by 11.50, misplaced by an intern apparently, I've barely got the lightest understanding of what Dunreddy do so I'm going to let Devon talk his spiel until hopefully 1.57. And with every push against a pedal, I can imagine Ben's tie getting caught up in the spinning disc in front of me and very quickly – and agonizingly – squeezing his windpipe. Hah.

'And your thoughts?' Devon murmurs over the computerized music.

'All about platform,' I say with a wry smile. This is a pretty useful cover-all statement.

'Of course.' Devon shrugs and stands up on his pedals, ready for the next blast. My skin is safe for the next day, but I can't say the same for Ben's.

—

In the locker room at the gym, I check my work phone first, on impulse. An email from Ben. Pfft.

From: Ben

To: Delilah

Blackthorn, what's the situation with your family emergency? We're all concerned.

As if I'd give him more intel to trip me up with. I almost want to reply: got to try harder than that. But instead I'll take the high road and just delete it – 23 emails needing a reply have come in over the last hour and a half. It'll be the late train back to the shop tonight, then.

On my personal phone there's a short message from JP visible on the lock screen. *Comments!* it says. And that's it. Doesn't seem to be a cry for help, so that's a relief. Unless he used voice dictation again and it really is 'comets'. A deadly meteor shower seems a bit random for Fenwild.

Then another message comes through. *Vlog!* I open up my browser and google his YouTube channel. It's the vid I helped him brush up for yesterday, titled, 'Crafters unite! A tiny baby needs you!' In his usual unrehearsed, slightly sloppy style, JP had explained his accident (leaving the bunting bit out – quite wisely) and that he couldn't knit anything for Chester, but would anyone else be able to help out? I'd found, under his instruction, a free pattern online for tiny baby hats and pasted it into the description bar.

When I scroll down through the messages posted underneath, there are 17 already. And they all say yes!

Standing there in my Sweaty Betty leggings, I lean back against the locker door for a moment. It's amazing to think there are 17 people ready to knit Becky a tiny hat that will fit. Kind people who'll happily help a stranger in need.

I reply, *Crafters are the best! Becky is going to love this. Clever bro.*

And he replies, with his limited skill, *Yaaas.*

But then my work phone buzzes in my other hand and I switch back from knitting and purling to the here and now. Devon is asking for a full report on Dunreddy by first thing tomorrow. Definitely the late train then.

Chapter 4

When I open the side door to the flat behind the shop, I hear an odd thing: Maggie, but squeaky. It's been a week since I first raced back here to find JP plastered up and immobile and so far the arrangements for Maggie and me to share giving him our helping hands (since his are about as useful as a cheese calculator right now) is working out just about OK. Getting the late train back is a bit wearing when there's so much to do at work. I swear something is going bonkers with the email server as new messages and tasks pop up without me seeing them and then are super urgent: 'Do this by the end of the day or my head will explode' kind of things. Clive is on the case with the IT guys but so far no luck as to why. And it's hardly giving Devon any joy that I've missed a few emails from him. Pretty shitty timing. Maybe the email exchange has it in for me.

But at least when I do get back to the row of thatched cottages and the funny little house names – Ramblers' Rutt, Spiggle Cottage and Durr Barn – I know I am far from the City and all that stuff is just going to have to wait for twelve hours, explosions or not.

Maggie's voice is coming from the kitchen and I listen in as I hang my coat on the overloaded hooks. She's gone all high-pitched, like she's trying to hit a difficult note in *The Sound of Music*. But she's not describing hills and goatherds, she's detailing the recipe for her pesto sauce.

'Sit down, Auntie,' I hear JP say.

And then another male voice, one I don't know, saying, 'Please, do have a seat. I assure you it's fine. It's just lovely of you to offer in the first place.'

Maggie then goes super trill and giggles, punctuated by the odd snort. She jumps another foot in the air when she sees me in the living-room doorway. 'Another late arrival! Now, I really must cook you both something.' She turns to a tall, skinny cupboard wedged next to the oven and starts to dig around. 'What kind of young man doesn't have pine nuts close at hand?'

I can sense JP is opening his gob to give a cheeky reply to that so I shoot him the big-sister look and his teeth clamp shut.

It's gone ten p.m. so I have no idea who this bloke is, crammed on to the tiny sofa next to JP. His balding hair is neatly cropped and he has two leather bracelets on his wrist. Maybe he's a knitting crony? Though I can't see a crocheted belt or Fair Isle socks from where I'm standing.

Bracelet man hefts himself up into a standing position, and puts out his hand. 'I'm Stan. JP's OT. Ha! That's a mouthful, isn't it? I'm his occupational therapist, here to help while his arms are healing. Sorry it's so late, but I wanted to check he's doing OK with his bedtime routine.'

I wince. With Devon's surprise deadline thrown at me, I'd been working so hard all night that I'd forgotten my role of pants-puller-upper to my dear little bro. I don't want him to struggle, of course, but it doesn't mean I have to enjoy being that close to his boxers. Or his bum. Thank God he can just about manage his bathroom business alone. I mean, seriously: thank God. Sign me up for a monthly donation to whichever church we have in the village, because I could not go that far even for my beloved brother.

'But by the sounds of it, you have him all sorted between you. Which is great. It doesn't get better than family.' He winks at Mags and she almost melts into the tea towel she's been wringing in her twitchy hands. Oh, I get it: Mags fancies him! Man, my brain is slow tonight. I have to shake my head to dislodge the Dunreddy stats and take in this fit-to-bursting room properly.

'Have you got a cup of tea, Stan?' When my frontal lobe kicks in, it takes me back to my Brownies hostess badge.

He sits back down. 'I've had two, thank you, care of your very kind aunt. And she's been offering me a late dinner, which sadly I have to turn down this time.' Out of the corner of my eye, I can see Mags lift on to her toes when he says 'this time'.

I perch on the side of the armchair. 'To get back to...?' Maybe JP isn't the only one I can help while I'm staying.

'Just Matilda. My cat. Right, fella. You've got my number if you have any problems before my next visit. And if the pain gets too much, you know what to do, right?' They nod in a manly fashion at each other and Stan waves us all a jolly goodbye and says he's happy to see himself out. In this flat, you can see everything from everywhere so it does seem a bit weird to follow him to the door.

Maggie turns back to the bubbling water on the hob. 'Well. Well,' she says into the rising steam, I think to cover her very pink cheeks.

I'm going to file this in the back of my head for the weekend, when my brain isn't quite so scrambled. We should make sure Mags is coming over the next time Stan is. Just coincidentally, like. But now to shovel in some carbs and flop down in front of some fancy Scandi crime box set. Wait, that requires too much thinking. Maybe a *Come Dine with Me* rerun.

JP tries to hook one of his casts round my neck in a clunky hug. 'Aah, sister. So glad you're home at last.'

'What do you need?'

He tries to look aghast. But the smile pokes through. 'Couldn't borrow your awesome touch-typing skills for half an hour, could I? There's been so much response to the blog post, and loads of emails pinging through to the shop account.' He drops his voice to a gravelly whisper. 'I did ask Mags but she opened up a browser and just typed *EMAILS* into Google. She didn't even hit return. She just sat there for five minutes wondering why my laptop was so slow. I can't break it to her, sis. I just said, "Yeah, it's the Wi-Fi. Bit bunged up tonight."'

I punch him in the thigh to stop us both cracking up. 'Fine. But just half an hour, OK?'

—

It's now 1.00 in the morning. I've gone past that stage of being dog tired and have circled back into hysterically alert. I'm fuelling this with coffee and adrenalin.

I really didn't mind typing up emails for JP – I just sort of went into a trance and let my fingers fly as he dictated. Lots of messages to his online craftaholic mates who've said they'll repost his hat appeal to their blogs, replies to suppliers asking how his arms are doing and does he still need a job lot of stitch markers for Friday. But we very easily went past thirty minutes into sixty, then ninety, and then I realized I had taken up the challenge of weeding his inbox of loads of spam and newsletters. When I turned round to ask him if he ever read the daily bulletins from Wow Wools, JP's chin was resting on his chest and a pool of dribble was leaving a dark patch on his T-shirt. I pulled the crocheted blanket from the end of the sofa over his legs and kept going. I knew my brain was too buzzy to stop there.

His junk mail is stupidly full so I have a trawl through. Nigerian princes, poorly designed phishing, and so many emails with the subject 'Hello' that I almost miss a gem.

It's the email address I recognize, from a Bloomberg article the other week – MCJ Invest. A really progressive investment firm with a squeaky clean reputation for ethical and environmentally-friendly business affairs. I've heard they are so committed to being a paperless office that the CEO has even banned Post-its.

Maybe JP has a mate there, from his time in London? He wouldn't want to miss the message being gobbled up by junk, so I take the risk that I'm not about to read anything too grossly laddish or abuse JP's trust. (I mean, just tonight I've helped him in and out of a bath, so no one could accuse me of not being kind to my little brother.) I click open the email and quickly read through the scant paragraphs. No friendly chat, just a business introduction. It's from a junior exec called Lorraine, so no big cheese but still, what she is saying is interesting – they are looking to invest in small craft businesses outside London and want to meet JP. Very interesting. JP is happy with how things are going, and if he's happy then I'm always happy, but sometimes I worry about what might happen to the shop – and more importantly, him – if the craft trend dies down and the stress of a failing business sends him into another spiral of anxiety. A solid investment could be just the right kind of safety net.

I leave JP a note for the morning:

> *Look at the starred email in your inbox. I'm going to do some research on MCJ but let's talk? Be back late. Maggie's coming to help you get dressed xxxx*

–

I suppose I don't really take much time to look around me when I'm in London: I wake up early, do some HIIT at the gym, slide into my office chair at eight a.m. with a sweaty glow and a flat white, leave at eight p.m., grey and with flat energy levels, and in between all that my eyes are glued to my phones for any news or client contact. I hardly notice my shoes, let alone the streets or the scenery or the weather. But shivering on the Fenwild train station platform, I can't look away from the sunrise that's making the most incredible silhouette of the copse and the thatched roofs beyond. The sky is inky blue at the top, turning violet and then burning with a rosy pink at the bottom, with the trees and houses so black they look like an illustration from my childhood copy of *1,001 Arabian Nights*. I am a city girl, through and through, but I can see why you might swap concrete streets and abandoned mattresses for this kind of countryside view. JP always says it helps keep him centred, calm and still.

And though I agree Fenwild is looking gorgeous at 7.03 a.m., I'm sadly anything but centred, calm or still. I don't like that I'm in Devon's bad books this week. It leaves me with a nervous jigging leg as I sit down on the empty train. The handful of other commuters promptly lean against windows and fall into deep snoozes, but I'm just too twitchy. Three hours of sleep before handing in a big report was not my best plan, but Michelangelo designed a helicopter and he only slept for 45 minutes at a time, right? Besides, the report is done, emailed over to my assistant late last night. Clive will have it printed and bound in the post room first thing, so I can hand over a sleek, polished article to Devon and get back all those Brownie points that are so rightly mine. And if Ben so much as raises an eyebrow in my direction about the office time I've been missing, I'll ask the post room if they can possibly fit his lips in the ring-binding machine too and shut him up for a while.

I'm at my desk at 8.30. I've chased off the lurking nerves with a cheeky croissant and downloaded a meditation app in the loos. Maggie is always telling me I should take a leaf out of her mindfulness book. Literally, she means that – she has so many self-help books and colouring books and books on tape, and each birthday and Christmas I get something similar. Whatever floats your boat, I say, though I've never found myself with ten spare minutes and thought, *I'll just colour in a picture of a Buddha and be Zen.* I usually think, God, the dry cleaners have had those shirts for three weeks now, better pick them up and be clean. The app didn't really seem to take the edge off, but it did give me an idea for one of our clients who runs business skills workshops and seminars – they should develop an app, get a third party involved to spread the cost. I email myself the idea and feel a glow of confidence which then squashes any leftover niggles about Devon's grump. He does this sometimes: if he's had a bad kickboxing class, he might criticize our choice of font on a PowerPoint. If he couldn't get the Nobu reservation he wanted, he might make us all stay late at work and order a Japanese takeaway around the boardroom table. But then the next day it's all forgotten and he's praising the inventive range of tropical fruit on display in reception. Swings and roundabouts. Underneath the ballsy business speak and expensive ski-and-surf tan, he's actually a kitten. A kitten who takes home a healthy six figures and has a house in Belsize Park.

Clive waves me a good morning as he puts his bag down. I open my mouth to ask a question, but he anticipates me before I've even said a word. 'Yup, the print room are on it and have promised to deliver copies directly to Devon, right about,' he looks at his iWatch, 'now. So he's got thirty minutes to read before your nine a.m. meeting. Tea, boss?'

I lean into my ergonomic office chair, enjoying with a childish thrill the way it stretches all the way back, almost to toppling point. I should have known that Clive would take the wobble out of today with his reliable perfectionism. He nails every task, usually before I've even finished asking him for something. 'You're a star! And yes, please, a strong builder's for me this morning.'

I turn back to my emails, whizzing off replies and reassurances and adding new jobs to my task list, pinging a few to Clive as well. When I see him out of the corner of my eye, standing at my shoulder, I smile. 'Just the ticket, cheers, chuck.'

'Well, that's a warm reception. Good morning to you too, Blackthorn.'

Balls, it's Ben. 'Morning, Cooper. Anything pressing you need to discuss? A new hair gel supply, as I assume you've emptied the Boots warehouse?' It's a bit personal, this kind of ribbing, but I'm now mixing sleep deprivation with excited adrenalin ahead of getting in with Devon and giving him the old Dee dazzle. So I'm feeling a bit bolshy.

Ben rolls his eyes, but colours slightly. 'Hilarious. Just wondered what the deal is with you and Devon? He seems like he's on the war path. Did his basement extension get denied again? He seems dead set on that disco room.' He folds his arms over his perfectly wrinkle-free suit. Ben is one of those people that you know comes from money: maybe it's his perfect skin and teeth, his non-stop confidence, the suit that clearly hasn't come from the sale rail, but he has private school written all over him. In fact, I think that's his school tie he's wearing. He's said more than once that he went to the same prep as the CEO's son. In fact, he shoehorned it in last week in the break room, as Brenda from accounts showed us a video of her daughter's cello recital. Apparently Ben is grade six. Whoop di do.

I'm not biased against Ben purely because he's posh, don't get me wrong. I have a list of legitimate reasons to dislike him that are unique to him and him alone (the over-gelled hair that he sweeps back dramatically when he's about to say something 'important'; the fact that he's always the first person to leave after work drinks, thereby avoiding his round; his sense of entitlement to power and leadership). But I suppose growing up the way we did, with no spare money for anything, it does put me on edge when I see someone flaunting their gold cufflinks and their fancy 'boys' club' maroon tie. There were some very lean years in the Blackthorn household when I was a teen, sadly because our chosen family business for generations had been an independent travel agent. When the bottom fell out of the high-street travel industry, our world bottomed out too – living with Gran temporarily in her little bungalow, selling the car, home-made birthday presents. My mum even pawned her engagement ring so we could have some sort of chicken at least for Christmas dinner. I watched my parents carry the weight of the world on their shoulders as the credit card bills came plopping through the door, but the job offers were sadly much scarcer. And I knew then that when I grew up, I'd earn my own money. I'd work hard, yes, just like Mum and Dad did to retrain as actuaries even though it bored the pants off them, and I'd make sure there was always a big fat turkey at Christmas. So seeing someone swan about without even an idea that nice things in life mean a lot of sacrifice and blood, sweat and tears, well, it doesn't make me warm to them, let's put it that way. And the only thing that sweats from Ben on a typical work day is his lemony aftershave as he rushes out to a lunch with one of his cronies, probably all put on Daddy's tab, I bet.

But today is not a day to think about Ben Cooper. Today is about smashing it in the meeting room, taking Devon through my concise yet carefully strategized document to push for maximum growth at Dunreddy (who, I discovered last night poring over the scant files, make pasties and pork pies for motorway services, and that's a valuable pie to have a slice of, even if your arteries won't thank you). I've hit on the core brand values they need to strengthen in their business approach. This is what I do. This is my bread and butter. Or pasty with cheese, if I ever get face to face with these new clients. In fact, if I push hard enough, this would be a great project for me to take the lead on. I have it in the bag.

-

'You've lost the plot.' Devon slaps the ring-bound report down on the shiny boardroom table, making me flinch just a little.

'I'm sorry?'

'This…' Devon gestures with one hand as if pointing to a discarded dog-poo bag in the park. 'This is not good enough, Delilah. Not good.'

My mouth goes dry and I reach for my green tea. 'I… I think this is a fair study within the time frame. I laid out…'

Devon snorts and rolls his eyes. It doesn't make for a pretty picture. 'This is the work of someone who threw together two ideas on the train and dropped in some Clip Art to pad it out. Nice try on the ring binding. For a second it made me believe this was the work of a professional. What's going on with you, Blackthorn? This is not like you. I'm starting to worry.'

I know by 'worry' he doesn't mean about me, but about his bottom line. He's worried I'm going to piss off a client, make a costly error of judgement. He's worried I'm going to do a Nigel from the second floor who broke down in tears in a client presentation to a cosmetics firm because his wife had just left him and theirs was her favourite hairspray. Devon deemed that was 'no grounds to scare off the cheque-signers'. And then he sacked him.

'Don't worry, sir. I will… redraft something for you. By end of play.'

His well-groomed eyebrows draw down into a wide V. 'I'm listening.'

Think, Dee, think. Thinking on your feet is your speciality, remember? Don't trip over your laces now, girl. But I'm struggling to see what I could do differently: I laid out the current market climate, the challenges and strengths, the key strategy to move forward and the kind of agencies we might use to help the company achieve that. It was like so many reports Devon has enthused about in the past. Could the basement thing be pissing him off so much? All I can do is play for time and hope he's calmer by six p.m.

I clear my throat and take a deep breath. 'I have a second strategy up my sleeve. I'll work it up and come back to you.'

Devon's frown is still there, angled right at me. 'Are you committed to this, Blackthorn? You ran out of the TechBank meeting, you claim some "family issues".' The air quotes tell me all I need to know about Devon's sympathies for that term. 'I've heard rumours of unpredictable behaviour for a little while now but I didn't want to believe them. But this seems to back it all up. Where's your head at?'

Rumours?! Unpredictable behaviour?! I'm so predictable, so reliable at work that the cleaners set their watches by me for the eight p.m. shift.

My lips move about uselessly, like I'm a ventriloquist's dummy and the person operating my mouth is just trying to scratch his thumb. I'm not thinking on my feet; I'm stumbling into panic.

Just then, my phone vibrates against the table. A picture of three lime-green baby hats lights up the screen. Perfect.

Before I can snatch it away and throw it out of the window, Devon's eyes dart down and take in the tiny knitted caps, each with a white bobble on top. And a few words of text that caption the image: *For us?!*

Oh, JP, your timing is sometimes not the greatest.

I'm trying to bluster out my reply. 'Devon, this is all actually simple to explain. I'm—'

He holds up his well-manicured hand and stands suddenly. 'I'm going to stop you right there. Whatever you're... doing, I from this point have no further vested interest. We're letting you go, Delilah. Right now. Due to disappointing performance. Within ten minutes security will be at your desk. I hope you remember that you can now no longer contact clients? Right, goodbye.'

And then it's quiet. Bar the subtle swish of Devon's expensive trousers and the clunk of the door closing behind him, it's quiet. I've never been so silent in my working life. My head goes blank, all the explanations and arguments floating off, above my head, like the smoke rings I tried to blow as a teenager. There's nothing. I'm blank.

I'm not sure how long I've been sitting in the leather chair, my hands leaving clammy circles on the chrome arms, when a cough from the doorway makes me leap out of my skin.

'Boss?' Clive's face is pale. 'Everything OK?'

All I can manage is to shake my head by half an inch. I slowly walk past him, down the hall to my desk, pick up my bag and without stopping march to the lift. I ignore the persistent deep voice behind me calling, 'Blackthorn? Blackthorn!'

I can't be here to see Ben's victory dance.

Chapter 5

'She won't even take a Jaffa Cake. I *know*. No, we'll be OK, Mum. Honest. Mags is taking great care of us. And I'm sure Dee just needs some time to come round. I'll keep wafting chocolate under her nose. Don't worry! You do not need to change your flights back. Please don't. Anyway, I don't think Dad would come with you by the sounds of it. He's loving the barbie life too much. Got to go, will email you tonight with an update.'

JP awkwardly brings his right hand down in a slow karate chop to his phone, just about brushing the screen with his little finger to end the call. It would be funny if I wasn't so numb. His phone has been on loudspeaker on the kitchen counter so of course I've heard all of Mum's nervous squeaks and worried objections. But I'm glad he put her off coming back early – I can't bear to see anyone right now.

Fired. Fired! Me. Me, fired!

That one clunky thought rattles around in my head like a pinball and I just can't seem to bat it away. On impulse I checked my work phone on the train home, only to find that I had no network access to my emails or files and even my password had been voided. I was shut out. I was gone. Devon has washed his hands of me because... because... I missed a meeting, a few emails went astray and he didn't like one report out of hundreds of brilliant ones?! It's utter crap. It's unfair. It's bullshit. But I know he can do it. Our company employment contracts are tailored to reflect the fact that we're expected to work round the clock, way above EU guidelines for acceptable working hours, and our commensurate pay and bonus schemes mean that the termination clause is pretty brutal. With no chance of appeals or tribunals, even. You can't have all carrot and no stick in this game. And now the stick has an imprint of my arse on it, as it whacked me out the door.

I hide my work phone under the sofa cushions. I'll post it back another day, or something. Whatever.

JP lowers himself onto the arm of the old sofa, his face creased with concern. 'Sis. Sis, what can I do? You've said three words to me since you've got back. How can they do this? You're such a badass! You've earned them millions. Not that they need more. You should get angry, tear some stuff up...' he turns his head around the room, looking for something breakable. 'I never liked those bookends, with the yarn balls glued on them? Dad's cousin sent them, remember? Bloody naff *and* a waste of yarn. Smash them! Pulverize them! And then I might need you to help me have a wee.'

The way he sneaks this last bit in starts a small laugh in me that becomes a big one. And soon I'm struggling to catch my breath.

'Well... that's something.' JP narrows his eyes at me. 'Something, at least. Right, our plan is loo break – I'm getting really good at sitting-down wees now, all on my own – tea break and then I'm going to take your mind off things.' He nods confidently and I think for once I'm going to let him be the big one between us. I'm just too poleaxed to think straight, let alone be the bossy sibling today.

Which is perhaps why he has managed to get me here sitting, his crocheted blanket over my knees, a big ball of thick navy wool by my feet and two smooth, cool knitting needles in my sweaty hands.

'So, just let the yarn hang between your fingers on your right hand and it'll feed through nicely. Then the needle goes in, yarn wrapped over, pull up and out and – there! There, see! You've made a new stitch.' With JP craned over me, I can see the flash of happiness in his eyes, and a little green shade of envy. The poor sod really misses his favourite hobby right now. He is living his craft passion vicariously through me, which is one sure sign of desperation. 'Now you try on your tod, no guidance.' He leans back against the wall, itching a shoulder blade on the door frame.

Trying to keep hold of the two needles, the wool itself and the soft rows of JP's knitting feels a bit like the panicky manoeuvre when someone passes you a tiny baby at a family do, and you have to concentrate so hard on supporting their head and not squashing a small arm and not dangling your hair in their mouth. So much going on at once, just a hair's breadth from everything unravelling.

I push the needle through the little hole that I *think* is the right one on the left-hand side. The wooden knitting needle is thick like a school paintbrush and I remember JP telling me that different yarns need differently sized needles. Each one has a perfect lifelong match, like penguins, apparently. This is a really chunky wool so it needs a chunky set of needles and JP said it was lucky he'd started this thick pullover before his accident, as chunky is good for beginners. He'd got about 30 centimetres in before he'd taken that tumble. His knitting is beautiful: soft, even, regular. It's actually mesmerizing how perfect it is.

So the needle is there, poking through, and now I have to wrap the yarn around it. But does it go over or under again? And am I supposed to be pulling hard like this? JP said something about tension and not making your work tight and inflexible but at the word 'work' all I could see in my head was that ring-bound presentation being slapped down in front of me on the boardroom table.

That was good work. I know it.

Well, the yarn is round. OK. Wait, what now?

What now? What will I do? I've lost my job. I got sacked! Me!

'That's a bit tight on the old tension,' I hear JP say, but I'm only half in the room. I'm thinking about what everyone will be saying in the office, right this minute. Any rumours about me being unpredictable are just going to seem valid, the way I ran out of there. Ben will be *lapping* this up, I bet. He'll be strutting about, pushing his oily hair off his forehead and doing that fake wincey smile people do when they're trying to give an impression of care and concern. 'I did think she was stretching herself too far,' he'll be saying. 'Not everyone is cut out for this kind of work, you know.' He'll wink at one of the interns who'll giggle in reply.

I'm not really seeing the needles move in front of me, but I can feel the awkward, lumpy movements in my hands as I struggle to pull the needle through and get the new stitches on the flaming stick. I'm seeing my flat up for repossession, my savings account withering away to nothing, I'm seeing cardboard boxes being loaded into

Mum and Dad's spare room. My eyes sting and I shake my head. No. No, it won't come to that.

'Just let the yarn go a bit there, sis. You're yanking it pretty hard, yeah?'

But I work hard and I work fast – I don't deserve this! What was Devon on?! And where did he hear these rumours? That's got to be my first mission: get to the bottom of this rubbish. Get my reputation back. Make Devon rue the day he pushed me out. Push him out, even! Yeah, get comfy in his seat. Send him out the door with his tub of protein powder and framed picture of his beloved speedboat. Hell, I'll have the damn boat too while I'm at it!

'Whoa there! Whoa!'

I feel JP nudge the back of my hand with his own and I look down to see a knotted, tangled mess on my lap.

His eyes wrinkle. 'I think you might have managed to knit four times into the same stitch. Five times over. Which is, weirdly, quite an advanced stitch but not what we were after here. You've gone so full on with the tension that you've left yourself almost no room to manoeuvre, Dee. We can start again.'

'Aargh!' My scream surprises even me. 'I don't want to start again! I had everything just the way I wanted it!' I drop the wonky knitting on the floor and kick the yarn ball under the TV stand.

'Hey!' JP admonishes. 'Respect British wools in my house! That's valuable stuff.'

'Ha! Ha, ha! That's perfect. Wool is valuable, OK, I see. Because I'm not, am I? All my work, all my career building, all my five a.m. alarms and working dinners and client parties, that all means nothing, that's not valuable.'

I can feel my neck flushing as my voice gets louder and hoarser.

JP nods. 'Now we're getting somewhere.'

'All that and – poof – I'm just gone. In the blink of an eye. How dare they? How *dare* they?! And now it's me who's got to start again. Brilliant!'

I seize my demented attempt at knitting, letting the needles clatter to the floor, and wrap the hanging yarn around my hand, pulling and pulling as one knotted stitch pings free after another. Soon I'm speedily unwinding through my rubbish stitches and I'm into JP's perfect ones. Ping ping ping, they're gone and they're nothing, the only proof they ever existed in the kinks of the thick wool as it pools on the sofa cushion. Not a jumper. Just a puddle of nothing.

And when there's nothing whatsoever left, I look at JP. He's smiling, just.

'Exactly!' he chirrups. 'That's better, right? Out is always better than in. A part of creating something is also, sometimes, destroying it. But you can always start again, with anything in fact. Knitting. Jobs. Stuff 'em, Dee. They're idiots. You're so much better than them.'

I realize that I need to catch my breath. I try to remember my Pilates rhythms and count out for five. 'I will try again. And this time I'll do even better.'

I might not be able to manipulate wool into anything pretty or useful or even closely resembling a pattern, but I can appreciate how lovely it is to hold. It's like having a little soft guinea pig in every colour of the rainbow, except yarn balls don't squeal and poo in your hand when you gently stroke them. Some of it is crazy fluffy, with a fine fuzz like a haze surrounding each ball. (Skein, I should say. I'm still getting to grips with the lingo.) Some of the yarns are tweedy and robust, with flecks of grey and brown sprinkled amongst racing green or navy blue. I can just imagine these being turned into a professor's cardigan, with elbow patches sewn on after. Some yarns are lighter, softer, and feel almost like cotton as I pick them from the cubbyholes and double-check the dye lot numbers before slipping them into a labelled envelope.

JP gave me a refresher on dye lots before letting me loose on his online orders this morning. He's happy to keep my hands occupied as a way to exorcize my stress and I'm happy to keep busy and not visualize different ways to remove Devon's stupid head from his orange body. Anyway, dye lots are a big deal to knitters, he said: you could order the exact same colour wool from the exact same brand from two different websites and if they weren't from the same batch of wool dyed together, the shades could be just that essential fraction out. Then you'd change over wool halfway through a project and be able to see the difference. JP says this is why he can't bear to see the purple cardigan he made Mags years ago now – his first full garment, when he was still learning the ropes – as on one sleeve there's a slight shift in colour. Invisible to anyone but a total perfectionist, but then JP and I definitely have that in common, so I can't really bring him up on it. Anyway, it's important I make sure that if someone has ordered four or five or fifteen of the same colour wool, that we're sending them all the same dye lot number. And given that customer satisfaction and online reviews are key to keeping a small online business like JP's afloat, I'm not going to skimp on these kinds of essential details.

With two orders packed up and ready for the post office, I'm enjoying finding a rhythm to this work. Scour the shelves for the right yarn, take in names like Angel, Snuggly and Super Chunky, check the numbers, double-check address label matches printed order, stick label on put it to one side, on to the next. I'm on my sixth order and rooting through a big clear plastic bag of small but perfectly formed balls of yarn for baby clothes with a mix of cashmere. To be honest, I'm rooting more than necessary but it's just so soft and smooth against my fingers. I'm searching for one last skein in a shade of the subtlest duck egg and when I go back to double-check the order, I see this customer has bought a pattern book too. So, over to the bookshelves and I'm looking for *Sweet Baby Knits to Treasure*. On the cover is a very apt sweet baby, rolls of fat forming lines at his wrists and neck. He's wearing a blue-and-white striped knitted romper and a matching hat.

Becky. In everything that happened at the office yesterday and my boiling rage that followed, I have completely forgotten about Becky and the hats! I whip my phone out from my back pocket and send her a speedy text.

Delilah

How's it going, love? I'm actually free and in the village all day today if you want to meet up? Or I could bring you some bits and pieces, if you like, just say a quick hello.

I wasn't expecting a reply; even with my scant knowledge of babies and motherhood I know that when you've got a newborn you're not exactly sitting pretty and waiting for a social event to kill time. And I don't know if Becky and her boy have got home yet – maybe if she's in the hospital her phone has to be switched off. But my phone buzzes almost as soon as I've put it down on the shop counter.

> **Becky**
>
> Yes, please! We're home! All the tests came back clear, thank God. I'm knackered and so messy but couldn't care less because we're home! Come and meet Chester. He's totally fine. Tiny still but we're working on that. Please come! Would love to see you, hun. xxxx

A warm tingle spreads out through my ribcage and up my arms. They're home. He's fine. This is greater than great. I look up at the ceiling and mutter a quiet 'thank you', I'm not sure to who exactly but maybe the knitting gods can have this one. Perhaps all those teeny hats waiting for Chester in the living room have brought us good luck. The positive karma JP put out into the world by calling on his crafty buddies has definitely reminded me that people can be kind and generous and trusting, at any rate, even if my working life would seem to prove otherwise. But today isn't a day to think about that. Today is a day to buy a bulk load of chocolate fingers and go and visit an old friend and a very new, box-fresh baby one.

My phone vibrates again with a ring this time, rumbling against the countertop: maybe Becky has a biscuit order for me? But the name *Ben* flashes on the screen and the phone starts to wiggle from side to side a little as I steadfastly ignore it, my breath held. Nope, not today.

Chapter 6

Chester may be small but he is perfection. Utter perfection. His fingers are pink and delicate but also have a kung-fu grip of steel when he winds them round your thumb. His cheeks are fuzzy, like one of those super-fluffy yarns at the shop and if I was going to pick a colour from the Baby Knits range to match his skin it would be Peaches and Cream. He is so wonderful, I could stare at him for hours.

'Say hello to Delilah,' Becky coos down at the baby as I sit with him held in my arms on their grey sofa, a muslin draped over each of my shoulders and a pack of baby wipes tucked under one elbow. I feel with all this kit, I should be bandaging soldiers alongside Florence Nightingale, rather than anticipating a milky burp. Mind you, the sitting room in front of me is its own kind of war zone: there's a torn-open gigantic pack of nappies spilling its contents all over the carpet; empty crisp packets and a pizza box are sticking out of the bin by the coffee table; and both Becky and her bloke Matt look like they've been on a hundred dawn raids in a row, with heavy grey bags hanging under their eyes. But this can't be a war because I've never seen two people look happier. Grey bags, yes, but their smiles are brilliant white and beaming. With every stretch or gurgle Chester makes they both jump up and down in excitement, marvelling at how that's his

49

seventh arm stretch, his tenth yawn so far and that they are almost certain he smiled at the cat yesterday so he's going to be a vet, probably. It is one of the most delightful things I've seen in a long, long time.

I brought chocolate fingers and tortilla chips with dip and some frozen pizzas for them to eat later and you'd think I'd just presented a fancy hamper by their cries of 'thank you'. They've been back for three days and hoovering up all the supplies friends and family drop over to keep their sleep-free bubble of love functioning. 'I brought something else, too. In my bag…' I gesture with my head towards my black leather bag, seeing as both my hands are full with the gorgeous Chester. I bought this particular bag on New Bond Street a few months ago because it was big, with enough room for a laptop, but also flashy, made out of the kind of slippery-soft leather that you know has cost big bucks. I wanted it to be a statement at work: I am here to win; remember me. I have to swallow suddenly, as I watch Becky root about, the bag conspicuously empty of a laptop now. I clear my throat awkwardly, 'There's a book bag in there – it says *Keep Calm and Carry Yarn*. It was the only spare bag JP had. Yup, that's it. Have a look!'

Becky squeezes the bag and gives a playful wiggle of her eyebrows as she brings it over. 'If all the stress and lack of sleep that comes with a baby means that you get presents, I can almost live with it.' Then she flops down on the sofa next to me and tips the contents onto her lap. It's like upending a bag of jelly beans for all the colours that come tumbling out. Seven tiny, knitted baby hats from JP's craft community: yellow and blue and green and even a pink-and-purple striped one. Her hands reach for the striped one first, feeling the fabric of closely knitted stitches under her thumbs, then tracing the delicate rows with one finger.

I laugh and set off a little startle in Chester who luckily recovers and drops back to sleep. 'Someone didn't read the notice about Chester being a boy, hope you don't mind. The thing is, JP so wanted to knit something himself, only he can't while he's stuck in the casts, so he asked his buddies that he knows through his vlog. And people sent these in just a week, can you believe it? More are coming soon, if you've got room for them.'

Becky looks at me, her face as pale as that day in the supermarket again, her mouth opening and closing without making a sound. Matt coughs behind me and as I look he's turned away and is furiously rubbing at his eyes in that way men do when they are trying to stop themselves crying.

'Dee,' she whispers, 'Dee.' She's still holding the stripy purple hat.

'You don't have to use *that* one, if it bothers you.'

Becky blinks. 'I will use it. We'll use them all. I just… I can't… someone made these – for us?'

I nod.

'Those weeks on the ward, you're stuck in this limbo. Will he be OK? Will we ever get home? And then you see a flash of real life – a bus going past the window, the shoppers with their trolleys, when I bumped into you that time. Normal people, doing what normal people do, while all the time your life is held together by a hope. You think no one knows what you're going through. They've got their ordinary, straightforward life and your heart is breaking quietly, out of the way. We were the lucky ones, Chester is fit and healthy, but we knew how close we were to being seriously not lucky. But these people, you told them about us and they made these?'

She grabs a handful of the hats now, holding them to her chest tightly.

'Yes. I don't know much about what these crafty people do, but I do know they're pretty generous.'

Tears are plopping down onto the red bobbly hat, the sunshine-yellow one. Becky smiles. 'You don't know how much this means. We needed tiny stuff but it's the idea that they've never met us and yet they'd spend their time making these. God, the stitches are so small! How do they do that?!'

I roll my eyes. 'I'm literally the last person to ask. But come by the shop soon with Chester, when you feel like a stroll with the pram. JP would *love* to tell you all about stocking stitch at great length.'

Becky laughs. 'I will. Blimey, if I tried to do something as complicated as this…'

'Um, I think you'll find making this,' I nod my chin down towards her darling son, 'trumps anything that can be put together on little bamboo sticks. You have made an entire human person! And he's perfect.'

The flush returns to Becky's face and she peers down at Chester, still snoozing with a face of utter Zen calm in my arms. 'He is, isn't he? Good things come in small packages, as my mum keeps reminding me. Who would have thought it was possible to swing from such total happiness to panic, to terror and then right back to blissful in about a fortnight?'

I would hug her right now if I had free arms. 'You're doing a great job, you know.'

She shakes her head and bats the idea away.

Matt coughs again. I've not met him before but I'm already picking up that he's a man of few words who prefers to use grunts to express himself. Fair enough. 'You are,' he says with a hoarse voice. 'You're an amazing mum.'

'I'm going to make us some tea before I cry again.' She hops up and heads to the kitchen.

I catch Matt's eye and he nods. 'Thank you,' he says. 'And please tell the others thank you. From the three of us.'

–

I leave with as much spring in my step as I've felt since heading into *that* meeting with Devon. Some things in life are bigger and I know I will remember that baby cuddle for the rest of my life. I'm going to see Becky at least once a week while I'm here, I vow to myself, and help her out with whatever she needs: biscuits, baby winding, a solid shoulder to absorb tears. She let me take a quick picture on my phone of Chester in one of his collection of new hats, with her and Matt leaning their faces in close and doing a big thumbs-up to the camera, the international hand gesture of, 'Thank you – we are chuffed to bits!' I can email it on behalf of JP to those kind knitters who sent in the mini beanies. I might get it printed and framed for JP's living room, too: a reminder of all the good he does for others. He's always been like that: when my favourite Cindy got run over on the drive and totally crushed when I was seven, he pulled the head off his GI Joe doll and put Cindy's head on its body so I could have a replacement. OK, so he had been the one to put Cindy just behind Mum's car wheel to see if she would survive but at least he had the compassion to make

53

amends. He's a gentle soul. I'm not sure I'll ever grow out of feeling like I should protect him because of it. These thoughts are tumbling around in my head as I approach the shop on the way back from Becky's. Someone really should scout this place for a Dickensian drama set: the ancient higgledy-piggledy row of shops looks like a set of piano keys all out of place, black and white and jumbled. But somehow there is a beauty to it, even if the doorways are tiny and the window frames bow in the middle. The locals keep up the old traditions of black timber and white limewash, so that the postcards sold at the newsagents of *Fenwild in 1800* really don't look all that different, bar a lonely phone box in the here and now. It's exactly the kind of place you expect to find a haberdashery, if not a blacksmith and a shoeshine, and JP runs his shop with all the reverence to local tradition that the village requires. He hangs tasteful Christmas decorations in the window in December: berries and cinnamon twigs and the like. And he always knits a few things for the summer fete's tombola. He fits here like a hand-knitted glove.

I'm so relieved that JP found the thing that makes him truly happy. A hard bullet of guilt still sits under my ribcage that I helped him into a law career that ultimately caused him to have a breakdown, but at least I could help him get this shop up and running with some investment capital. But as I think of the day I happily wrote him that cheque from my ISA account, I start to see the pounds and pence draining away the longer I go without a job. My ISA, my current account, my credit limit all running away from me like a tap you can't switch off. I need a paycheque. I need to get back to work. I can't be a drain on JP or Mum and Dad – I have to get my career back on track, and fast.

With a new jar of instant coffee open on the kitchen counter, the kettle boiling and the toaster working on two slices of granary bread, I open up my iPad and my personal email account. Time to get cracking and send some feelers out for a new role. Wallowing will get me nowhere. I bought the iPad years ago, it's far from a new flashy model, but it will do the trick. I bought it to watch Netflix on work trips but then always seemed to have my head stuck in files and meeting prep, so I left it here with JP once and didn't realize it was missing. I think he's sneakily been enjoying the Netflix app still on here, but I can let that one slide seeing as he's giving me board and lodging right now. He's also lending me some of his hoodies seeing as I haven't brought all that many clothes with me. Once I have a few interviews lined up in London for this week, I'll sort out grabbing more stuff from my flat. And throwing away the milk and half a cucumber in my fridge that have probably started fermenting into something an East London restaurant would call a reimagined pickle yoghurt.

The problem with reaching out to my work friends at other companies is that all their email addresses were in my work account, which I am now locked out of. My *old* work account. I need to practise saying that. And I need to practise explaining why I left so suddenly, and why I won't be giving Devon as a reference. I'll also have to cleverly fudge it on LinkedIn.

I do a little detective work on the websites of my rivals, where some old uni mates now work. You take the URL of the helpdesk email address they give, then give it a bash with first initial dot surname and see what happens. With a few innocent but to the point: Hey, we should grab a sandwich, emails to old friends winging their way, it's time to take a gulp of boosting coffee and call the recruiters. Sometimes slippery devils, sometimes asking you to interview for a job you're clearly wrong for or that is wrong for you just to meet their target and therefore their bonus, recruiters can still do their bit – they are plugged into all the industry gossip and sometimes know about a role opening up before the poor blighter who's about to be booted. Though I'm not sure any of them could have had so much as a whiff of my departure, seeing as I went from hero to zero in a matter of days. I concentrate on slowing my breathing as I stir my coffee a bit more and check my alphabetized list of recruitment agencies to call. First up: Clara Ambrose.

She does some great 'professional listening' as I quickly breeze through my current situation: lots of 'ya-hah's and 'OK's punctuating my speech while all the time I can hear her keyboard click-clacking at her desk. But I don't begrudge the multitasking – it's exactly what I do in the office. The in-house masseuse refused to come and work on my neck knots anymore after he found me tweeting a client during a Zen head massage. But that's just how I find my own personal Zen!

I speedily – strategically speedily – explain that I had to leave my last job 'rather abruptly' but this doesn't seem to bother Amber. In my line of work people are canned for a poor quarterly report more often than you'd like to believe and it's professional courtesy to smooth over that and get on with what's next. After I give her the headlines of my education and experience, I can hear her typing speed pick up. 'Good, good,' she says. 'I'm sure we have something for you. In fact, I got a sense of something over at the big tech—' but the tippy-tappy rhythm abruptly stops. 'But maybe… ah… that might not be a smooth transition. Uh, yes. You know what? Leave it with me and I'll get back to you.' And just like that the line goes dead.

Not like a recruiter to want to end a call before you've agreed to interviews with at least five of their clients, but maybe she's having a manic-busy day. Fine. On to the next.

Zadie Benson says it's a quiet month and she'll add me to her list. Tristan Davies coughs quite a bit and then says he's needed on the other line. I get another half-hearted brush-off from a European recruiter who have been pestering me every month for the last three years. Weird. But then, Brexit has done weird things to us all, I suppose.

My list is struck through and I'm struggling to see the next steps from it. I was hoping for a notepad jammed full of times, addresses and company names. Half-promises of callbacks aren't much to go on. As I stare at my inbox and prune back a few emails, something much more promising pings in. From Peter Foster, an old economics buddy from uni who I used to bump into at mixer drinks and who now works for one of my old rivals in management consultancy. Originally a rangy guy from Yorkshire who'd leap at any free booze on the go until he was physically thrown out of a joint, now he's a respectable father of two and heads home to the suburbs each night, whether there's still red wine in the bottle or not.

To: Delilah Blackthorn

From: Peter Foster

Subject: Re: Hello stranger!

Listen, in a bit of a rush but just grabbed the head of recruiting on her way to a lunch and she says she'd love to meet you (her words not mine), they're on the hunt and coming from a rival doesn't hurt, eh? If you can hang out in the lobby tomorrow at 11, she's got half an hour free to talk. You can suss each other out. If you try and go through all the security crap to get inside the actual office, you'll miss your window with her. So grab a latte and she'll find you. Elaine Leibovitz.

Good luck! Would be excellent to have an old mate on board. And you must come out and have Sunday lunch with us soon, Susie would love it.

P

Now this is more like it – action, direction, opportunity. I know enough about the firm already to hold my own but I have tonight to revise and polish. Starting off with researching this recruitment head. And then over to Bloomberg to track the share value. And then checking out Peter's LinkedIn and who else from his team are on there.

–

'Earth to Dee! Earth to Dee!' Maggie is making a loudspeaker with her hands, leaning right into my line of sight, blocking the laptop.

'Hmm?'

'How long have you been sat here, darling?' Maggie's cheeks are flushed from her walk up the hill from her bungalow to here. Her hair is wispy around her face, the bulk of her unruly slate-grey tresses tied up with a tie-dye scrunchy. Mags has always had this giggly youthful spirit to her, 63 or not. She's an eternal optimist, which you'd have to be with all that she juggles – a poorly, elderly mum, a low income and now a godson in plaster. There are scant lines on her face, even around her eyes, and she's always put her perfect complexion down to a lack of a man in her life to cause her worry. Maybe if that's the secret to great skin I should delete my dating apps. Mind you, I haven't been on them in six months, so I've probably been frozen out by now.

I stretch one arm up over my head, then the other. My shoulders are heavy and stiff. 'Just thought I'd look into a new job, over my lunch.'

She tsks. 'It's gone half five! All that screen time can't be good for you. I do wish you'd get outside a bit more – walk and get some air, maybe. Anything to stop you thinking about work. Or even a hobby like JP's, to take you out of yourself, hmm?' Mags dumps her Bag for Life on the kitchen counter and pulls out some celery.

I try my very best, because I love her so much, not to roll my eyes. 'Didn't JP tell you? Me attempting to knit ends up in attempted bodily harm. It works for JP, he's the chilled-out one. I chill out by... keeping very busy.'

She presses her lips together and raises her eyebrows. 'At least promise me you'll video-call your mother tonight. She's that worried! JP with broken wrists, you with—'

'A broken career?'

'That's not at all what I was going to say, young lady.' Mags is now pulling out courgettes and passata. I think her famous organic ratatouille might be on the cards tonight. Delish.

I get up and join her, pulling a chopping board from the middle drawer. 'I know, I'm just using humour to deflect. See it all the time at work. But no need to panic, I've got a great interview lined up for tomorrow. The Dee train is back on its tracks. Destination: The Big Smoke. JP's place is here, with his Zen knitting and alpaca yarns. My place is in the City with a nervous breakdown on every corner and every kind of sushi you could dream of. It's all going back to the way it's meant to be. Now, let me give you a hand with the slicing. Nice and thin for the ratatouille, yes?'

I know Mags is looking at me long after I finish talking, as I cut into courgettes and tomatoes and onions. But she's never really understood why I'd want to fling myself into the world of high-rise offices and even higher bonuses. She's always wanted me to be a garden designer, after my brief obsession with *Gardeners' World* when I was little. Her world is here, and the people in it. And thank goodness she is here to help JP while I get back to my nine to five. Or seven to nine, more likely. She can keep him fed and watered while I keep the bills paid. We've all got our roles and mine is to earn a whole bakery's worth of bread.

Chapter 7

The coffee shop in the basement of the Glenross building makes a pretty decent flat white. With each sip my spine is feeling that bit straighter, my nerves that bit steelier, as if the caffeine is my Popeye-like fuel for bringing out the big guns. And I got guns, baby. This interview is mine for the taking. In my head I see me doing a little Beyoncé hand gesture to Devon across the boardroom table. 'Boy, bye!'

I know just who I'm waiting for, thanks to Elaine's LinkedIn profile: curly brown hair and stylish tortoiseshell glasses. I'm scanning the glass lifts for a likely candidate, my carefully rehearsed but oh-so-casual sound bites about my career so far on a loop in my head: 'For me, it all starts with the client. Find their key need and the strategy writes itself. Of course, that's not something they teach at Trinity college!' *Cue good-humoured chuckling.* 'And now I'm ready to spread my wings, take what I've learned over my seven years and reach new clients, solve new problems. It's all about moving forward. You adapt or you get left behind.' *And then segue into a reference to Elaine's speech at the recent 'Recruitment in the Digital Sphere' conference. Nice.*

But as I mouth the last bits over and over to myself, checking for any leftover croissant on my Whistles skirt, I still can't see any curls, any angular specs. And it's getting on for five past eleven.

I check my watch against my iPhone – maybe it's fast? Might just hook my iPad up to the cafe Wi-Fi, so I can ping her my CV in an instant, when she asks for it.

'Hey.'

I hold my iPad to my chest, the nudge at my shoulder for a second putting me on bag-snatch alert. Once a London girl, always a London girl. 'Christ, Petey, you scared the breakfast out of me. Good to see you though!' I slip my iPad into my bag and smooth my hair quickly. 'Have you come for a debrief? I wouldn't mind an insight into Elaine's style – is she jokey, formal, does she like to be friendly or just cut the shit?' I look over Peter's shoulder, my eyes peeled for my interviewer in case she's hot on his heels.

'That's the thing, Delilah. Um, oh God, I don't know how to say this. Elaine's time is pretty rarefied, you know how it goes. She did some ringing round about you this morning and... and she's not coming down. I'm sorry.' He rubs his chin and I can see pinched lines at the corners of his eyes. It could be the sleepless nights of having several small kids. It could be that he knows he's about to ruin my day.

'What? Why?' Suddenly the caffeine has gone from giving me Popeye's killer muscles to Olive Oyl's knock knees. I can feel it rattling around my bloodstream with nowhere to go but jitter through my limbs.

Pete looks up into the tall, empty atrium. 'She didn't tell me much beyond headline but, but— hell, I know this can't be right, but what she heard is that you formed an unhealthy relationship with your client at TechBank. That you *went too far* and when the client pulled back, you freaked. There was talk...' His eyes flick pointedly to my stomach and back. 'But, I mean, that's what she heard from a contact. Sorry.'

I suddenly need to sit down. But I'll be damned if I give in to any Jane Austen style fainting right here, right now. Not while my peers stride around this marble floor, in between meetings or out to lunches or actually meeting interviewers in the flesh. And that would definitely only feed any crazy thoughts that I might be pregnant!

Unhealthy relationship? I sold my soul for that client. The squash I learned to play, the weird Swedish cuisine the director was into (fermented fish is not my idea of an ideal business lunch), but more importantly the brilliant plan I masterminded over months and months of laboured research and expert insight: none of that was unhealthy, none of that was improper. That was my job! And just what is 'unhealthy' meant to mean? Romantic? Sexy? Stalkerish? Just because I'm a woman working with a man it's suddenly got to get filthy? Bloody *Fifty Shades of* 'sodding' *Grey* has a lot to answer for. How could anyone assume that kind of thing from the professional work I was doing? Who in their right mind would leap to all those conclusions, rumours that paint me in such a bad light? Unless they weren't misunderstanding, because they wanted to spin it. Oh.

Oh.

Ben.

He knew about the squash games. He knew I wanted to take the client on solo, no longer teaming up with Devon, and that freaked him out. That threatened his fragile public-schoolboy ego. And so he painted me as the crazy lady of Canary Wharf. Bloody Ben! With having to miss just one meeting and seeing those baby hats on my phone, Devon was ready to forget all my pedigree and believe I could be having a client's baby, for Christ's sake. No wonder he booted me out the door before I had the time to say anything – just in case I wanted to take a year of maternity leave and really mess with his profitability. And now he's been spreading it around his executive friends, for good measure. Bloody Ben and bloody Devon and the bloody bullshit of being a woman in business!

I would love to scream at the top of my lungs right now, to blow out this steam, but instead I take a deep breath. 'Well, that is not true. *Any* of it.'

Peter shifts from foot to foot. 'Then take them to court, Dee, give them what for and make the lawyers sweat. And then pay.'

I shake my head. 'I signed things in my contract that stop me doing exactly that. I've seen a few old colleagues try it but get bled dry by the legal fees and then end up precisely nowhere. Just an even more tarnished reputation to take home. Nope, I'll have to think of another way.'

Peter makes his uncomfortable apologies and leaves me to ruminate over the last cold dregs of my flat white. I should make a move, back to the village. I should swing by my flat and pick up more clothes. I should do something, anything productive, but my white-hot rage has me glued to the spot, as though my best block heels are shod in lead all of a sudden.

How dare he? And how stupid are people for believing him?! I know my industry isn't the most forgiving to women, but I genuinely thought if I did my share of the toil that no one would ever try these kinds of petty games on me. And now it seems I've been blacklisted, through the careful whispers in some elite drinking club I wouldn't be allowed into, because my chromosomes aren't quite the ticket. Well, I won't have it. I bloody well won't.

Somehow… I mean, I literally have no clue how because I'm just jelly-like with shock and anger right now… but somehow this is going to be put right. And Devon and Ben will be put right out on the street, with tears staining their Italian leather loafers.

I purse my lips together as tightly as I can, an old childhood trick to stop myself even leaking one tiny tear. If I'm spotted weeping in the ground floor of the Glenross building it will not help turn the tide on my tarnished name. I put my coffee cup in the bin, smooth my skirt down at the sides and pull my shoulders right back. This is one 'filly' they won't see broken.

I'm two steps towards the revolving doors when I nearly trip and face-plant onto the hard, shiny floor. Easy, Dee, easy.

Coming through the highly polished glass is a highly polished smile. One I wish I didn't know so well. And he's actually smiling at *me*, with everything he's done.

Ben waves at me. He actually waves, like we're meeting up for tennis at his arsing country club with Tarquin and Jemima. 'Dee!' I hear him call as the large revolving circle comes close to spitting him out near me. *He* must be here for *my* interview. Sod this. I'm not having a showdown before I'm well and truly ready for it. You don't see a Western ending with a gunslinger at noon mumbling to his opponent, 'Oh, hang on, I left the bullets in my other pair of chaps.' He'll get his comeuppance, but only when I'm good and ready. I'll keep this short and sweet. So I leap into the next opening before he can walk out of his and I jab against the wood, causing the door to hit its automatic stop.

It's something JP and I used to do to wind each other up in department stores when we were bored tweens, trapping each other in the revolving set of doors while Dad was too busy looking for marked-down shirts. We were once in there for a full ten minutes, before a security guard grassed us up.

Ben's not expecting the sudden halt and clonks his nose against the glass in front of him. Ha!

'Right,' I say between clenched teeth. 'One, you don't call me by my nickname. It's only for friends and family. Two, actually, you just don't talk to me full stop. I know your game, Ben. I know what goes on in that pretty head of yours. And it's not cool. So enjoy your little victory. Because it's going to be a short one.' I narrow my eyes and turn my back on him, waiting for the doors to kick back into life.

'Delilah,' I hear him say flatly, 'I don't even—'

But as the wood and glass starts to swing away in front of me, I'm out of there and his words spin in the air behind me.

—

When I get back to Fenwild, my hands red from dragging my little wheeled suitcase on the Tube and the train and then the cobbled streets, and my cheeks still ruby red from the anger boiling my blood. I need some of JP's words of wisdom to give me perspective. Maybe he has a loom I can smash this time; I feel like something big needs to absorb all this rage. I may be the family organizer in our set-up, but he's the sympathizer. If I'm CFO of our sibling relationship, he's the HR director. I'm Martin the Money-Saving Expert and he's Dear Deirdre. Actually, we'd make a great crime-fighting duo.

The image of us in coordinating cape and tights has chilled me out somewhat as I sling my suitcase down in the living room.

'JP? Are you in?'

But he's not. Which is odd, because he doesn't have a hospital appointment. In fact, according to his wall calendar (one I found him for Christmas of a WI chapter in Devon who posed nude, except for carefully placed balls of yarn – 'My dream combination, skin and skeins!' he'd happily chirruped when he opened it) he had his OT appointment with Stan here this morning, so he had no need to go out. And a man with two broken forearms can't get all that far on his own. Unless the bus driver is willing to dig the change out of JP's back pocket, which I doubt. So he must be local. The pub will be open by now; maybe he's telling a slightly adapted story of how he got his casts to the regulars at the Witch's Nose. Seeing as he's been re-watching a lot of action movies recently to kill time, it might involve terror plots, exposed plutonium and a hot girl running through the woods.

I quickly get changed into my comfiest jeans. I had to dig deep back in my flat to find them, seeing as my usual rotation of clothes goes work-suit-pyjamas-work-suit-pyjamas with no time in between working and sleeping for anything like casual wear. But it's nice to feel the stretchy denim around my waist. A lot more forgiving that a dry-clean-only outfit, anyway. And in my head it means I'm far, far away from the City and today's lump of humiliation. I stuff my keys in one back pocket and my bank card in the other. I'll think about my budget after I've treated myself and JP, and whoever else is at the bar, to a couple of dangerously strong G & Ts. Jeez, I need one.

But I'm only a few steps from the front door when I recognize a tall guy and two arms in casts, through the window of Picture Perfect, the framers two doors down from JP's shop. The old door creaks and the bell above it tinkles as I push my way inside. The narrow shop has the same floor footprint as our haberdashery but instead of being stuffed with racks of buttons and displays of seam rippers, this shop is one big open space. The only thing busy and full are its walls: bursting with framed charcoal sketches and oil paintings. A woman at the counter looks up through her floppy grey fringe. She's got that really amazing dyed-grey hair that's almost ash blonde, and it turns into a powder blue at the ends. Way too cool to be a Fenwild local – she must have got lost on the way from London to somewhere amazing. I nudge JP in the hip. 'Hey, I've been looking for you.'

He jumps about a metre in the air, which is impressive for someone carrying round two stone in plaster at the moment. He looks between me and the girl at the counter. 'My sister,' he blurts quickly. 'This is my sister. Dee.'

The girl nods, making her fringe bounce. 'Hey. I'm Patti.' She has a small, but very sweet smile.

I nod back. 'I'm actually Delilah, Dee, most days. Dee. Our parents didn't really think through the names thing. Though you can't deny Juli—'

'Ha ha!' JP barks loudly. 'Anyway, sis. How was London? You look tired! Maybe go and have a sit-down and I'll see you in a bit?' His eyes are wide and I can see just a few beads of sweat at his hairline.

'Um, are you OK though? You haven't been overdoing it? I was a bit worried when I saw you weren't at home.'

He lifts his chin just a fraction. 'I'm totally fine getting about, thanks. Stan said I'm smashing it. And besides, I really wanted to talk to Patti about getting this artwork framed for the shop. More of an atmosphere, you know?'

I peer at the, um, artwork. It's two A3 Rothko prints, dog-eared and crumpled in places. I think they're the ones Mum and Dad gave JP when they changed their dining room from cream and red to cream and green. Nice, but hardly worth splashing cash on having them properly framed beyond the usual IKEA jobs. It looks like he's just grabbed any old thing to be framed. Patti seems just as doubtful, keeping them at arm's length and cordoned off by different wood samples, while fiddling with her bottom lip.

'I was just telling your brother that we can definitely frame them. If he's sure. It's my uncle's shop, so he'll actually do the framing. I'm just here for a bit of work experience before I head to a postgraduate art school, in Berlin.'

Yup. Knew it. She's super cool. Never mind too cool for school, she's too cool for a regular university – she's going to one in Berlin.

Patti gives me a look beneath lashes slicked in electric-blue mascara which seems to signal, Is he for real?

Time for some careful diplomacy. I'm a part-owner of the shop, after all, I should give JP a steer if he's about to make it look like a dentist's waiting area. 'This is definitely one way to go,' I start, 'but I wonder if there's something that would fit the place that bit better? Reflect what you do there, you know. Oh!' I poke JP on the shoulder and he winces. 'Those vintage patterns you found in the attic, that got you into knitting! They would look awesome.'

Patti crinkles her very delicate eyebrows. 'You knit? You run the haberdashery?'

JP sucks in a deep breath. 'Yup. That's me.'

She waits a beat, then says, 'Cool.'

He nods. 'Yeah.'

She flicks her fringe out of her eyes. 'So if you want to take these samples back with you, compare them to the patterns and your shop interior, let us know what you think. And we can get busy. OK?'

JP's cheeks colour. 'I don't suppose you'd carry them round, would you? I'm a bit... er...' he smiles his charming little-boy smile, 'incapacitated right now. Fell off a ladder. An eight-foot ladder.' His eyes slide to mine and I get the distinct impression that I shouldn't add any more accurate detail to that story.

'Pfft. I'll do that,' I grab the sticks of varnished and painted wood. 'I'm sure Patti can't just leave the shop on its own. Don't be a pain, JP.' I roll my eyes apologetically at her.

She smiles again. 'Well, it's not like anyone could make off with much. Unless they crave Plexiglas. Let me know what you decide. Bye, guys.'

–

I can tell from the way my brother huffs his way through both shop doors and kicks his boots off against the *Welcome Knitters: Come Yarn, Come All* welcome mat with two more huffs that he's far from happy. I think if he could dramatically drop into the wooden chair behind the till and cross his arms, he would. As it is, he settles for accidentally knocking a revolving display of embroidery threads, so that it spins in waves of rainbow colours. I follow him to the counter.

'What? I'm sorry I didn't like your prints but they are a bit,' I drop to a whisper, 'middle-aged. Dude, Dad only chose them in the nineties because they went with his favourite shade of magnolia.'

But as I say this, I look around me and clock just the same dull shade of beige on the shop walls too. It's not the first thing you notice when you enter Blackthorn Haberdashery: it's a tiny shop but filled with an incredible volume of craft stuff. There are twenty kinds of scissors, to start with: from tiny to crinkly to lethal-looking. Along both walls, up to chin height, are wooden pigeonholes stuffed with balls of wool, tubes of buttons, bolts of cotton fabrics and lots of colourful hardback books called things like *Knit Me a New One* and *What a Stitch*. The display units that run like two stripes up to the till have zips of five lengths, cottons in every shade (plus metallic ones that I can't believe actually hold anything together), tailor's chalk, pins, needles, sewing machine feet and then – bewilderingly – shoulder pads. I defy anyone with any kind of haberdashery conundrum not to come in here and have all their wishes made true. It is a little cluttered, if I'm going to be picky, and the decoration could definitely do with a spruce but I can tell JP is hardly in the mood to hear that now. I think he might actually be pouting. I haven't seen him do that since the dog peed on his Tracy Island.

'Argh! Dee!' By the look of JP's grimace, I'd be getting a dead arm now if he had any sort of flexibility. 'I didn't care about the stupid prints, I just…'

'What?!'

'Isn't it obvious? Cute art girl. Brother in the prime of life. Ringing any bells? Or do you need it in an email?'

Oh. Ohhh. 'God, sorry! That was you chatting her up, then?'

He puffs and fidgets on the spot. 'Yes. No. Not exactly. I was warming up to it. I was finding an "in".'

I lean forward on my elbows, careful not to scatter a pile of invoices. 'Dude, Rothko prints are probably not your "in" with a super-cool art girl. If you want my advice…'

JP scowls. 'I don't. But what is it?'

I walk around to him and gently lay my hand on his shoulders. 'I don't want to sound weird, being your sister, but to an art girl *you* are hot property. Just as you are. You are a bloke that crafts. You make stuff. You know the value of creating things. Most guys she meets probably scoff at an art installation made of Kinder Eggs but you could stare at that kind of thing all day, genuinely into it.'

'Unless I got peckish.'

I wag a finger. 'Stay with me here. Just be yourself. Get her round to the shop, not just as a packhorse, but the next time you're running a class. Let her see you in your element. And that way you can tell whether she's really for you or not. Let's face it, she's got to be down with the yarn if she's going to be a keeper, right?'

'Hmm,' JP narrows his eyes, 'and you *won't* interfere if I do invite her over? You nearly said my bloody name over there just now.'

I clamp my hands over my mouth. 'Shit. Sorry. Won't do it again, Guides' Honour. I will leave you to make your best moves in peace.'

He eyes his arms. 'Can't really make any sort of move like this, so it's going to be a right old slow seduction.'

'JP! I don't want to think about you groping anyone, thanks.'

He tsks. 'I would never *grope*! But knitting doesn't deplete your testosterone – I still actually fancy girls. Now, if only there was a fancy watch shop round here where we could pick you up some loaded suit who can talk synergy all day, then we'd both have found our perfect types. Your hormones could do with a bit of a reboot, Dee. The last time I heard you speak to a guy you fancied on the phone it was to confirm what time you were headed to the sixth form leavers' ball.'

I flop down on the saggy sofa. 'Well, if you believe the rumours going round Canary Wharf, I can't keep my hands to myself these days.'

'Eh?'

I feel to check my bank card is still in my pocket. 'Don't suppose you fancy a late lunch consisting of Gordon's gin, do you?'

Chapter 8

'Fuck a duck.' JP gulps down some more of his double through a long straw.

'I feel like Mum is halfway round the world, shuddering but not knowing why. But in this case, the language is pretty spot on.' I chase the ice cubes round my glass with my green plastic stirrer. Three gins in and I'm not feeling cheered. Maybe I should have asked for a piña colada but that might have thrown Big Brian behind the bar.

We're pretty much the only people in the Witch's Nose at three p.m. on a Tuesday, apart from Brian and someone's grandpa doing a sudoku over a pint of stout in the corner. It's the kind of dark, fusty pub that never seems to change and that kind of permanence is just what I need right now. Even if the chintzy carpets are a bit mossy in places.

'So what will you do? I mean, you know you can stay with me as long as you want. And not just because I need you to butter my toast. Stan's doing his best to teach me to do these things with my casts on, but any chance to be spoilt and I'm happy.'

This at least makes me half-smile. 'Thanks. I think, to be safe, I'd better find a tenant for my flat to cover the mortgage. I might need to see a career consultant. If my name really is as muddy as a rugby pitch in consultancy then I might need to… branch out. And careers consultants are not cheap. So I've got to watch my bank balance and think of a way to bring in some cash flow until I'm back on course. And to keep busy, to stop myself going on a murderous rampage with those super-sharp dressmaking scissors you sell.' I let out a long, slow, Pilates breath.

'I can deflect Mum for you, save her worrying too much and you going even more murderous with her ten missed calls a day. You've never been so lucky to have her in a whole other time zone.'

I clink my glass against his. 'Cheers to that. God love her, but I'm grateful for the headspace right now. And if she does manage to get me on the phone I'll just change the subject to your poor broken bones.'

JP licks his lips and nods. 'Throw me under the bus. I can take it.'

I turn my phone over from where JP relegated it to when we got here: hiding upside down, under a Smelly Goat beer mat. Just what I expected: five missed calls. But when I scroll through the list, only one is from Mum: there's one from Clive and three from Ben. Well, that is just a flaming cheek. I open up his contact and quickly press *Block*. I'm not giving him the chance to gloat over 4G any time soon. But sweet of Clive to call – I must drop him an email tomorrow and reassure him I'm fine and all these rumours are a load of old toss. Maybe I can persuade him to drop a little salt in Ben's tea, the next time he's passing…

But I'm not falling down that jagged rabbit hole again today – being angry just slows me down. It doesn't butter any parsnips. It definitely doesn't pay any bills. I need distraction. I need movement.

I shake my head and hide the phone back under its beer-mat blanket. 'Right, let's talk about something else. Quick. Keep me distracted, little brother. I need my brain to be deep into something productive.'

JP drops the straw from between his teeth. He's getting quite good at managing to do things with two arms out of action. His teeth are like a Swiss Army Knife these days, picking things up, tearing open post, and he's perfected pushing down a door handle with his behind, which is a sight to see.

'Well, since you mentioned inviting Patti to one of my classes at the shop, I was going to ask... would you help me run one? I can still do all the talking, but I need a willing puppet to demonstrate things. And, weirdly, you being useless at anything crafty is a real bonus. Because some of my class feedback is that as a pro I make it look easy, and go too fast. You'll do well if you complete a row without creating twenty new super-tight stitches and turning a scarf into a doorstop. Ha!'

I kick him under the table. 'Nice way to ask for a favour, but yes. OK. Whatever you and the shop need. I'm there. Can you handle another drink?'

He shrugs. 'Go on, then. Call it ongoing pain management.'

'And I don't have work tomorrow.' I try to say this with a sardonic air but instead it comes out a bit mopey. Maybe three G & Ts was not my best call. 'Hey, did you look at that email I starred for you, by the way? Before I got... before I left work, I spotted that email from MCJ.'

'I've had too much booze to try and pretend I know what you're talking about. Sorry.'

I flick him on the forehead. 'You should wake up every day overjoyed you have a sister as amazing as me to keep you on the straight and narrow. It's an investment firm and they reached out to you because it seems they're interested in making some small-scale investments in start-up craft companies. I know you've been going a few years, and you know what you're doing, but a jolt of cash could help you take things to the next level, expand a little.'

JP frowns. 'I don't know. That's not my world, Dee – it's all gibberish to me. That's your gaff.'

'I'm going to take that as a compliment. Well, shall I talk to them? Another distraction technique for me, anyway.'

'Yeah, whatever you think. Sounds good. You're the money. Now, how do you feel about feeding me dry-roast peanuts in a public place?'

-

I might be the first person to ever draft a business plan on a Costco bench.

But something I was taught on a 'Disrupt and Conquer' working methods course in my *old* job was that if you want to break out of old, familiar patterns of thought, you need to break out of old, familiar places and practices. So Costco it is. And they sell a decent hot dog in their cafe, it turns out.

I had to stock up on loo roll, teabags and Bourbon biscuits ahead of this class I'll be running with JP. Who am I kidding? I'm running it as much as a poor little guinea pig in a lab runs the trial of lipstick it's wearing. But nevertheless, I'm going to do my bit – for the good of JP, for the good of the shop. So that means making sure we're ready to host eight keen but green crafters to learn how to knit a hat, keeping them fed, watered and cosy; hopefully these classes will soon run regularly enough to eat through all our biscuits and plump up the bank balance. There was a really quick response when JP posted a new blog after we got back from the pub a few days ago: he slurred out the words and I typed them up, not quite as wobbly as him but still feeling a nice level of numbness from plenty of gin. We also put a sign in the window with a big neon-pink frame, which certainly caught the eye. JP harrumphed that it was too girly but I told him to get real and respect his key demographic. Yes, some men do craft but the audience is 99.99 per cent female and I'll eat my hat if another man turns up on the night.

I ran through a stock check at the haberdashery, under JP's careful eye, and pinged over a quick order to the supplier for the bits and pieces we needed: some 5-millimetre knitting needles and tapestry needles for sewing up after. I actually didn't realize hats needed sewing up; I thought they were just made as one whole thing. JP scoffed at this and said, 'You have years of work ahead of you before you're ready for knitting "In the Round",' but I was too busy digging out all his carrier bags from under the sink to ask what that entailed. Sounded like a terrible knit-to-the-death joust with giant needles slung on your shoulder. And God knows I can do enough damage with normal knitting as it is.

Mags very kindly drove me over to Costco this morning in her reliable little Skoda and since we've pushed the huge trolley round together and paid for our bulky bargains, she's mooched off to inspect their range of potted plants while I whipped out the old iPad and started to put together a flow chart.

After JP gave me the nod to get in touch with MCJ the other night, I replied to them, filling them in on how my brother and I were joint owners and, though I was the silent partner, I certainly knew my way around a profit-and-loss account and so any investment discussions could come through me. I want to plant my flag very firmly at their feet – I know business. Don't think I'm a woolly wool fan that you can bamboozle into terrible terms. They came back almost immediately with renewed enthusiasm, so I'm impressed by how they operate. The woman emailing, Lorraine, asked if I could share our original business plan plus any updated headline stats on the shop, its retail website and the tied-in blog. Fair enough. They want to see what they'd be putting their money behind.

The only dropped stitch in the whole enterprise (JP is having a worrying influence on my turn of phrase already) is that our original business plan was a walk around the park near Mum and Dad's that JP and I took after one of Dad's spectacularly huge Sunday lunches. We never wrote anything down, per se. JP was coming back to himself after his breakdown at that time, really enjoying his new crafty pursuits but floundering in the face of an uncertain future. He didn't want to stay on Mum and Dad's sofa bed for ever, but he didn't like the idea of moving in with me because that meant a hectic city life again. He knew he wanted to keep exploring these new passions but he also knew he couldn't shut out 'real life' for the rest of time: he needed to earn a living. As he spoke into the foggy, chilly air that day, I remembered a TED talk I'd had playing through my headphones on the treadmill once: if you're at a career crossroads, if you don't see the way forward, start with the things you love in your life. Build a career from those pointers. Love rugby? Ring up the national Rugby Federation, see if they have any marketing openings. Used to be a big tap dancer as a kid? Even stage schools need finance officers. Surround yourself with what you love. It might not make you a pile, but the happiness that follows is priceless. When I'd heard that talk, I'd shrugged it off as I was already in a career that satisfied me, but back then seeing JP wring his hands and chew on the ties from his hoodie, I saw that we had to create a new path for him, starting with what he loved.

'If you could paint the scene of your perfect day job, crazy as you like, what would that look like?' I'd asked him.

'Being surrounded, like wall to wall, with amazing yarns. Maybe even learning how to dye my own? And being with other people who like the same stuff as me, who get me. Not an office. But lots of tea still. That's essential. It wouldn't matter if I was paid much, really.'

When we got back to our parents' and stamped the mud off our boots at the back under Mum's scrutiny, I launched into a plan over walnut cake and instant coffee: I'd put up the money if JP, Mum and Dad could pool their know-how to get an amazing haberdashery up and running. Mum and Dad might have had to fold their own business years ago but they still knew everything about how to find premises, organize the running of a shop and, crucially, make accurate change. That was as far as our plan went back then and the rest of it grew organically, with plenty of trial and error but luckily avoiding any major disasters or acts of God. Unless you count JP's falling off a ladder wrapped in chintzy bunting as a sign from Above that my brother needs to get out more.

I decided to call on Mum and Dad to email through a rough idea of what we spent to start with, any mission statements they may have scribbled on the back of a cardigan pattern, and the rest we can fudge with jargon. This is my 'gaff', as JP pointed out the other day. But the real fun for me is this headline document. I told Lorraine I'd get something over to her in a fortnight, once I'd had time to review data, but what she doesn't know is that I could write a kick-ass document standing in the Costco queue to pay for the 2 kilogram gross of Premium Chocolate Flavour Bourbon Biscuits. I need two weeks to just subtly polish the stats themselves a bit...

I want JP's hard work to be shown to its full advantage when these investors appraise him so they can see he's someone to really get behind. With a solid investment, he could be set for the next few years. At the rate I'm going, I won't be able to stand him another big cheque any time soon. And it *is* a great business, it's just still in that chrysalis stage that any relatively new company is in: about to break out into the big time and show its beautiful self, but on the edge of something new and daunting. Plus, it's both the perfect distraction for me and an ideal way to keep my business and consulting skills sharp, all the way out in the Shires. I can feel a trusty tingle of energy flow down into my fingers as I type, edit, annotate. This is going to be *good*.

There are a few blocks in my flow chart: digital presence; bricks and mortar retail space; brand strength. Digitally, JP is already streets ahead of most other businesses like his because he has a well-followed blog and uses his genuine passion to reach people online. It's a brilliant way to forge customer loyalty. But the skin of the blog and the shop's site need a refresh; the design feels a bit tired and amateurish if I'm being blunt. Which in this case it's my job to be. I'm sure I have a contact who could do this for me on the cheap, to expand their portfolio. I also need to make sure JP is planning his posts, so they're regular and don't repeat themselves. I'll map them out on the nudie knitting calendar if I have to. Pulling knitting and sewing enthusiasts in via JP's blog is great, but they need an easy digital journey over to the shop section so they can click away and add lots of lovely crafty must-haves to their cart. I unpacked a boxful of pom-pom makers the other day. JP reassured me they're amazing fun and people buy them in all sizes to add to their stash, but the odd plastic curves looked like they could just as likely be sold by JVC to peel eggs, so I'm staying out of product selection myself. JP's been reluctant to get on to Instagram so far, claiming it's all about avocados and perfect butts, but the number of users doesn't lie – the future is Insta. I'll get him on there and his account synced up with his other social media accounts for the shop. If I can get his Follows and Likes boosted in the next two weeks, not to mention the click-through rates of purchases in the online shop, it's going to make him seem all that more appealing to MCJ.

Now, my plans for the physical shop itself have less to do with my day job and more to having good taste. I love my brother, always have, always will, but interiors are not his thing. The shop has everything a craft nerd could dream of – but can they find it in all the clutter? And when you're persuading people to make a non-essential purchase in a tough economic climate, the whole shopping experience should feel inviting, like a treat, something special they deserve to give themselves. The stuffed-full look of the shop at the moment can be overwhelming to newbies (I know from experience) and the bad lighting along with the dingy magnolia walls doesn't exactly shout 'boutique'. But that's nothing some studious rearranging and a trip to B&Q can't solve. Plus, with JP's arms out of action, he can't stop me introducing a new organizational system, even if he wants to! I'm going to go through his ordering system: see what products turn over most quickly and which are slow to shift. Those slow sellers will get a more prominent spot in the new layout. With a lick of vibrant paint – maybe a cool vintage turquoise – a few scented candles and those original 1950s knitting patterns framed artfully around the place, the shop will feel like a destination, rather than just a storage shed. And it will make for a much more relaxed atmosphere during the classes. When people are relaxed, they shop. And higher takings through the shop over the next few weeks are going to look great in my headline stats presentation to Lorraine.

I'm not going to share this whole plan with JP, not exactly as I'm writing it, anyhow, as a phrase like 'brand strength' will send him into a spasm of fake gagging noises. But it isn't just wanky business jargon – JP is not making the most of his brand, and that's bad business sense. He's a young guy who knits. That's a better USP than I've seen in a long time, and my brother could be doing so much more with it. The blog name – *About a (Knitting) Boy* – is catchy and fun, and I think JP just needs a bit more of a nudge to put himself front and centre. He does vlog and it's always from the heart, so he has some great subscriber numbers on YouTube, but he could be pushing himself more as the face of the business. He's a single and (although it pains me to say it) attractive guy, with a talent most ladies would find heart-melting. He could do a lot for the reputation of knitting, if he just stepped into the limelight. So I'm going to train that spotlight on him in the next few weeks, and he'll just *have* to get ready for his close-up. I know what his potential is, even if he doesn't.

'That all looks rather flash.' Mags smiles down at me, a wilting begonia tucked under each arm.

'Thanks, Auntie. Nearly done. Can I get you a coffee?'

She shakes her head, getting the voluminous sky-blue scarf wound around and around her neck caught up in the flower heads. 'You keep at it, I'll get one. No night nurse tonight for mum so I will have to be alert, should Extra Granny need me!' Her smile dips a little. 'Oh. I forget you haven't called her that in ages.'

'She'll always be our Extra Granny,' I smile. 'I can come one night, you know. We could swap charges now and then? You yourself always say a change is as good as a rest.'

Maggie rolls her eyes, the twinkle back once again. 'No, no. You have your busy work to do, and I know all of Mum's ways by now. She'd miss me, I think. So what is all this you're doing?' She nods down at my screen. 'Looks swish. Is it part of a job application? A new role, Delilah?'

I look down at my plans. 'You could say that, Mags. You could say that.'

Chapter 9

A circle of chairs is one of those odd things in life that can have two opposing meanings at the same time. On one hand, it's the sign of social togetherness and ease and unity; on the other hand, it's the sign of social togetherness and anxiety and awkward coughing. But love it or hate it, a circle of chairs is what we have smack bang in the middle of Blackthorn Haberdashery tonight. Tonight is the night of the class and I've been busy all afternoon getting things just so. I've hefted the display units to one side to make room, but rotated them so that products related to tonight's projects are still reachable. The tape measures in a range of jazzy prints and with funny animal-shaped cases are my favourite at the moment, I think because they remind me of the *Mary Poppins* film, which I loved so much when I was little. If she had her tape measure on me tonight, my height would probably read, *Delilah Blackthorn: laughs in the face of adversity, but is strangely intimidated by knitting enthusiasts.* Because, weirdly, I am. I'm not nervous about giving presentations to company CEOs or talks to lecture halls full of MBA students. But I have got the right collywobbles about eight strangers staring me in the face while I try to clumsily knit one and purl the other. I could barely force down my second Jaffa Cake with tea this afternoon. Maggie double-checked the expiration date on the packet, she was that thrown by my lack of appetite as we packed up Internet orders together.

I just feel… out of sorts. Out of my depth. Out of place. I suppose, when I'm in a public speaking role in my professional life, I know just what's required of me. Like any good consultant I know my client's needs and I address them. But what do these beginner knitters need? Not an economics graduate who can speak some light Swedish but who knits as though she's angry with the wool. Still, I can make them tea and hide behind the kettle if I get flustered.

'Tea monitor reporting for duty!' Maggie salutes as she shuffles her boots on the welcome mat. Oh, poo. There goes my alibi. 'I have the night off,' she wiggles her head, 'so I thought I'd come back and help out with tonight. Stick my oar in!' Her tinkling laugh fills the shops. 'I'm actually not a bad knitter myself,' she says quietly, out of the corner of her mouth, so JP doesn't hear from his position in the living room.

'Thank you,' I breathe, clasping my hands in front of me. 'It's still all Greek to me.'

'Mags!' JP calls from the back. 'Sorry to be a berk but can you put my bobble hat on for me? It's really hard without thumbs!'

–

Most of our students are now sitting in the circle, half staring down into their laps and half happily rubbing their knees while making idle chit-chat, proving the circle has two sides. We have three teens, bubbly friends with a stack of woven bracelets each at their wrists, clearly loving the crafty trend of the moment. Two forty-something women who look like they could be sisters and are both poring over a phone screen, whispering and giggling. I catch sight of a celeb nip slip on the display – maybe they're here not so much for a craft trend as a cheeky night away from mum duty, which is fair enough. Two empty seats to fill and we can kick off. Why do I feel like I'm about to sit finals again?

I rearrange the biscuits on their plate for the fifteenth time. I tighten my ponytail. A part of me is enjoying not having to worry about proper blow dries while I'm temporarily away from office life, just strapping my hair up in a hair tie and forgetting about it. And I can definitely forget about getting my highlights redone for the foreseeable future, not until I have a new wage packet on the way. One trip to Benito's salon in the next town, would take out about a month's worth of groceries.

'Hello, everyone! I'm JP, great to meet you.' JP crab-walks sideways through the back entrance, into the shop. The casts make his frame wider than usual and the narrow doorways of this old building aren't cooperating. He's got a neon-green bobble hat pulled down at a funny angle and a smile bright enough to power the Blackpool Tower. This is JP's happy place. He takes everyone in. 'Have we all got tea before we kick off?'

I see the teens and mums take in his two broken arms with wide eyes and open mouths. JP laughs it off. 'Slight mishap, er, rescuing a cat from a tree. It was a heavy cat. But I have my trusty assistants tonight, my sister Dee is here, for starters, to supply all the drinks and help you through our project. Speaking of which…' He dances his chin up and down, to make the bobble wobble. It does the job of changing the subject. 'This is what we'll be making. Your very own bobble hat!' The girls gasp in awe, one even gives a squeal. 'I went for Incredible Hulk green, but you are free to pick your own colour. What you want to do is grab a ball you like from that pigeonhole over there.' He nods vaguely so I help out by pointing at the right cubby. 'You want it to say Chunky Feel, Extra Thick on the label.'

The two older ladies explode into laughter behind their hands, as the teen gang rush to pore over the yarns. We have inky blues, hot fiesta pinks, sunset yellows and some charcoal grey which I'm eyeing for myself. I'm hoping a neutral, less attention-grabbing colour like that might be more forgiving of the bad knit job I'm about to perform. For an audience. Christ.

JP supervises the yarn rummaging and the laughter is replaced by a burble of happy nattering and murmurs of approval as wools are held up to the light or against coats to check for clashes. With this backdrop of contented activity, the shop door opens with a whoosh of head-clearing fresh air.

'Room for a little one?' Becky is pink-cheeked and shiny-eyed, dressed in a big khaki anorak with a furry hood.

'Hey! This is a nice surprise. But what about Chester?' I quickly catch myself up for blurting out something that sounds so judgey. I sound like I'm accusing her of abandoning her baby. 'Sorry, no, I meant...'

But as she unzips her coat I can see exactly where Chester is: wrapped up tight in a stretchy bandage-type sling on Becky's front, happily snoozing and occasionally snoring for good measure.

'He's been such a peach, honestly, just feeding and sleeping, feeding and sleeping. So Matt said, why not get out? I can feed him anywhere and he's happy sleeping on me. I love it too, if I'm honest.' She rubs one finger along the gingery fuzz covering the top of his head and then kisses him. All our students make sighing noises from the corner. Clearly a cute baby as shop dressing is an added bonus to the crafting experience. I'm definitely not complaining: a chance to see Becky and her boy, plus an ally in the wings should I get things hideously wrong and end up with some demented sock instead of a hat.

I take her coat to the hat stand. 'If you want to go into the flat to feed him or change him, just go through, whenever you need to. Mags's hanging about back there. I don't know if you remember her, but she's our unofficial aunt and she's lovely. She'll show you where everything is.' I put my arm around her shoulders. 'I am seriously happy to see you!'

She leans her head down onto my shoulder just briefly. 'Me too. Ever since you brought us those hats I have been dying to understand how they come together, so I could make one myself. Speaking of which, come here, you!' Her hazel eyes fill with tears and she approaches JP. Their hug is like a complex origami challenge: folding around his plaster casts and not squishing Chester, nestled by her cleavage. But some kind of hug is eventually achieved and as Becky wipes away a few tears I can see JP is blinking back some of his own.

'Thank you, thank you,' she says into his jumper.

'S'nothing, yeah, you're welcome,' he mumbles quietly.

She leans back and looks up at him. 'It's not nothing! It's amazing!' Becky turns around to the huddle of students at the pigeonholes. They are drinking in this emotional scene, clearly delighted to get biscuits *and* a show in their ticket price. 'This guy got his knitting buddies to make little hats for my boy, when he was born prematurely.

It's… it's so brilliant because it's vitally important premmie babies stay very warm at all times and it can be hard to find things small enough to fit properly. And besides that, in a really scary time, people were thinking of us. And that means the world.' She sniffs. 'Come on, Becks, hold it together. No crying on your first night out!' she admonishes herself with a sardonic smile.

'That is amazing,' one of the crafty teens says, a girl with long jet-black hair and perfect cat-flick eyeliner. 'Can we make little baby hats? Tonight, I mean, instead of grown-up ones? Then we could give them to you.' She smiles at Becky just as Chester lets out a deep snuffle of a snore. More and more I'm understanding why JP has found himself so at peace in this craft community: people create and share, just for the fun of it. There's no competition, no point-scoring, no ulterior motives. It's like a cult without the bad bits and with added frequent tea breaks.

Becky blushes and shakes her head, causing Chester's to wobble just a fraction. 'Don't, you're going to make me go again. JP and Dee have already given me seven hats – Chester has got one for every day of the week! Including a jazzy purple one for dress-down Fridays.' She sneaks another kiss onto his sweet little head. 'But if you did want to make one, I kept in touch with two other mums from the neonatal ward. I bet they'd love them!'

The teens clap like happy high-school seals and the two mum friends nod vigorously. 'Count us in,' one of them calls, pushing up the sleeves of her red polo-neck jumper, ready for crafty action.

JP clears his throat to find his teacher voice again. 'Well. Brilliant! In that case, let's move away from the Chunky yarns and down here to the Double Knitting, which is just right for finer things and baby stuff. We'll have to work off my sister's iPad for the pattern, if you don't mind, as I don't have a handout ready. But the good news is that these are possibly one of the quickest things to do – you can plunge straight in easily, and the feeling of satisfaction is immense!'

There's another minor eruption of laughter as the class move further into the shop to look at the finer yarns and I decide to keep my eye on the two mum friends. They are incorrigible.

I sidle over to JP, who is discreetly scratching his back on the corner of the counter. 'So, do you think Patti might come?'

He raises an eyebrow. 'I asked her, she said it sounded sweet. Which could mean any one of 10,000 things in the language of women, I've come to learn.' He lets out a low sigh. 'I kept a spot open for her tonight. So we'll see. If you're right and I've got to work my arty boy angle, then I really, really hope she comes. She's so *cool*. And I think I'm at that point where I want a proper relationship, you know? I want to meet the parents, share a starter, get a mortgage. All that stuff, do you know what I mean?' His blue eyes are very still as they catch mine.

'Um, I suppose. But that's great, bro. I hope she turns out to be the One. And how could she not fall for the hottest male crafter of the decade? If not the centu—'

Just then a flash of a black leather jacket against a brilliant white T-shirt catches my eye at the doorway. For a second I feel like I'm in that Levi's ad in the laundrette, the one that helped me through puberty. Pushing through the door is a guy with a lean figure and a jaw that looks like it could slice bread. He could be lost on his way to a casting call, his steely grey eyes moving around the shop as if looking for a street sign. The teens almost seem to synchronize their drooling.

'Can I help you, mate?' JP asks.

'Hi!' His smile is twinkly, lifting up on one side more than the other. Oh, boy. 'I'm here for the class?'

'Perfect.' JP forces the word out through teeth clamped shut. 'Come in and choose your wool. What's your skill level, can I ask?'

The model takes off his perfectly supple jacket and places it on the back of a chair. 'I'd say intermediate, warming up to good. But I'm self-taught, so I thought I'd come and get some expert guidance. I love your vlogs, mate. *About a (Knitting) Boy*, right? I totally get what you mean about doing something with your hands being so soothing, there's nothing that chills me out more.'

The mum mates look ready to explode as they each grab two red balls of wool and make googly eyes.

'Yeah, yeah.' JP nods and turns on the spot, to grumpily mouth at me, 'No way!'

Can you still say you have a USP if there's just one more person with those same qualities? You are still 99.99 per cent unique, really, amongst the general population. The bad news for JP right now is that in this room, 100 per cent of the men are exactly like him. He's about as unique as a Starbucks latte.

The door opens again and Patti slips in, her dip-dyed hair in two loose braids, giving her a perfectly dishevelled look against a faded Metallica T-shirt. 'Sorry I'm a bit late, I was getting a lesson on canvas stretching from my uncle.' She rolls her eyes. 'Where shall I sit?'

I pretty much leap on her, pulling her away from the hunk and towards the back of the shop. 'This way! Let's hang your coat up and get you a cup of tea.'

'Do you have any fresh mint?' Patti asks, hopeful.

'That sounds great. I'll have the same!' the hunk chips in.

Right. He's going to be a problem.

Chapter 10

'I am ridiculously proud of myself.' I hold my three rows of knitting up to the shop light, double-checking again that there aren't any rogue holes I've not spotted. I managed to cast on ten perfectly good stitches, on just my fourth go, in the class and then I knitted three rows of stocking stitch! JP was right, I was the perfect test case: once the others found out I was a total newbie, the floodgates of questions and queries opened, and JP fielded them all with a calm, confident manner. When we got on to decreasing, though, my head hurt and I had to quit while I was ahead, going to wash the cups up for a new tea round and slice up the coffee and carrot cakes. Mags had been busy in the flat during the class, I think putting away JP's clean underwear for him while he couldn't see, to save them both an awkward moment. I took her an extra big bit of cake for her efforts. I think we're all looking forward to JP regaining the full use of his arms and taking back control of his unmentionables. Four weeks to go.

It's just JP, Becky and me on the shop floor now, them 'supervising' while I put the chairs and display units back to their rightful places. The chairs fold up and live in the shed; the display units need a gentle push or else a show-ering of needle cases, pinking shears and snap fasteners will scatter everywhere – I've already learned at my cost. The class pupils said their goodbyes half an hour ago, floating out the door on a cloud of warm chatter and a puff of pride; all of them proudly clutching their half-finished hats, eager to get home and complete them. Hopefully they'll come good on the rest of the knitting and the sewing up (JP recommended they check out his vlog tutorial on the subject or pop back in for guidance), and send the hats on to Becky's mates. What was really sweet was that one of the teens circulated a sign-up sheet, torn from her diary, so everyone could swap numbers and keep track of their crafty efforts. Whether it was a nifty ploy to get the hunk's digits it's hard to say, but even if it was, I liked her chutzpah.

The leather-jacketed stud didn't prove to be as much of a distraction to Patti as I thought he might: it was like she was blind to his perfect hotness, and kept her eyes trained instead on JP's slightly ill-fitting T-shirt and the way he'd close his eyes when getting excited about teaching the next step of the process. She managed a swift bit of knitting, which makes me think she's had some childhood training from a granny that she's keeping on the down-low. The hunk himself – Marcus – was fairly confident but easily distracted by questions from the rest of the class: 'Are you a model?'; 'Does your girlfriend knit too?'; 'Do you want a lift home?'. After that last one, the mum who asked the question got a slap on the arm from her mate who whispered, 'Married! Remember?' into her ear. I think he's quite used to the attention and thrives on it.

Once I stepped back from guinea-pig duties and serving snacks, I also got busy taking some pictures of the class. Something to help spruce up the site and a nice visual to drop into my presentation to MCJ, showing the diverse nature of the business: retail, online and events.

At Blackthorn Haberdashery, we've got it all… I'm still mulling over a good branding line as I set the shop back to rights and fish out JP's broom for a quick sweep.

'Your hobbies all sewn up… hmm. Cheesy, but might work.' I push the odds and ends of snipped yarns into one multicoloured pile.

'What are you muttering in there?' Becky has taken up a comfy pose on the sofa, Chester propped on loads of cushions on her lap as she feeds him. True to her word, he didn't let out a peep all evening, he just fed and slept, on repeat. She seems to read him instantly: feeding, burping, changing, singing just as he needs it, so he doesn't ever really have cause to get frustrated and reach police-siren levels. Becky is a natural at all this mum business. It's weird on one hand to see someone who you mostly associate with alcopops and watching *Titanic* at the cinema for the eighth time now become a parent and responsible for a whole other human being, but on the other hand it fits Becky so well and she seems so in her element that it makes perfect sense to me.

'Oh, um, nothing. Do you need anything in there?'

'I'm set, thanks. Still full of tea and cake. I should get out of your hair, though, it's nineish, I think.'

'Nah,' JP butts in, 'stay as long as you like. We're sick of each other by now. This is the most time we've spent under one roof since Eurocamp when we were kids. Though that was worse, because the roof was made of tarpaulin and there was no escaping Dee's sleep-talking.'

I swipe gently at his feet with the broom. 'I do not sleep-talk.'

'You do. You used to sing B*Witched songs. In a bad Irish accent.' Becky laughs. 'Well, your pain is my gain. I love having you back in town, Dee. All the other mums

I've met have these giant, full-term babies that make me feel self-conscious about Chester still being teeny weeny. And everyone else is at work— Oh God, sorry.'

I rest the broom against the wall. 'Don't worry, it's fine. I'm really happy to be here too. Otherwise I probably wouldn't have had the time to have seen Chester till his first year of school, let alone in his first month of life. I love working, I love what I do, but it's not exactly easy to fit a life around a 70-hour week.'

'Any nibbles at all on the interview front?' JP asks in a soft voice.

'Nope. But it's fine. I've found someone to rent my flat, so that's the mortgage covered for now. I'm on the waiting list for the most recommended career consultant. And while I'm working things out, I can help you with the shop, maybe see if we can get you a bit of investment, hmm?'

'And you're learning to knit,' Becky interjects.

'I will remember to add that to my CV,' I deadpan.

'I'm not sure I'm a natural knitter myself,' she goes on, as she walks back onto the shop floor with Chester now over her shoulder and a muslin cloth underneath his chin, rubbing gentle circles on his back. 'But I love having a goal in mind, to achieve. The thing about a newborn is that you don't get anything *done*. Your day is just a blur of feeds and poos. And a literal blur on the poo front – that stuff gets everywhere. Even six rows of stitches is an achievement to me. And if I can knit a hat to help another baby like Chessie, another mum like me, then that feels pretty great. Though they might only get it next Christmas, at my rate.'

JP smiles. 'The completion of a task is a big appeal to me too. A little feeling of control in a mad world. That's why I'm so fed up of being Mr Lego arms. I look like a Lego man, don't I?'

'You don't!' I reassure him emphatically. (He does.)

'Thing is, knitting a tiny hat is an evening's work, a nice pause in the middle of a bigger knit. All the serious knitters I know can do them with their eyes closed. You saw how quickly they came rolling in for Chester. It's a shame those other mums going through the same thing don't know anyone with a knitting blog to put the shout out for them.'

I take an escaped ball of ruby-red yarn back to its rightful pigeonhole, neatening the others there so they're also facing label out. 'That's why I want us to work on the site, make it more visible and appealing, so more people find you.'

'To knit baby hats for us?' JP asks.

'Yes, that and buy stuff. It's good for everyone.'

'Good for everyone,' he echoes, his voice tapering off into a dreamy whisper. He's cooking something up in that crafty brain of his. It was a look in his eyes like that which ended up with me getting a knitted phone case last Christmas. To be fair it was beautifully done and in my favourite cobalt blue.

'What?' Becky blinks, a micro-burp coming from Chester as she finishes winding.

JP starts to nod to himself. 'We put the knitters in touch with the mums. Those who have the skill linked up with those that have the need. If it only took a week to get Chester kitted out with hats, imagine how many other babies we could help.'

Becky nods. 'A nurse told me there are something like 60,000 babies born prematurely in the UK every year. I just had no idea of the scale of it, how many people are affected. One day on the ward, I was trying to distract myself and I worked out that that's 165 every single *day*.'

I put my arm around her shoulder and squeeze her in tight just briefly.

JP joins us and leans his head on the top of Becks's. 'So many people, and they need a bit of help, even if it's just a tiny thing. And you saw how the class reacted – other people love to be involved, people genuinely love to do a good deed. They're paying it forward. And we could do it all through my website!'

There's a flash of excitement in my brother's eyes as he paces up and down the empty shop. 'It could be a collective, a craft collective. Like the pink hats thousands of women knitted to march against Trump, you know? That movement actually saw a huge spike in the sale of hot-pink yarns. I was sold out for a week.'

'Keep talking, I'm listening.' I hop up onto the counter and lean forwards on my elbows to give him my full attention.

'We can supply the pattern, free of charge. Maybe even patterns for tiny cardigans and socks too. And then advise on the best yarns to use for people who are still beginners.'

Becky starts swaying side to side – either she needs a wee or she's getting Chester off to sleep. 'That's important, actually, the kind of wool you use. Because you need to be able to chuck the lot in the washing machine. There's no spare time, or sanity come to think of it, to handwash when you have a tiny baby.'

JP points at her, his fingers in a gun shape. 'Yes! Brilliant. That's the kind of insight we need to do it properly. Becks, you are officially our Mum Ambassador.' She dips into a jokey curtsey, mid-sway, but JP's already back in his train of thought and on to the next stage. 'A cotton-mix yarn would work nicely, something with a subtle acrylic mix. Just not that foul Wow Wools stuff from the States – it goes all scratchy and baggy after one wash, so I've stopped stocking it now. Too many customer complaints.' He awkwardly rubs his chin with a heavy arm. 'We could aim for 165 hats – only a day's worth of premmie babies, but it's a start. I could do a video tutorial for new knitters to explain about yarn choice, recommend a few, and in case they get stuck do a demo... well, not straight away, but eventually.' He looks mournfully at his two rigid fore-arms.

'And 165, that's not... a bit ambitious?' I ask, cautiously.

'If we think little, we do little, sis.'

'OK, you're starting to sound like a management training day now, but I'm with you. It's a shame we can't hold one ginormous class, really,' I say, thinking how great for the cash flow it would be if you could squeeze 100 people in here at once and up-sell them all a ball of wool, some fancy bamboo needles and a Liberty knitting needle case.

JP spins on the spot to look at me. 'But who says you can't?!' he says in one breath. 'Quick! Get my laptop! Sis, we're vlogging.'

–

It turns out, if I can't get my career up and running again (the waiting list I'm on for the fancy consultant is seven weeks long, so I'm uneasily treading water till then, seeing as I'm blacklisted by recruiters and old colleagues), I could make an entire shift and work as a make-up artist or hairdresser. Or film set designer or lighting expert. Because just filming a ten-minute vlog with JP involves me checking over his face for any spots or bits of tooth-paste, fluffing up his hair *just so* at the front and smoothing it down at the back with some styling gum I think he's had since his gap year. I then have to check the 'back of shot' to make sure we haven't left any old coffee cups or spare socks hanging about in the living room and angle three different desk lamps with mega-strong bulbs towards JP's chair, so he's well lit. All this for him to gabble on in front of his iPhone.

I never knew how vain my brother really was. It's pretty shocking. I know he's kind of helpless right now and he can only do these things if I chip in, otherwise he'd want his privacy and fair enough. But that doesn't mean I'm not storing this away to wind him up with at some future time when he has four functioning limbs and isn't such a sad little puppy. He actually said, when I queried the need for hair fluffing, 'My subscribers expect me to look a certain way.' Bieber, eat your heart out.

I stand back, having clipped the iPhone into JP's rickety tripod. When I get back to earning, I'm buying him a proper one, and a light box. If he loves this, he should do it properly. But for now my role is to stand silently and make sure the stand for the phone doesn't keel over mid-chat.

JP nods and finds a big grin. 'GUYS!' he shouts, making me jump out of my trainers. 'Big news, super big. So, remember how I said I wouldn't be at CraftCon, because of these fellas?' He winks down at his casts. 'Well, sod it. I'll be there and I want to see you, all of you, because I'm planning something BIG and I need you all to be part of it. So, check out the description box for my stand number and swing by and say hello. Milton Keynes, make the trek – it'll be worth it. Don't forget to book your tickets! I'll be there with stuff you can buy from my shop as well as some of my favourite things I've made over the years, just to show off a bit really. Ten per cent discount for anyone wearing a pussy hat!' I'm waving my arms in a big cross and mouthing, 'No!' at the mention of a discount, but JP carries on regardless. 'Because it's time to knit again for a worthy cause, for something that matters.' His eyes glitter in the bright lights. 'We're going to make a difference. You game?' He smiles his charming schoolboy smile. It's really no surprise he has such high subscriber numbers amongst the loyal male craft contingent and hormonal teenage girls, not to mention randy grans.

For a moment he freezes, his beaming smile fixed and looking straight down into the camera. Before he mutters through his frozen lips, 'That's it,' and I realize he's waiting for me to hit the off switch.

'Cup of tea and then an editing session, yeah?' JP is so keyed up, I don't really want to admit that I was looking forward to a head-clearing run around the village, maybe down to the river and pounding it out for a good hour. Running is the only way I've found in the last few weeks to burn up the energy I would have usually poured into work and clients. And if I can knacker my muscles to the point of being jellyfish-like, it also helps me conk out at bedtime and not spend the night on the edge of the single mattress, thinking about overdraft limits and interview techniques. I can always run tomorrow. Besides, if this idea of JP's, whatever it might be, means he's going to put even more of himself into the site and the shop, that can only be a good thing for his happiness and his future stability. Stan has been keeping an eye on JP feeling busy and fulfilled enough while he's all bound up in plaster –

it's an important part of healing and bouncing back into regular life.

I flick on the kettle and plug the laptop in to charge at the little kitchen table. 'So what's CraftCon when it's at home? I'm guessing like Comic Con but without the dressing up?'

'Yes and no.' JP gets up, stretches his legs and arches his back. 'No cos play and no bright green wigs. But people do wear the stuff they've made, as a badge of honour. Mind you, in a big, stuffy arena with the heating on that's not always a wise move. I did some permanent damage to my Spider-Man pullover the first year I went. You never really feel the same again about clothes that you've really *sweated* into.' I'm not going to dwell on that image, though I do remember JP modelling a jumper he'd designed and knitted, in bold red and black, the Spider-Man logo central on his chest. It seemed to say, I'm a badass knitter, but also still a pubescent boy at heart. Take me or leave me. 'Anyway, yeah, it's a big craft convention with loads of stalls selling stuff, plus demonstrations going on all the time. I was going to cancel my stall, seeing as standing up for eight hours isn't much fun for me right now. Plus, I can't do the demo I was booked on, "Manly Makes with *About a (Knitting) Boy*". Shame. But, when you said about getting loads of knitters together for our collective it just popped into my head – it's where *all* the knitters are! If I want to reach them, that's where I start. And you can come along and lend me your hands, right?'

I start to feel a panicky thump in my heart at the idea of clumsily knitting under a spotlight in front of hundreds of old pros.

JP must see the perspiration beginning to ping onto my forehead. 'Not to do the demo, you plonker! To carry the boxes and stuff. Jesus, calm down, sis. You're not a knitting savant. You can't go from butchering stocking stitch to mastering Fair Isle in a few days. No, I'll just have to let them down on the demo front, which is a shame. But you're up for it, yeah?'

I pause, the bullet points of my Negotiating in Business training flashing before my eyes. Lesson number 3: when you have an advantage, use it. 'I will help you. If,' I point a finger at him, 'and only if you let me have free rein in re-merchandizing the shop?' I'm happy that JP wants to get out and take his project to loads of others – it can only be a good thing for him and the business – but I'm not forgetting the nuts and bolts of good economics, either. And I'm starting to get twitchy for a project; without a hundred emails to plough through and a target to hit, I have all this leftover energy. And there are only so many times JP's DVDs can take alphabetizing.

'Sure,' JP nods. 'Knock yourself out. Tidy away.'

'It's a bit more than tidying, but thanks.'

My phone buzzes on the arm of the sofa.

Clive

Hey, Delilah, just wondering how you're getting on? Are you still in London? I don't know if this is the right thing to do, but Ben has been asking me about you and how he can get in touch. I've been fobbing him off but just thought you should know. It would be great to catch up if you are still in town.

C

Good old Clive, still running the defensive for me, even when I'm no longer his boss. He knows me well: I'd rather put a cute kitten pic as my LinkedIn profile than have any sort of contact with Ben right now. He's not getting the chance to gloat to my face: he can gloat alone in his swanky Mayfair apartment or wherever it is that Daddy's money has set him up. I hope he chokes on his beluga caviar and spews on his old school tie.

But other than that, I'm totally over it.

Chapter 11

'Who buys this stuff?!' Becky is trying not to laugh out loud; Chester is asleep in the pram by the shop's front door. She has two cream shoulder pads held up by just her fingers, as if they are physically repulsive. 'Hasn't anyone told the craft world that shoulder pads went out with *Dallas*?'

I am kneeling in the middle of a mountain of stock, like a mini tornado has ripped through John Lewis and we are the only survivors. It may have been a mistake, in hindsight, to take everything down at once before starting to re-merchandize. But I'm committed now. And the pincushions actually make for a comfy knee pad of sorts.

'JP says there are just some boring essentials you have to stock, so people can mend things and trust that you carry everything. It builds loyalty. And I say fair enough, but it doesn't mean the boring stuff should get pride of place at the front of the store. The best stuff should go at eye height, then everything else can go in rows below, in order of how well they sell or how high the unit price.'

'So there's method to your madness, then?' Becky chucks the shoulder pads onto my pile, where they start a mini landslide of button cards and seam rippers.

I look at her over the heap of stock. 'Have you ever known me to do something without thinking it through?'

She chews her bottom lip. 'White flares with red pants underneath?'

'Oh God, I hate your perfect recall of the late '90s. In my defence, I was 14 and by the time I realized my pants were showing, I was already on the bus, halfway to the cinema. So I thought it was better to style it out.'

'Style is not what we called it.'

I couldn't help but laugh, the memory of persuading Dwayne Carver to lend me his plaid shirt to tie round my waist coming back to me. I'd had to give him half my pick 'n' mix.

'Are you sure this isn't boring, Becks? I could go and get you a magazine from the corner shop, you know. You, me and Chester in the shop must be boring for you. Not much of a day out, but I just really want to get this place in order as soon as I can.'

She waves her hands in front of her face. 'Tsk! This is absolutely perfect. The boy's asleep, I didn't have to make my own cup of tea, I'm not staring at my own walls but a whole other set of walls. If I have to change one more nappy with a backing track of *Judge Rinder* and someone saying they don't want to pay back the £12.50 they borrowed off their aunt… Well, it won't be pretty. I'm just happy you're back in town.' She pauses to take a sip of her tea. 'Not to get too hormonal, but I missed you, you know.'

I put down the ribbons I'm untangling. 'I've been a bit of a crap friend, haven't I?'

Becks scrunches up her lips and looks at the ceiling.

'You don't have to say it and you don't have to be polite and deny it. I should have been better at staying in touch; I got obsessed with studying and working and promotions and I forgot about the best people in my life.'

Her lips unscrunch into a small smile. ''S OK. I used to feel pretty hurt by it, when you went off to your fancy uni and no one heard from you again. But then I realized it wasn't just me you weren't in touch with, so I figured it wasn't massively personal. I was busy too and maybe I could have reached out a bit more. What matters, in the big scheme of life, is that right here, right now, we're together and we're mates. And you can make up those lost years with some laughs and the odd nappy change.'

My shoulders shiver. 'Um, could I choose making a prat out of myself a thousand times over a nappy change? I love Chester but just the colour of that stuff I've seen you wipe off him is terrifying. You know, we never wet the baby's head, did we? Seeing as I missed your baby shower, we should steal the drinking booze ritual from the men and get a bit tipsy in a nice gastro pub or something.'

Becky bites the inside of her cheek. 'Tipsy is not great a thing when you're making milk and you haven't slept for five weeks straight. Besides, I didn't have a baby shower. Chester turned up before I could have it! Cheeky monkey.'

I lay down a fistful of zips. 'Well, that won't do. We *have* to have one. I will organize it and pay for it, as part of my grand apology for being a dickhead of a friend. Who do you want to invite? Your work mates, new mum mates?'

'Nah. I'd rather keep it just us, maybe JP too. I like my friends and the other mums I've met too, but when I catch up with people and at the baby groups everyone keeps making sympathetic, floppy faces when they hear Chester was premature. I like being with you – you're just you, you're not floppy at me.'

I put the pads onto the shoulders of my hoodie and wrap three tape measures around my neck with a flourish,

108

like a feather boa. With a strawberry-shaped pincushion held on my head like a fascinator, I drawl, 'How dare you! Ah'm the floppiest woman in ahll of Dallas!'

Becky snorts, a little tea coming out of her nose. 'Still a better look than the white flares.'

'Oi!'

There's a knock at the back door. Maybe JP forgot his keys. He went out with Stan this morning, in order to build his confidence at being out and about in his condition. Apparently Stan's keen he doesn't rely too much on Mags or me, which is music to my ears at this stage. I'd rather scour his company accounts than scour another scrambled-eggs pan.

I dash to the door, flicking it open while at the same time turning back to Becky. 'Come in, you arse. I'm busy.'

'Really?'

The voice makes me stop dead in my tracks, just behind the shop counter. One shoulder pad slips off with the jerky movement and hits the tiled floor noiselessly.

It's not JP.

I snatch the tapes from my neck as I feel an angry heat rise from my stomach and into my cheeks. But they get tangled and I'm somehow garrotting myself. Ben steps forward in an instant to untie them but I bat his hands away.

'What…' I try and spit out, as air enters my lungs again, 'are… you doing… *here*?'

Ben's face is stony and serious. I've never seen him in jeans before, and it's weirdly unnerving. He's never seen me wearing sewing accessories before but I doubt the effect is anything similar.

He grimaces. 'I think we have a few things to sort out. Is now a good time?'

'I'll... er... get my muslin and go.' Becky leaps up and gets behind the pram, wheeling it out of the shop door even as I protest.

'No, no. You stay. Becks! Becks?'

I narrow my eyes at my former colleague; the only good thing about being fired was that I'd never see him again and I've been in the same space, with him, twice now in a week. Talk about insult to injury. 'How did you know where I was?'

He has the good sense to look sheepish and inspect his black trainers. 'Rumour went round that one of the interns was subletting your flat for a while. I bought him a few beers and he told me what he knew. A quick Web search of your name and the village, and I found this shop.' He peers around, taking in the landslide of items on the maroon carpet, the bare, faded walls in desperate need of a new paint job. Well, that *is* next on my To Do list. 'Not what I expected.'

That little barb is like a shovelful of coal in my furnace. 'I didn't expect to get unfairly canned by Devon, but we can't have everything we want in life, it seems. Now, is there something you actually wanted to achieve by coming here? If it's to revel in my downfall then you can piss off.' I say this very deliberately, maybe a little too loudly. All the while, Ben has his eyebrows knitted in my direction.

'Why do you always think I'm out to get you, Blackthorn? I'm here to help.'

Good manners would dictate that I offer Ben a hot beverage in my house but sod that – I can't even bear the idea of him sipping from one of JP's chipped *Reading Town FC* mugs. So Cheeky's Greasy Spoon it is. I march along the narrow path ahead of him and push open the steamed-up door.

Fenwild might be picture-postcard perfect in lots of ways – we get our fair share of coach tours taking a break from a trip out to the Cotswolds, and warming up their shutter speeds to capture the thatched roofs, hedgerows, and cute little doorways better suited to a Hobbit than a twenty-first-century person. But Cheeky's didn't get that memo: it's a concrete block of a building, built during some rushed development in the '70s. Along with the laundromat, it's a throwback to a bygone age, and I doubt the menu has changed much since they first opened. I doubt the vat of tartare sauce has ever been changed since, either. But it does a thick, syrupy hot chocolate and a wicked fry-up, and you are guaranteed to have it to yourself most days, unless the Costa in the next town over has a power cut all of a sudden.

I resist letting the door slam back into Ben's face. 'What do you want to drink?'

'Flat white.'

'Two white coffees, please, Bob.' I find a smile for Bob, the owner, at least. Cheeky's is a traditional kind of place – the only flat and white things come pressed around sandwich fillings.

Bob nods and clinks two mugs together as he grabs them off a high shelf. 'Right you are. Take a seat, pet.'

I sit down by the floor-to-ceiling window, the tiny table Ben has chosen meaning I have to sit opposite and face him. Or not. I'm looking out of the window, appearing to be fascinated by the post office van pulled up outside. Childish, yes, but effective. Tantrums on the supermarket floor are childish but they get you a Lion bar, right? Sometimes it's good to go low.

'Dee—'

I whip my head round and give him a warning look.

'Delilah. I haven't come all this way to have a row, OK? I don't know what you think of me—' I snort through my nose at this and turn back to examining the window. 'Right. I'm guessing it's not good, then. I'm guessing you think I had something to do with Devon… Devon firing you. But I didn't. And I've been trying to get in touch with you and tell you that.'

Bob places two mugs down in front of us. 'Anything else? Any food for you?'

I shake my head, enjoying the idea of how revolted Ben must feel at being asked to eat in a greasy spoon. He's all organic soda bread and organic jam, I bet. His public-schoolboy values must be in a right pickle.

'I could kill a sausage bap. Butter and brown sauce, please.' Ben rubs his stomach emphatically. 'Missed breakfast at the B and B.'

'Oh, up Hollyhock Lane? My mate Bev runs that. Say hello to her when you get back! And for you?'

My brain is too busy trying to de-code what's going on here and my stomach is too knotted with anger for me to make a decision on food, so I dumbly shake my head.

'Okey-doke.'

'So, as I was saying. This whole thing with Devon is just not right. And I don't know why it happened, why he chose to push you out, but a) I want you to know it's not me. And b) I want to help.'

I blink, the steam from my coffee tickling my nose.

'Hang on. Wait a second. Are you staying here, in Fenwild?'

Ben looks perplexed for a second, the corners of his eyes wrinkling slightly. 'Yes, of course.'

'But why come out here?'

He looks me straight in the eye. 'Because after that dressing-down in the revolving doors, the penny dropped that you thought I'd been part of the… decisions. Which I wasn't. The first inkling I got was hearing Clive talk about it in the canteen, then I checked your desk and sure enough you were gone.'

I push a lonely toast crumb around the tabletop, avoiding his direct stare. I don't really believe him, but I want to see if I can catch him out. 'So you didn't know about these rumours? That I'd had some sort of inappropriate relationship with a client? That I might be,' I drop my voice to a whisper, '*pregnant*.'

'What?!' he hisses back, his eyes wide with shock. 'Are you… I mean, is it…?'

'No! No, I'm not. Not even close. But it's apparently part of the same rumour mill about me.'

'Christ. That is extreme. All I'd heard was the same old rumours about you being next for the top job. About how you worked inhuman hours and once floored the operations director in a kick-boxing workshop.'

My leg twitches at the memory of connecting with David Butler's cheekbone. My defence is that I assumed he was a lot taller than he really was. And he was only out cold for a few minutes, five tops. The sad thing was, it was supposed to be a team-building away day. He would never get into a lift with me after that, let alone an in-depth business discussion.

'So maybe Devon pushed me out because he thought I was coming for his job?' I ask it out loud more for myself to mull over than for Ben to answer.

He nods thoughtfully. 'It's not unreasonable. You're bloody well intimidating.' I snort through my nose at that and he looks incredulous. 'Don't even deny it, Blackthorn. You're scary. You scare me, at least.'

'Oh, yeah, you were so scared by me in the office that you felt the need to undermine everything I said, smarm up to Devon right in front of me, pressuring me about missing that last meeting to make me look inept…'

I trail off as Ben's face gets cloudier and cloudier: his eyebrows are lowered, his mouth dropping into a frown and I could swear he's gone a little bit grey too. 'I was only ever trying to play up my position to our boss because you had me running for the hills – you clearly outstrip me. And when you had to leg it out of that meeting I was genuinely concerned for you! Why, Blackthorn, why do you think I'm some Machiavellian villain in a Savile Row suit? What have I ever done to offend you so badly? I'm here because the idea that someone is walking around, thinking I got them fired, is pretty upsetting to me. I want to sort that out, but you keep making out I'm the Moriarty to your Sherlock or something.' The storm on his face has well and truly broken, with an angry flush creeping up his neck.

I feel a rush of panic hit my heart and it beats like a punk-rock drummer. 'What… er… didn't you ever get ribbed at Eton? Hit a bit too close to home, have I? Oh dear, better blow off some steam at polo this weekend.'

Ben slams his coffee cup down on the Formica just a bit too forcefully, and a splash of coffee hits the table. 'Right, let's just get some things straight, I'm not posh, OK? I went to a public school, yes, but there are things called *scholarships*, Delilah, especially when you're in a single-parent family of limited means but you somehow have a weird affinity for trigonometry. But even if I was Lord Fancy Pants McGee, why would that bother you? Why should that matter? And you're one to talk, with your Oxbridge connections opening doors for you.'

I open my mouth, but there's no good rebuttal to fill it. Ben rolls on.

'The thing is, you've never given me a chance, right from the minute I joined. You just made all these assumptions. Whereas, I would try and hang around your desk, shadow you on a few projects even, to *get to know you*.' The flush has made it all the way to his ears now, and I get the feeling there's plenty more steam to erupt. 'But… I don't… I came here to clear the air but I'm in danger of turning it blue right now. So I'm going to leave you my number,' he pulls a business card out of his wallet, from his jacket pocket, and spins it across the table at me, 'and maybe when you've had a chance to let the facts filter down into that apparently sharp but stubborn brain of yours, we can talk tomorrow. Yes?'

Without waiting for a response, Ben leaps up and heads for the door.

'Oh,' he says from the doorway, a chilly breeze rushing in between his legs, 'since you now know I'm not rolling in posh-boy cash, you can pay for the coffees.'

–

JP is pushing leaves around his postage-stamp garden with his wellies. Stan suggested he find a way to achieve some activity – however small – so he doesn't lose his sense of self-worth. Tidying up the fallen leaves with his feet is the only thing we could think of.

'So, you thought he was your nemesis but it turns out you were his. Wow.'

115

'Hmm.' I hold my warm mug closer to my chest. I couldn't face the rest of my coffee at Cheeky's and retreated home for a hot chocolate instead, care of JP's larder. 'I'm still not sold. OK, so maybe me working round the clock put pressure on others to do the same. I see that, and I'm not exactly proud. I mean, it's weirdly fun for me to work like a dog but it's not everyone's cup of tea.'

'Trust me – you *are* the weirdo there, sis. All work and no play is very bad for the soul.'

'Fine. But I still think he had too much to gain from me leaving to be totally innocent. We'll see. We've agreed to meet again tomorrow. I'm prepping my interview for him now.'

'Always a barrel of laughs,' JP mutters, pushing three wet leaves into a yellow bucket lying on its side.

'What was that?'

'Nothing. Just… it's been a laugh, seeing the responses to my last vlog, about the CraftCon meet-up. Loads of people are into it, the mystery. The stall might well get swamped at this rate. Bring a big stick for beating people back with. Or maybe I could.' He turns on the spot suddenly, swiping his casts from side to side as if cutting in a cornfield. But the weight of the plaster sends him slightly off balance, and he ends up slumped against the already bowed fence with next door.

'Steady!' I yell, hearing more of Mum in my tone than I'd like. That reminds me, I owe her an email update, to save her wasting her entire holiday in an angsty panic about her two offspring. 'Are you sure we'll be able to manage, then, just the two of us?'

He bites his top lip. 'It was always pretty mad when it was just me, without trying to create a craft movement at the same time. My advice is wear flat shoes and block off the whole of the next day for sleeping.'

'Right.' I can't say I'm exactly looking forward to this craft expo thing. But if it's motivating JP and it looks like it will up the shop's profile, I'll dig deep.

'Just wish these guys were loose,' he wiggles his fingers at the ends of the plaster casts. 'So I could still do my demo. I had to pull out at such short notice they haven't been able to fill the slot. That sucks. We need to encourage all the blokes out there to craft, by showing them it's not totally girly and that men can do it. They just need to pick up their first set of needles and try it. There just aren't that many willing male guinea pigs to demonstrate it, beyond me.'

The last mouthful of my hot chocolate slips down deliciously, but the warm glow I'm feeling is less to do with sugar rush and all about the crafty idea that's just hit me. And crafty as in a fox, not a fox-doing-crochet.

Chapter 12

Becky had taken a little bit of persuading to agree to let me use her conservatory. But in the end, when I pointed out it would be more entertaining than yet more daytime TV, and I'd take Chester out for a long walk afterwards so she could have half an hour to herself, she bit my hand off like it was a cheese toastie.

I just couldn't face the idea of having Ben back at the flat, or in the shop, not when he still felt half like an enemy and the other half a baffling riddle. OK, so maybe I saw his smooth looks, refined accent and old-school tie and made a few assumptions about him, but no matter what, we were in competition with each other and he can't honestly say he 'just wants to get along'. I'm going to get to the bottom of his involvement in me getting the sack – using some pretty basic but crafty techniques.

I'm pulling two wicker chairs to face each other in the small lean-to conservatory, when the doorbell goes. I can hear Becky's jolly, high-pitched tone and then Ben's lower, less confident one following her. Ha. He has no idea what's going on.

'She's through here. There you are, Dee. Your guest has arrived.'

Ben nods a hello as he takes in the room. The late September sun is glittering through the floor-to-ceiling windows and glass roof, making it eye-wincingly bright as well as sticky hot. Not at all comfortable or relaxing. Perfect.

'And here's your referee.' Becky ducks into the living room and comes back holding a baby bouncing chair. With a sleeping baby inside it. She places it facing away from the windows and the glare, and sets Chester off with a gentle jiggle, just for good measure.

Ben is pulling at the neckline of his T-shirt now and keeping a wary eye on Chester.

'Right,' Becky wags a finger at us both, 'no loud noises, OK? This chap needs to sleep and I need to catch up on some Internet shopping. My new mum boobs don't fit into my old clothes.' She rubs her hands together. Ben looks as though he'd like to duck his whole head inside his T-shirt and hide. 'See you later.'

'Thanks for coming.' I point to the chairs. 'Take your pick.' My voice is barely above a whisper and Ben responds in the same.

'Why exactly is there a baby here?'

'Just giving my friend Becky a break. Why, it doesn't stress you out, does it?' I already know it does. The idea of waking a baby and dealing with the screams that follow is the perfect heightened stress situation to really crack someone. Add in the sunlight making him blink and the climbing temperature and I have Ben just where I want him – too distracted, stressed and uncomfortable to think of anything clever. He's going to blurt the truth whether he wants to or not.

'So, I have a few questions for you. And we can keep them short and sweet, as I'm sure you'll want to get back to London at some point today, have Sunday at home before a *gruelling* work day tomorrow.' Before Ben can chip in, I press on, 'So just answer the questions in as few words as possible, yup?'

'Um, yeah, sure.'

Chester gives a piggy snort in his sleep, as if ratifying our agreement.

'OK. Here goes. Why did you come here?'

'To clear the air.'

'Did you start rumours about me?'

'No.'

'Did you know I was getting fired?'

'No.' Ben's voice is so definite it's a little too loud, and the baby flinches in his zoo-print chair.

'Have you benefited from me leaving the company?'

'Er...'

'Answer the question.' I'm leaning forward on my knees, my legs just inches from his.

'Yes,' he concedes. 'I've inherited your client list.'

'Aha!' I jab at the air with one triumphant finger. I knew it.

'Which was hardly my decision. And I'm not a villain in this, Blackthorn, but I'm also not an idiot. I was told to take up more responsibility and I'm going to do it. I want job security, just like everyone else.'

I can't really get him there. I mean, if the loafer was on the other foot, I'd do it too.

'Did you get a pay rise?'

His eyes narrow. 'Yes, they *matched* what they had already been paying you.'

Interesting.

'But you say you feel bad about what's happened?'

'Yes.'

'And you want to help me?'

'Yes.'

'Do you have limits on that offer?'

'Limits?' Ben blinks in confusion. 'Well, I won't do anything illegal.'

'How do you feel about knitting?'

'Er...'

'And public humiliation?'

'Uh, Blackthorn—'

'Didn't you say you wanted to help?'

'I did, but—'

'But nothing. There's a crucial task you can help me with. And then you're off the hook and you no longer have any implied guilt or sense of obligation towards me. You never even have to see me again. OK?'

'Yes.'

'Ha HA!' My gleeful bark of laughter unfortunately wakes up Chester who makes a sweet little mewling noise in complaint.

Becky's head pops round the doorway. 'Oh, you sod, Dee. I haven't even checked out my online shopping. You'd better get him in the pram and out the door before he has a chance to work up into a full lather.' She looks between Ben and me: his pale, sweaty face and my beaming, victorious one. 'Maybe you can walk your guest here back to the station?'

-

It seems I'm not as talented at manipulating a shop display into looking half decent as I am at manipulating grown men into doing my bidding. I had this plan that I was going to recreate an autumnal scene with all different kinds of wool in yellows, oranges, reds and even the few specialist metallic gold ones we stock. *Simple*, I thought,

I'll unravel each one a bit so they can dangle from the ceiling on the loose bit of yarn. Then they'll look like falling leaves. But what I hadn't factored in was there was nothing for me to hang them from. And when I finally had taped them awkwardly to the small plasterboard ceiling in the tall bay window that served as our shop window, they hung limply and lamely. Less like a tumble of crisp, colourful leaves and more like pants on the washing line that have just been caught in a surprise shower.

I hate to say it, but I'm out of ideas. This visual stuff has never been my forte. I was always asking to do Cubism in my art lessons at school because at least that way I got to use a ruler. This is definitely JP's arena but neither does he have a literal free hand to help me nor can he physically fit into this cramped space with his plaster casts. So, I'm sitting cross-legged in the window, head in hands and wishing I could outsource this for free. This needs to get done as part of the shop's reboot – having a few balls of wool in a wicker basket is not eye-catching enough, as much as JP says he hates to put his lovely wares in the sun and risk them fading. A bit of fading is worth it to bring in more trade and make for more desirable pictures of the website, too. I want a damn flashy picture to go with my presentation to MCJ. From a quick bit of competitor stalking online, I've seen chic London haberdasheries with window displays that look like underwater scenes, pearlescent fabrics shimmering against crocheted fish, or sweet shop jars full of colourful treats good enough to eat and certainly good enough to splurge cash on. I want our shop window to be an experience for our shoppers, to put a spring in their step and entice craft nerds, not just be a mostly empty space to catch dust bunnies.

At work, if I ever came across part of a project that wasn't in my skill set, I was mature enough to recognize my limits and scour my contacts for someone who could do the job perfectly. Nothing wrong with delegation. In fact, it's one of the key skills all my business books give as essential for entering the management level before you're 40 – not that that's looking likely for me right now. All I manage at the moment is JP's washing and the loo roll supplies in the flat. But I *will* come back fighting – you can't keep Delilah Blackthorn down. No, sir.

I'm lost in a thought of how much fun it would be to wrap Devon's car up in wool, like those Yarn Bombers JP showed me online last night, when a gentle knock behind me brings me back to the less fun here and now. I twist round awkwardly from my spot and see Patti tapping the window pane with a circle of wire.

'Want a hand?' she mouths through the thick glass.

I scramble towards the door before she has time to reconsider.

–

Once I've explained my idea to Patti, she nods thought-fully, her fingers twirling in her soft grey hair all the while, and says, 'That's doable. Sure.' I could kiss her, if that wouldn't be a total thunder-stealer for JP.

We twist lengths of the wire she's brought from the framing shop with the loose lengths of wool, so the wire is almost invisible, leaving one end hooked deep inside the ball. That gives us the strength to angle the falling 'leaves' in a way that actually looks like it has some movement behind it, some sort of design, rather than soggy laundry. Patti asks if I have any old newspapers lying around, and offers to put the kettle on.

Now this is a brother's girlfriend I could be happy with, I think. I'm quite parched from all my muttered swears in the stuffy window. But rather than brewing me a cuppa, Patti starts making a big bowlful of tea. Maybe it's a hipster thing? I mull. Then she grabs a pencil from the middle kitchen drawer (always guaranteed, in any kitchen, to be full of random junk and at least one pencil) and sketches out a rough leaf shape. 'We cut these out,' she says, 'scrunch them a little and dip them in the tea. Leave them to dry on your radiator and you've got some extra russet foliage, for a contrast of texture. And to fill the space up a bit more.' I gaze at her in full-on wonder. How has she turned something so basic into something so striking? I could do with her in my contacts list.

So now it's two hours later and we've scattered the leaves on the floor of the bay window and Blu-Tacked a few reaching up the walls, too. It really does add the finishing touch and as we unfold ourselves from the teeny space and file out to admire it from the other side of the road, I hear a pair of granny-aged ladies coo, 'Now isn't that something!' Bingo. Objective achieved.

I turn to Patti once the ladies are out of earshot. 'Some happy would-be customers there, I think. I really owe you one, Patti. I would have shoved everything in the bin by now and given up, without you.'

She shrugs nonchalantly. 'Real art takes a bit of perspiration. You had the vision – I just helped it come alive.'

'It really does seem alive, doesn't it?' I say out loud, before I pull myself up. That is not a Delilah thing to say. This is not a skirt-suit, professional, get-shit-done thing to say. Clearly I have travelled too far into the craft rabbit hole and it has turned me loopy. On the other hand, this is the most creative I think I've ever been, and I'm proud of it. But to stop myself suddenly banging on about harmony and mindfulness – which would be the sign of a complete brain transplant with JP, worthy of an '80s movie – I change the subject. 'Do you do installations as part of your art studies? Is that how you knew about the wire and the tea?'

A small smile curves her lips. 'Yeah, pretty much. The average student art room these days doesn't have the funding for cows in formaldehyde or skulls encrusted with jewels. So you learn how to be pretty creative with the contents of the garage. And you should *see* what I can do with a hot glue gun.' She flicks up her dainty eyebrows and I can't help but laugh.

'So our knitting class must have seemed pretty tame by comparison, then?'

'I wouldn't say that. I'm in awe of anyone who has that kind of skill, where someone has invested hundreds of hours to master something. In that respect, knitting is no different from sculpture, or sketching, or painting.'

Interesting. I might press the point while it's presenting itself. 'I know what you mean. Some people might get into these crafts because they're suddenly *trendy*,' I'm thinking of a perfect black leather jacket slung over a chair. 'But JP has this amazing dedication to what he does beyond fads. He loves how it can change people, centre them, mellow them out. Well, anyone but me. Knitting makes me feel like I've got goalkeeper's gloves on and I have to diffuse a bomb. But he's the real deal. He has an artist's soul, he's very intuitive, very sensitive.' She's lowered her eyebrows now and I can tell she's scrutinizing me. I might have pushed the little-brother PR a bit too eagerly. Another subject change, quick. 'So do you think you might knit a hat for our campaign, for a premature baby?'

Patti's face brightens just a touch. 'I'm bloody well going to try. And if I end up with random holes, I'll just say it's an intentional post-modern design.' She winks and I see a swipe of emerald eyeliner on her lids. She really is so very cool, but now not disarmingly so. JP'd better get cracking on his charm offensive before she moves abroad and gets seduced by a German video-artist-slash-beard-model.

There's a sharp whistle behind me, a three-note signal that our mum used to use to call us in for dinner. I turn and there's JP, happily walking up the street, going as fast as his plaster casts will allow.

'Hello there,' he nods to us both, his eyes stopping on Patti.

'We've just been talking about you,' I say, and JP looks at me with narrowed eyes which seem to mutter, 'You'd better not have been.'

'Yes, about the woolly hat campaign,' Patti chimes in, unaware of the thousands of tiny daggers hitting me in the face. 'Your sister was telling me about it. I'm in. And anything else you need, by the way, just shout. I love a community project.'

JP murmurs, 'You're awesome,' and Patti blinks a few times before quickly inspecting her gold lamé trainers.

A desperate cough is in order. 'Ahem, sorry, frog in my throat.'

From the very visible whites in JP's eyes, I can tell he didn't mean to say that out loud and now he's panicking more than a kid who's forgotten his PE kit and is about to do three laps in his underwear.

'You are... awesomely generous, to give some of your time to our campaign. And actually, we could use an artist's eye on designing some posters to gather support? We'll put some up locally but the main audience is online, so it's got to be something that would work on small screens too. Does that sound like something you could get involved with? I mean, this is all JP's baby, of course, so...'

JP breaks off from nervously chewing the inside of his cheek. 'Uh, yeah. Yeah. That would be... awesome.' Obviously having a major crush turns my brother's vocab into that of a Mutant Turtle.

I point between the two of them, a big dumb frown plastered strategically on my face. 'Actually, do we have your number, Patti? So we could map something out?'

–

Ten minutes later, I'm holding the door open for JP's lumbering frame and his phone is holding the digits for Patti Saunders.

'You're welcome,' I smile as I help him negotiate the shop and take up his spot on the stool behind the till.

'Welcome?!' JP splutters, his cheeks going red. 'You want me to be grateful?! You should be grateful I don't have two hands free to give you a serious Chinese burn. Especially without Mum here to hold me back.'

I plant my hands on my hips. 'Uh, excuse me, but did you not just go into that conversation a bumbling fool and yet come out of it with a cool girl's number, thanks to my steering? That kind of consulting work usually costs about £200 an hour at work, thanks.'

JP blows out a big puff of angry air, his cheeks momentarily looking like two fat tomatoes being squeezed of their juice. 'Yes, but that's the thing – you *managed* me in front of Patti. So now she'll think I'm a hopeless loser who needs his sister to get him a date.'

'If the woolly hat fits…' I whisper, as I tuck an errant skein of lavender-coloured wool back into its correct place in the colour spectrum. All the wools, within their thickness and brand groups, are now stacked in the rainbow spectrum. JP might have thought it a naff thing to do, but he can't deny it brings a new feeling of beautiful symmetry to the shop.

'Watch it. I may be two workable thumbs down but I'm not a total idiot.'

'But before I stepped in you didn't even have her number, or a way to see her again! I've got you a guaranteed two or maybe three chances to hang out and show off how dedicated you are to your craft. Which she really digs, by the way.'

'Really?' The flustered wind leaks out of JP's sails for a second and his eyebrows dart up in surprise. 'She said that?'

I turn my back and stalk to the other end of the shop, pretending to inspect the new zip layout, again in a rainbow arrangement and sizes clearly distinguished. Not the dump bin of tangled horror JP had in place before. 'But I don't want to *interfere*…'

'Too late. You have. But at least something good has come of it.' He pulls a sulky bottom lip arrangement, one he knew was bound to charm football stickers from our mum in the early '90s.

I bark out a short laugh. 'I don't get it! I was helping you, pretty effectively as it turns out, and you're in a mope. Men are weird.'

JP shakes his head mournfully. 'That's just it. You don't get men. A brother or a male friend would never have done that, right in front of me. They would have let me do my thing, in my time. You... you just don't get how men think.'

OK, my sense of humour is rapidly diminishing, like a pack of digestives on a Sunday afternoon.

'Excuse me, I know just how men think. I have spent many hours of my life poring over market research reports that show how men view themselves, their families, their careers, their disposable income, their... needs for a triple-blade razor, for Christ's sakes! Men are not as complicated as you want to believe, sunshine.'

'Yeah? When's the last time you had a boyfriend then, sis?'

I let the long zip that I've been playing with fall back against the display. 'Very mature. Nice one.'

JP's voice goes croaky. 'I'm sorry, Dee. I didn't... I shouldn't...'

I clear my throat and straighten my shoulders. 'Well, if you're so desperate for more male company, I have good news for you.'

–

It's hard to give someone the cold shoulder when you're helping them fold their laundry so I have decided to forget JP's little dig in the shop and focus on the bigger picture. Sure, my love life has taken a back seat to my career. Way back. Like my career is driving the coach and my love life is uncomfortably perched over the revving engine at the back, trying not to heave. But that's just temporary. Everyone knows you have to establish yourself in your career in your 20s and 30s, then you can do the lovey-dovey stuff. And to be honest, I haven't felt like I've ever been missing out. Some of my uni mates went through horrific break-ups either right after graduation or just before turning 30 and hitting the old 'What does it even mean?!' roadblocks of life. They lost weight, they stopped paying attention at work, they got seriously bad haircuts... Clarissa even got a really regrettable tattoo that said *Dance like no one's watching* across her lower back. It looked like it had been tattooed with no one watching, not even the tattoo artist, and she had to save for two very painful years to get it very, very painfully removed. Ouch.

Just the memory of it makes me rub my back above my jeans, or maybe it's aching because I've been sitting at the rickety kitchen table again and lost track of time. It's 1.23 a.m. but only now are my eyes starting to get dry and scratchy from all the screen time. I've been dropping pictures of the newly organized and painted shop into a document and putting in some convincing but short blurb about how the bricks-and-mortar side of the business acts as a community hub, combined with an event space – I'll put a picture of our baby-hat class in just under the text. I'm deliberating on whether to mention the campaign to knit the premmie baby hats in the pitch document; it's great for social and community engagement but I don't want MCJ to think JP is distracted by too many good causes to run a tight ship too.

It can't be denied that JP's blog views and social media followings have rocketed since he put the shout out about the big mystery event he's planning, and he's been reminding everyone online to come and see him at the fair for the big reveal so there's been a brilliant rate of engagement. It's only led to a small bump in online sales at the shop, though, so that's something I need to work on. And we've had some feedback from loyal fans that they miss his YouTube tutorials going up. The whole site has been reskinned thanks to an old contact in Web design passing my details to a student she taught, who was eager to get something on her portfolio. I briefed the design to be clean and modern, but with hints of the same vintage turquoise colour I'd painted the shop walls. And it's come together really beautifully: it's easy to navigate between the retail site, JP's blog and all his archived tutorials. If you want to buy all the kit for a cabled jumper then watch someone talk you through using a fiddly cable needle in person – we are your one-stop shop!

We're on our way to where I want us to be, where I want JP to be comfortably established, but we're not there yet. And so MCJ are just going to have to wait a bit longer to see my wares. I think a few weeks just after CraftCon should do it, when JP will be riding the buzz of his big event announcement. Which reminds me. I open up Safari on my iPad and google 'CraftCon tickets'. I need to buy a few extra exhibitor tickets, for what we've got planned. It's not going to do any wonders for my bank balance, another few hundred pounds whizzing out, taking me perilously close to the bottom of my pot, but it's an investment. And you've got to speculate to accumulate. Even if right now I'm only accumulating nervous eels in my stomach.

I take a screen grab of the payment confirmation, so it can later go against company taxes, and switch over to my email. There's something in my inbox that quickly quietens the anxiety eels thrashing about in my system and hissing that I'll never work again: an email from Douglas McNaulty, the career consultant I've been so desperate to see these past weeks. He's got a last-minute appointment in four weeks' time. I'd still rather it was tomorrow, so I can figure out just how I get my life back on track but it'll have to do. I've been lucky, he says, because someone has dropped out in favour of rehab. I kind of know how they feel, a little bit. But hopefully seeing Douglas for an intense three-hour session will put everything right. It'd better bloody do, coming in at almost four figures, not including VAT.

The four weeks I have to wait give me plenty of time to think through my options and for this stupid rumour about me to bog off and die. Though it's still bothering me how it even came about. It wasn't Ben – so who was it? If it was just Devon who wanted me out, he wouldn't have needed a rumour – the firing power was his and his alone. But someone must have got to him...

The screen starts to wobble before my eyes. It's not the time to unravel sabotage schemes. It's time to hit the hay, before my head hits the Formica.

Chapter 13

'Am I doing this right?' Ben's voice is gravelly, but uncertain.

'You're asking the wrong girl. But if it feels right, go with it,' I reassure him.

'I don't know... and I'm not all that comfortable being filmed. You haven't even let me change out of my work suit...'

I straighten up from my position behind the video camera and give him the Look. The Look he's seen me give clients who dare to dispute my advice. The Look I give the coffee vendor when he says three extra shots in a macchiato is a bad idea. The Look that says Delilah Blackthorn doesn't take any shit, thank you. He's had a few days to take in the proposal I put to him at Beck's place and if he's come back to the village I take that as a full-on yes, so he'd better get with the programme.

'OK! OK! I'll try again. So I push it in here, but not too hard, and then I move my fingers around like this... oh, fuck, I've lost it. Nope, I've lost it.'

I can hear JP sniggering from the kitchen, when he should have his lips clamped around the straw of his protein shake.

'Anything to add, *Julian*?' I call.

He sheepishly edges into the room and stands in the doorway. 'Sorry, guys. It sounded a bit porny from in there. Like you were making *Debbie Does Double Knitting*. Not that I don't appreciate what you're trying to do, mate, seriously. Coming out of town after work like this. Very generous.' He makes a little head dip in Ben's direction. 'It will be great to get a new vid up there, after such a lull. I juuuuuuust…' He looks to the ceiling as he tries to squeak out an objection.

'What?' Ben and I snap in unison. Clearly craft doesn't bring out the Zen in him, either. I mean, to be fair, he's even more of a newbie than me. Before I roped him into this at our conservatory showdown, he'd never heard of an alpaca yarn, let alone tried to do stocking stitch with it. I had to explain that he wouldn't *actually* be making stockings, after he went a bit pale at the term.

'I just… I don't think that anyone will buy it's me, even with some fancy editing and my voiceover put on later. An hour is not long enough to be able to fool the crafters out there that you're an old pro. It's in the confidence of your fingers, you see.'

I think Ben and I managed to sync our eye rolls then, too.

I hit pause on the video. 'We know we're taking a hit because you haven't added anything to your YouTube channel in weeks and seeing as Ben is so keen to be helpful right now,' I pull a wry smile. 'I thought this made sense.'

'Nope. It doesn't. Sorry. Besides, the YouTubers don't just love me for my hands, they love my face.' He throws me a pouty look.

'God help us.' I slump back onto the arm of the sofa, and Ben happily drops the needles and wool he's awkwardly holding, as if the yarn has been woven out of asbestos.

'You can't fake it, chaps. I'm the real deal. And you're clueless.' JP nods smugly.

'Then sodding well teach me!' Ben snaps. Hmm. Now this is one man I *definitely* understand – because he's basically the male version of me. He's been trained to hate failure, to tackle it and wrestle it to the ground until it says Uncle. To be the best at anything he chooses to take on. I can use this. I can make this work to my advantage.

'Um, if you've forgotten or temporarily lost your powers of sight, I don't have a free hand – never mind two – to teach you with, Ben,' JP deadpans.

'Now, now,' I hold out my arms between them, 'it's not a terrible idea. OK, so JP, you can't hold the needles and show him yourself, but wouldn't it make a great spot on your channel if you were teaching a newbie face to face? *About a (Knitting) Boy* meets… Beginner Ben?'

'Erm…' Ben begins to object, but I keep talking.

'It could really work. It would be… a journey. Something for the fans to follow. A real-time crafting education!'

There's a flash of excitement in JP's eyes. 'Yes, I get it! And people could comment with what they want to see him tackle next – socks or variegated yarns or super chunky…'

'What words are you even saying right now?' Ben tries to join in, but the Blackthorns are hatching a plan and it's a family affair.

'Yes! Brilliant, bro! And he could be working on a baby hat, all along, so we always bring it back to the campaign. I like it. A great way to bring other craft wannabes into the fold. I'll get some graphics going. So what's the first step – what should he start with?'

'Casting on, definitely.'

'Oh, like fishing?' Ben chips in happily. 'I can do that, my grandad taught me.'

JP just lets out a low, mirthless laugh in reply. 'Fishing? You wish. No, this is real men's work, Beginner Ben. This is knitting.'

—

I have been looking forward to seeing Ben break during the teaching process, I have to admit: I smugly sit back behind the camera and wait for his own yarn meltdown, much like mine. But weirdly, and disappointingly, it doesn't happen. JP tells me to switch the video on to time lapse, so that the early part of the lesson can be turned into a good opening sequence, and after I have done that there isn't all that much to do except make tea and observe. Observe the most intense budding bromance Fenwild has ever seen. It's like Pitt and Clooney reborn, right here in this little sitting room, locking eyes over cream wool and a pair of 4-millimetre needles. Sparks have been flying, shoulders punched, winks exchanged.

These were the last two men on earth I'd ever put together as BFFs. JP: into meditation, knitting and long walks. Ben: into career success... Well, that is all I know about him, to be fair. I suppose I never did pause long enough to share any small talk in the office corridors. He could be a mindfulness junkie for all I know; he could have hiking boots in his battered record bag, slung down by the back door. But still, the idea of Ben in my head – suited and sharp – just doesn't fit in the haberdashery. As though a puzzle piece from the wrong box has found its way into our lives. But here he is, fitting perfectly with my little brother. Curiouser and curiouser.

I might not have been able to call it, but if they do hit it off it's only going to make my next plan to cash in Ben's offer to help that bit easier.

'Look!' Ben snaps me out of my calculating daydreams, by waving two centimetres' worth of knitting in my direction. 'Cast on and four rows in! Niiiice!' His smile is genuinely wide, ear to ear, and he turns to JP to high-five, bringing his hand down to squeeze my brother's shoulder instead 'You were right, mate, if you haven't got those initial foundation stitches right, you've just got to rip 'em out and keep trying until they are spot on. Totally see the difference in the spacing and the tension now. It was worth that seventh attempt. Definitely.' Ben is turning his handicraft this way and that, like it's solid gold and he's looking for the gleam.

'Great effort!' Despite the fact that they've been at this for about 90 minutes now, JP looks full of bounce and vigour, like a spaniel on a dogfood advert.

'Shall we break for some dinner?' Ben looks between me and my brother. 'I could go and get us a takeaway. Do you guys fancy Thai or Mexican maybe? I can do us a Deliveroo.'

JP is frowning like Ben has just switched into speaking Cantonese.

'Lovely in theory,' I say, 'but Deliveroo hasn't reached us out here in the sticks. There's a decent fish-and-chip shop down the road, though. I'll nip out – I should just make it before it closes.'

'Shit, it's nearly nine!' Ben checks his chunky chrome watch. 'Time flies when you're casting on, huh? But I can go, Dee – Delilah. I'm happy to.'

I'm already shrugging on my coat by the back door. 'By the time I've explained the weird cut-throughs and dead-end streets of the village, I can just be there and back. But thanks.'

Despite this, Ben is grabbing his coat from the hook next to me. 'I really insist. Besides, I'm here to *help*, remember? And that includes carrying greasy fish suppers along country lanes.'

'Mine's a double battered sausage!' JP shouts out as we close the door behind us. 'And a Lilt!'

–

Walking down the dim, narrow streets of Fenwild alone with Ben is even weirder than seeing him bonding with my brother on the little tattered sofa. It's not that he's the wrong jigsaw piece, but now for some reason I feel like the one that doesn't fit, here or even in my own skin. I am weirdly self-conscious about how I'm walking – is it too quick? Does it seem like I'm trying to ditch him? – and the fact that there's just a silence hanging in the crisp, autumnal air between us. Should I be saying something? Am I being rude? Why doesn't he talk, though? I'm so jangled by his presence that I spend the whole walk to the chippie tied up in my own thoughts and before I know it, we've joined a short queue and are waiting to order. The radio in the kitchen cuts through my tension a little, and the smell of frying chips instantly soothes me, as it would any sane person, but I'm still stumped as to what to say.

'So how are we standing on the friend-or-foe status?' Ben asks me, keeping his eyes on the front of the queue.

Straight to the point. Fair enough. 'Let's just say you are no longer on my blacklist.' I fiddle with the loose change in my purse, on the surface counting it but really just wanting to avoid eye contact. 'You've been open to humiliation and learning a skill most people associate with blue-rinse grannies, so I'm starting to think you *don't* have a master plan to ruin me.'

He laughs a big, throaty laugh and it hits me that I've never heard him properly laugh before – besides a quiet, polite chuckle for clients when they tell their mother-in-law jokes. It's a robust noise and a few of the other customers turn to look at us briefly.

'Well, thank Christ for that. No sniper sights trained on my back to worry about, then.'

'No. If I wanted to hurt you I'd just unravel your four rows.'

'Oi!' He turns to look at me, smiling. 'Below the belt, Blackthorn. Below the belt.' He nudges me with his elbow.

We shuffle forward a step as the queue moves.

'Just to get something clear in my head, I offered to help you and I was thinking you'd want me to see what I could find out about new job openings, or thinking of a way to quash these stupid rumours. But you ask me to help your brother with his craft business. I'm not complaining, casting on was tricky but it's a damn sight easier than networking with drunk buffoons in a members' club. But how was all that,' he mimes moving two knitting needles around with his hands, 'helping *you*, rather than JP?'

Blimey. It hadn't even crossed my mind when Ben offered to help that I'd use it for my career.

'Well, JP's business is my business – we co-own it. I'm the sleeping partner. And recently JP's had an approach from MCJ about a possible investment, so I'm looking into that for him.'

Ben rubs at his chin, a hint of five o'clock shadow appearing in the twilight. 'Right. I know their stuff. Pretty ethical, all round. Sounds promising.'

'That's what I'm hoping. So I'm giving the business – the shop, the website, JP's social media platform – as much of a boost as I can in a small timeframe to really show it to its full advantage. Hopefully get a sizeable investment that can help him grow it and really make a secure future for him.'

Ben looks at me. 'You're the older one, aren't you?'

'How can you tell? Have you got a big sister?'

'No, it was just me and Mum. But the protective thing, it's written on your face. You'd fight to the death for him.'

We move forward, closer to the counter.

'Pretty much.' Being this open and real with Ben is so out of sorts I feel like I'm drunk on just the smell of chip fat. So I try and change the subject. 'Any ideas you have, by the way, I'd love to hear them. For boosting the business. There might be low-hanging fruit I'm missing here.'

A wry smile spreads across Ben's face. 'Well, there's the Blackthorn of old. I feel like I could be sitting opposite you in a boardroom with chat like that.'

Now it's my turn to elbow him. 'Shut up! You know what I mean. And if I remember rightly, you're pretty fond of some jargon yourself. Didn't you once tell TechBank they could be the Netflix of banks?!'

Ben shakes his head shamefully and looks at the floor. 'All true, all true. But most of the time I was just clutching at straws, trying to stay in a conversation that was going 100 miles an hour. And there was me, on an old moped, trying to keep up with your Ferrari. It bugs me that you thought I was trying to undercut you in front of Devon.

Really, I think I was just trying to stay with the pack. Chip in with "the bants". Eurgh. I'm pretty much the weak one in the team.'

I can't stop the unattractive snort of air leaving my lips. 'Not true!'

He looks up to the ceiling and squints. 'True. And you know what? It's OK. I don't think this is going to be me for ever.' He waves down at his charcoal-grey suit. 'Not this exact job, anyway.'

'But then what's your plan? Where will you go?'

'We don't all have the big five-year plans like you, Delilah. Some of us are just making it up as we go along and trying not to fuck up too badly. Two cod suppers and two battered sausages, please, mate. Three Lilts too, ta.'

I'm gawping as I take this in. 'But what... so what do you *want* out of life?' I splutter.

Ben watches the food being assembled and takes the cream paper parcels that are handed over, a little puff of steam escaping as he takes hold. 'Blimey. That's a bit deep to tackle over fish and chips, don't you think? That's more of a Sunday-roast kind of question, with a cheese course thrown in. And besides, if you're going to chuck that conversational grenade at me, I'm going to lob it right back, what do *you* want out of life?'

I pick up the three cans of Lilt on the counter – putting two in my coat pockets and quickly opening the third. The fizz tickles my nose as I glug it down and the synthetic sweetness makes my teeth throb, but I'm desperately stalling. My life has gone from perfectly on track to permanently in a ditch in the last few weeks, and I have no idea how I am going to get it going in the right direction again. But I don't want Ben to know that.

I do love a good wallop of endorphins. And with everything swirling about in my head at the moment, exercise is just what I need to bring back my laser focus, not to mention combat all the amazing comfort food that Mags keeps delivering to our door, to aid JP's recovery. Cottage pie, Chelsea buns, bread and butter pudding: all the carby, buttery delights I'd normally eschew in London for something with endives and celeriac – but seeing as I really can't cook and don't have the patience for it, I'll take a home-cooked meal any day, regardless of the fat content.

I've been running every chance I get, looking to exhaust my twitchy muscles and my twitchy mind in equal measures. And when Becks messages me to ask if I'll come along to a new exercise class she wants to try, it seems to come at the perfect time – a Thursday morning when I have exactly zero tasks on my To Do list. The flat is clean; JP's out with Stan again; I've done all I can to date on the MCJ presentation; and staring at the clock wasn't going to speed up time and make my appointment with Douglas come any sooner. I've even been forced to pick up my sorry attempt at knitting a baby hat: JP says if I'm truly going to get behind him and his craft collective, I have to live the cause. So over three days I've managed to cast on the 71 stitches necessary and so far I've done half a painstaking row. It's given me two migraines, concentrating so hard. How JP does this every sodding day when he's fit as a fiddle, I do not know. But when my phone bleeps with a message, I let my knitting drop and bolt upstairs for my gym gear.

But there's one key piece of equipment Becky has failed to tell me I'll need for this class: a baby. It's just gone two p.m. and I'm standing with a clutch of about 20 women in the park, each with a brightly-coloured pram by her side.

'Sorry,' Becky whispers out of a tiny corner of her mouth. 'Um, can I blame it on sleep deprivation? I felt a bit too nervous to come on my own, so I thought of you. But I forgot that you need one of these to push about. Apparently the resistance is really good for you?' She points down at her sleek lime-green pram. It has massive wheels and a sturdy frame, like it was built to compete in monster-truck rallies rather than just scoot up and down pavements. Chester is tucked up under a thin blanket inside, snoozing with his sunny-yellow woolly hat pulled down over his sweet little head. It's impossible to be cross with someone when they have their cute baby in tow.

'That's... cool. No worries.' I smile through gritted teeth. I can take a few weird looks in the name of friendship. And besides, any kind of workout is a good workout. With all the energy fizzing through me today, I could offer to push two prams at once, if any of the mums need a breather.

'Afternoon, ladies!' Oh God, it's the hunk from the knitting class. He's the instructor. Perfect. 'Everyone find a space, get behind your buggies!'

Becky is just mouthing an 'Oh my God!' accompanied by a lavish, lusty eye roll as everyone finds their spot. And suddenly my buggy-less-ness is pretty obvious.

'Oh, hi!' Marcus spots me and waves. 'From the knitting class, right? Ladies, if you want to learn how to make your little one a hat from scratch, get over to the haberdashery in the village. They run amazing classes. I went to one last week.' The collective hormonal sigh from the group nearly blows me off my feet. No wonder this class is so well attended. Hot guy who is sensitive to your baby and can knit? I think most new mums would happily pay for six sessions of that, and then some.

'Blackthorn Haberdashery, that's us!' I try to stop my embarrassment making my voice squeaky. I try to channel professional Delilah, who can keep herself steady in the most stressful situations, because I actually feel more like 14-year-old Dee who once forgot her Home Ec ingredients and the hacked-off teacher made her whip air in an empty bowl for an hour, while tears brimmed in her eyes. But Marcus has given me an opportunity to get the shop name out to potential customers, and I can't let that slip.

'Yes, my boy is modelling one right now! It's gorgeous!' Becks does a big wave to catch everyone's attention, hearing the wobble in my voice and taking the spotlight instead. There are a few murmurs of interest so I vow to myself to hang around afterwards and make sure they remember to drop in and see us.

'But no baby with you this week?' Marcus frowns good-naturedly.

'Um, no.' I hold my hands open by my sides, as if to prove there isn't a set of twins hidden in my palms.

'Well, every mum needs a day off! Good for you.' He smiles. The mum next to me looks like she wants to choke me with her baby's teething necklace. 'You don't have your pram in your car, do you? Because that really helps in the class.' He's looking at me like I'm a total idiot, and maybe he's worried about me being allowed to drive a vehicle at all.

'Again… no. Sorry. I'm not actually…' The teenage me takes over and my voice disintegrates into a mumble.

'Sorry, can't hear you. What was that?'

'I'm actually not... a mum.'

'She's my friend! She's super sporty!' Becky chimes in loudly.

I can now tell I'm being mentally labelled by all the other women here: Bloody Show-Off. Maybe I'll just go at a half-pace today, then.

–

Marcus has got the ladies squatting at their prams, holding on to the handles for support, so I'm left crouching down on my tod, not going as deep as I maybe could because I don't really want to be lynched by women who are operating on four hours' sleep. God only knows how feral they feel right now.

Becky winces with each dip. 'I know this is... good for me. But why can't it be easy?!' She wheezes on the last word. Chester's hands flick open and then closed as the buggy jerks a little, but it doesn't seem to wake him. He is truly a poppet.

'It'll get easier, before you know it.' I feel my muscles complain and push against them even more. It's all part of the process, even if it hurts like a mother.

'O... K.' She wobbles as she heads down into another squat.

'And let's break for five minutes before a bit of High Intensity!' Marcus yells, and I'm the only one not to answer him with a groan. You can't beat a bit of HIIT for brain-numbing exhaustion.

Becks folds onto the grass like a damp towel. 'Jeez!' She prods her tummy. 'Abdominals, I'm sorry! I know I stretched you beyond all recognition with this kid, but do me a favour! Come back to meeeee.' She stage-weeps and flings her hand over her eyes.

I laugh and flop down next to her. 'Worth it, though.'

Becky pulls herself up into a kneel to check on Chester. 'That's true.'

'I've booked your post-baby shower, by the way – the fanciest afternoon tea money can buy. At Cheeky's!'

Becky hoots with laughter.

'I'm serious! Bob has agreed to let me order in a really fancy cake from a patisserie and he'll even get out nice tablecloths and bunting. You, me and JP. You don't have to invite anyone else if you don't want to.'

'That sounds like bliss. Thanks, love. The thought of fancy cake will get me through this sweaty hell. Oh, and I meant to say – my other premmie mum mates would love a few hats, when JP gets any more in the post. And when my health visitor admired Chessie's red beanie, I told her about what you guys are up to and it was like she'd won the lottery or something. Apparently, some of the health visitors run a scheme where they redistribute clothes to mums in need. And premmie clothes are high on their wish list. She said any that we can't find homes for she would gladly take off our hands. So that's good for JP's craft collective, right?'

I'm stretching my arms above my head as I listen. 'That's brilliant. I was getting a bit worried about JP's plans to get the hats out to new mums, how it would work in practice. Had visions of our living room filling up with towers of hats without homes. Like fluffy stalagmites everywhere.'

'Ha!' Becks flops back onto the grass.

I look at the mums huddled in little clusters around us, swigging water and blowing out their cheeks in exhaustion. On a normal Tuesday, I would be in an office, barely looking out of the window let alone watching a Buggy Fit class taking place. You can get so lost in what you're doing, in keeping your head down and working, that you can forget thousands of other lives are going on around you. My head turns to Becks, her arms spread wide in a position of total abandonment. People are having really tough times, right under your nose, and if you don't look up now and then, you can totally miss it. They can just be struggling, silently, and you'd never know if you didn't look out for it. If JP hadn't broken his arms, if I hadn't lost my job, I'd never have known the worry, the heartbreak that Becky went through, all squeezed into just a few short weeks. I wouldn't have been able to help, even if it was just delivering junk food and woolly hats. And if I hadn't been hanging around Fenwild for a prolonged, enforced stay, I wouldn't have been here to witness her coming out the other side, happy, and making her way forward in a new way of life.

'OK, up and at them!' Marcus claps and rubs his hands together. I think the only thing motivating Becky to get up from her recumbent position is the thought of his tight running shorts and toned legs. Hey, whatever works. An increased heart rate – however you get it pumping – is a good thing.

As we start a march on the spot to warm up for bouts of sprint pram races (or pretend-pram gentle jogs in my case), Becks leans against me for a beat. 'Actually, the health visitor lady asked me if your brother knew how to knit a perfectly working incubator, because that's something else they really need. But you can't knit everything, hey? There's only so much a gang of knitters can do.'

As my legs stamp out a steady rhythm, my brain gets thinking at full speed: if only we could take that crafty passion, that community spirit and turn it into cash. We'd be able to kit out a million hospitals if we could.

Chapter 14

'Has anyone helped to strap in JP?' Stan calls gently from the driver's seat. He has the kind of always-level voice that can get loud, but never cross. Not that I can imagine Stan ever being cross, at all, in fact: every time I've seen him he has a gentle smile and a new load of praise to heap on JP. Not only has he taken to the challenges of keeping hygienically sound with two wrists in plaster but, apparently, he's one of the most well-adjusted young men Stan has ever come across. My brother, of course, emailed this straight to my mum, which I think shaves a few 'well-adjusted' points off his score. But I'll keep that to myself. For now.

The one thing I didn't imagine super-chilled Stan to be was a van owner. But when JP told him about CraftCon and what a juggling act it would be to get all our helpers, stock and display kit in Mags's Skoda, he volunteered his vehicle for the day. It's a VW camper, so I suppose it does fit a little with his hippie vibe, though there's an AA sticker in the back window rather than a surfer slogan. I'm just super grateful not to be doing three round trips to the centre in Milton Keynes with pom-poms stacked in their hundreds on my lap while I read out instructions to Mags. She's never liked satnavs and worries she'll get distracted by the screen like it's an episode of *Shetland*, then crash into a tree or something. So it's me reading out loud from my iPhone if we go on any long distances together.

Stan's van means we can fit in JP, myself, Ben, Mags and Patti. I'd thrown an invite open to Becky but she said she hadn't done a car trip longer than ten minutes with Chester, and just in case he hated the whole thing and screamed the roof off the place, for this time, she'd stay at home. But she wanted an almost live stream of pictures and messages to keep her in the loop, especially at the big reveal moment. JP was going to unleash his plans for a national craft collective when he had a big enough gathering at the stall and beyond recruiting the passionate crafters there in the flesh, the coverage on social media should pull in loads more all over the UK, maybe even beyond. We'd soon have a truckload of premature baby hats to donate to the health visitors and, as a lovely by-product, a website chock-a-block with traffic that would send JP's stats soaring. This is what you call a win-win in my book.

'I've strapped JP in,' Ben reports, saluting Stan in the rear-view mirror.

'I feel like one of the X-Men about to take off in their special jet,' I say, pulling my belt around me. I certainly feel like we are about to set off on a special, if slightly unreal, mission. The problem is, JP is the only one amongst us with any special powers and he's bound up in plaster; it's like someone has stuck Wolverine on a giant magnet.

'It's called the *Blackbird*,' JP and Ben say in the same moment. And then they both crack up and yell, 'Jinx!' at each other.

I should have seen that one coming: introducing comic-book references to a couple of blokes and they're right back to puberty. If they ever left it.

'Room for one more? I've brought sausage rolls!' Mags's profile bounces along the van's windows until she reaches the open door at the back. There is room for one more back here, but I want her up in the passenger seat next to Stan. Firstly, because I think they might hit it off, and Mags has certainly been going all fluttery around him. And secondly, because I'm keeping this back seat free for Patti so JP can work his supposed magic over her during the journey. I don't necessarily get his point that I overstepped the mark the other day but it can't hurt to put things right and let him stand on his own two feet. I'll keep my lip buttoned. And then catch up with him later for sisterly feedback. I mean, I can't just switch off the habits of a lifetime!

But before I can say anything, Stan sing-songs, 'I'd love a map-reader! I just can't be doing with these little satnavs, with their funny robot voices. If you don't mind.' Mags is in the front seat and buckled up before I can even open my trap. Well, there's a turn-up. That skips about three steps in my plan for getting Aunt Mags back onto the dating scene. She's not had any time for herself over the last… well, decades, really, and I think it's high time she had some fun, as well as realizing how special she is.

Patti joins us soon after, climbing into the back wearing faded denim dungarees and carrying a red patent rucksack. JP introduces Ben to Patti and vice versa, with a swift look passing between the men. They've already talked about her, I can tell. Ben is fully briefed about JP's big crush. A pang hits my stomach, a small and childish one – I want to be the person that JP talks to about girls. But I can't begrudge him more friends in life. He's never been a beer-swilling macho man so hasn't always easily found his tribe. And Ben is at least sensible, I'll give him that.

'Let's hit the road. Milton Keyes, we're coming for you, baby!' JP shouts.

And with a whoop from Stan, we pull out onto the road.

—

If you squint a bit and don't notice every single detail, CraftCon could be a fashion week in some slick city: there are vivid colours and striking prints everywhere, bolts of fabulous fabric draping like sails on a big trendy ship and there are legions of leggy teens inspecting the stalls. Except that they don't want to buy a pinafore dress in acid-lemon corduroy, they want to buy the *pattern* to make it themselves. Personally, I love the instant gratification of seeing an outfit on a dummy and then – whoosh goes the debit card – and I'm taking it home twenty minutes later. Dressmaking seems like it's a whole lot of investment for an unpredictable return. I drop by a demo in the next hall to the stallholders, to see what kind of thing goes on, and it's all about pattern cutting. Forty-five minutes spent on how to accurately cut out the fabric pieces, before anything even begins to get sewn up! So God knows how long making an actual dress from start to finish would take. And then if you haven't cut the pieces the right way or in the right size, or if you've accidentally sewn a gusset where your elbow should be, the bloody thing might not even be wearable.

But I can't fault the energetic buzz here, along with the bright colours and interesting textures on display, there are all sorts of people starting to fill the corridors: young, old, mostly female but the odd perky-looking bloke getting stuck in; goths and pop kids, and hipsters and grans. All clutching their free tote bags and stuffing them with yarns, patchwork fabric rolls, card-making kits and more besides. We luckily bagged a stall that's a quarter of a big central block, so each stall has its own 'back room' – about as big as a shoe cupboard, but still somewhere to take a breather from customers and a space for me to set up the iPad. I splashed out on a wireless keyboard last week, seeing as I was doing so much work on it and my fingers were getting numb from speed-typing on the hard touchscreen. The keyboard makes a satisfying clicky sound as I log into JP's YouTube and Twitter accounts, then his Facebook page for the shop. It's linked to his personal profile, but he trusts me enough not to snoop. He wouldn't have trusted the 18-year-old me to do the same, and neither would I, frankly. But now he knows my interests are purely professional. And he can be snogging whoever he likes behind the Cineplex these days.

I'm interested to keep a watch on the hashtag JP put out with his vlog about his big reveal – #AboutAKnit – and see how it spreads throughout the day. Plus, I want to take plenty of pictures of the stall when it's full of happy, money-paying visitors for future PR and maybe get some informal customer feedback in person, too: why people love JP's blog so much, what they might want him to do more of, any products we don't stock that they'd like us to. It's all helpful. Plus, it's all free. The best kind of market research.

Patti volunteered alongside Ben to get merchandizing the stock we've brought for sale when we arrived. Our theme is that we're the yarn greengrocer. It kind of boggled my mind a bit when JP outlined his idea to me over Frosties and tea one morning, but he reassured me that you have to have an 'angle' at these things or you're just one of 100 haberdashery businesses blurring into the backdrop. Having a USP and strong branding always makes good business sense, so I went with it and sourced some big wicker baskets and a black foam board for us to write up our 'chalkboard' signs. Patti gave us lots of direction about how to go about creating the look in practical ways – we didn't have to fill the big baskets up entirely with wool, if we didn't want to lug that much with us to the venue; they could be half filled with a cushion, then twenty or so skeins could top up the rest. Green balls looking like apples, rose-pink ones like peaches and long yellow skeins could be hung from clips along the front of the stall like bananas. She stamped paper bags with BH, the shop's initials, and was adamant that the little chalkboard signs we wrote with the wool prices were authentic with greengrocer's apostrophes all over the place. That part kind of irked me, but she's the creative, not me. I'm quite literally keeping the back end of the business shipshape, tucked away in the cupboard while more crafters pour into the venue and the noise levels creep up.

JP pops his head round the doorway. There's a tweed flat cap on his head.

'What do you think? Patti brought it, to complete the look. I'm going to start calling out my wares. Cotton mix, two for a pahhhnd!'

I bite down my smile. 'You look great. But don't get carried away and undersell your stock. It's two for £5, remember? And only because it's being discontinued.'

'It's a shame, too. From a nice little British company who were making no-nonsense yarns until they had to wind things up. It's a jungle out there.'

I really want to laugh. 'Out there' is one of the friendliest customer groups I could ever imagine – crafters. But, yes, times are tough for any business, especially small start-ups. 'Everything looking OK out front?'

JP nods and the cap slips over one eye. 'Oh, bugger.'

I'm about to leap up and fix it for him when he steps back and says, 'Patti, my accessories aren't behaving. Could you lend me a hand?' And disappears back to the stall.

When I creep out and admire what the guys have done from a distance, ten minutes later, I am sincerely impressed. What I couldn't visualize from JP's description, Patti and Ben have totally brought to life: it really does have the feel of a fruit and veg market stall, complete with real bowls of fruit dotted around the place to blur the lines and give out a fresh, inviting scent of strawberries and lemons. You just want to reach out and help yourself to a handful of squashy, ripe wools in red and green and orange and plum tones. And Patti saved the biggest bit of foam board in our arsenal to write in beautiful hand lettering, *A Yarn a Day Keeps the Doctor Away!* with JP's Twitter handle and the hashtag below, in small letters. She's done the initial letters of each word in that fancy tattoo-style lettering, which gives it just the hint of an edge and means it doesn't look like a cheesy, inspirational, kitten-in-a tree poster.

I'm dead impressed. I'm still drinking it all in, struggling to find any criticism or bit of advice I could offer up to make it better, when something nudges my shoulder.

Ben is holding a wide cardboard tray full of hot drinks.

'I thought it was high time for a brew. Sadly, the guy on the coffee stand hadn't heard of a macchiato, let alone an "extra shot" so I got you a latte. That one, on the left.'

I prise it gingerly from its slot. 'Cheers. Very kind. And thanks for all this, too. I know I'm stretching your favour pretty far here. In fact, I hereby release you from your obligation from close of play.' I tap the rim of my coffee cup against one in the tray he's carefully balancing.

'Well,' he frowns, 'I'd hardly say I'm *obliged* as such… I've really enjoyed… enjoyed hanging out with JP. He's my kind of guy. No pretensions, just cool, just himself. I'm happy to be here, favour or no favour. And now I can knit. I can consult with a business, I can plaster a wall and I can knit a square. All bases covered.'

'Can you really plaster a wall?'

He nods. 'My uncle is a plasterer. He makes about twice what I do but it's bloody knackering work.' He puts on a rough cockney accent: 'You've got ta move quick, 'cause the very air is against yah, drying up what you want to be wet, lad.'

I raise my eyebrows. 'You're a bag of tricks, Cooper.'

'You know, plastering would be an excellent trade for you – you move fast, you're strong and you like to earn a lot in one day, am I right?' His tongue is in his cheek. He knows he's walking a fine line, but it's actually pretty funny in this instance.

'I'll be sure to raise that with my careers consultant in a few weeks' time, thanks. Though I worry about how I'd pull off overalls as day-to-day work wear.'

'I think you could wear just about anything and make it look great.' As Ben's last words leave his mouth he suddenly looks at anything but me, and I can feel an odd sensation creeping up my neck. Like I'm hot and cold at the same time. Must be all this recycled air in the exhibition centre. Or something.

I laugh lamely and get us back on to solid ground. 'Not sure JP's pulling off that cap.' I point with my cardboard cup. 'But the sales are starting to roll in.'

We watch JP give some schmooze to a gaggle of grans who are loading up on baby-soft peach yarns, while Mags puts their purchases into paper bags and Patti doles out change.

'Quite a team you've assembled here,' Ben says.

'I wouldn't say I've assembled them,' I reply. 'That would make me Professor X, which I am not cool with. JP knows exactly what he's doing. I just… facilitate things. But seeing as everything's ticking along nicely, I might have a look around, scope out the competition.'

'Good idea. I had a quick explore on my way to do the coffee run. There's an amazing range of stuff here – small purchases, serious big bits of kit over there by the sewing machine displays. Services, too. Someone who'll turn your family photos into embroidery patterns. And some of the workshops they're running cover turning your hobby into a business and monetizing an Instagram following. It's fascinating that it all comes under one industry's umbrella. Talk about diversifying. Wait. We're shop talking again, aren't we?'

'Yup.'

He points his tray towards the fruit 'n' yarn stall. 'Then I'll let you get on. Or I won't get taken on as a proper barrow boy at this rate.'

That hot-and-cold feeling follows me as I walk off in the opposite direction, the coffee not really doing much to even me out. What's that all about? Maybe I'm still adjusting to seeing Ben not as an irksome colleague but as… a friend, I suppose. Competition, I think. I'll find our competition.

But the old professional Delilah gets lost pretty quickly and a sillier, less focused Dee is soon trailing from stall to stall, her eyes wide with the very beautiful garments and cushions and jewellery at every turn. Modern designs in blocky, clashing colours; simple and traditional quilts that could grace a rocking chair or a three-piece suite just as happily; cross-stitch patterns that say *Bite Me* within a border of repeating roses or *Death to the Patriarchy* with a line of hot-pink skulls underneath. It's like being in a huge sweet shop with none of the calories but all of the colours and flashes of excitement. There's a big display of the original Cambridge Satchel company and I stand agog not just at their gorgeous, well-made bags but in awe of their pluck and profit. Plus, I really fancy a little one in cobalt blue. Well, maybe once I have a new job. If I ever have a new job…

I push the negative away and trundle on to the next company. For a minute I think I've caught the stallholder on the hop – there are long poles of wood on the floor, like she's still erecting her canopy, and she's bent over them. But with a closer look I realize they're broom handles. And they… they have cast-on stitches on them. Stitches from the thickest wool I've ever seen, like a ship's rope! I grab a flier from the little patchwork pouffe at the front of her tent.

> *GiganKnit: Big Knitting in the Extreme! We make rugs, blankets and all sorts with our uber-chunky wool and a lot of muscle! Come and take a workshop with us today. Info@giganknit.*

'Fancy a go?' The business owner catches my eye and I stumble over my reply.

'I'm not… I don't really… I'm a total beginner!' But she's already gently pulled me by the arm and pushed me down to sit on a squashy leather pouffe.

'Nonsense!' she trills, pushing a dreadlock out of her eye. 'This is perfect for beginners. Fewer stitches, at the very least! And you'll find it so easy to see where you're going. So, take up the needles, great. And then… yup. Push through and then round. Hey, I think someone's having me on! You're a seasoned pro!'

I blush a little and shake my head. 'I'm really not. But this is my kind of knitting – fast.'

She crouches down beside me and I get a wave of peony perfume. 'Yup. Fast and extreme. Not all knitters are quiet grannies, you know.' She winks and moves on to another interested-looking party.

'Do you want me to—?' I gesture at the knitting and start to stand up.

But she waves her hands, her silver rings catching the light. 'No, no. You feel your rhythm, girl. That canary yellow has your name on it, I'd say. See where it takes you.' And because I know JP is in his element, and I have nowhere else specifically to be, I do. I knit seven rows in the blink of an eye, with an even tension and each stitch suddenly appearing on my needle perfectly, as if by magic. I lay the seven rows on my lap and pass the flat of my hand over their measured, undulating surface. It's soft but substantial – delicate but strong, and I love that contrast. And I love that I made it. I did. Without blood, sweat, tears or bad language. I am stupidly proud of myself.

'Have I won you over?' The stallholder approaches her hands held behind her back and a broad grin on her face.

'We sell starter kits, you know. And I'm doing 10 per cent off, just today…'

I'm suddenly acutely aware of my purse in my back pocket.

–

When I do extract myself reluctantly from the extreme knitting, I mooch further along and see even weirder and more wonderful things: a collection of patterns for dog knits, some modelled by two very superior-looking dachshunds trotting about a mini raised catwalk; and a company selling huge reels of a sort of fabric yarn, made from the excess trimmed from big industrial bolts of jersey that make up T-shirts and the like. Because it's so stretchy, the three-centimetre-wide trimmed strips roll up into a round sausage shape and can be knitted beautifully. And because clothes come in all patterns and colours, so do their fabric yarns. I'm super impressed by how someone has taken what is essentially a waste product and turned it into a desirable one. And, yes, a profitable one. A little bit of crafty business in both senses of the word.

Just as I'm running out of steam and feeling like I might need to find an obliging panini and maybe stock up on a job lot for the others manning the stall, I get to the last exhibit of the row. Not as flashy, not as buzzing as some of the others maybe. But still intriguing. The display boards are big landscape images of a rural idyll with horses in a little paddock. Funny horses, though. Or not. As I get closer, I can see they're too furry to be horses – they're alpacas. Sort of like ponies with perms, I think, as I take in pictures of them standing in neat little rows, their curly fringes almost completely obscuring their vision. Or a giraffe crossed with a sheep. There doesn't seem to be anyone around and I spot a handwritten sign scrawled on an envelope and propped up against a 'Knitters Do it With Both Hands' mug: *Loo break. Back in ten!*

So I pick up a few leaflets and start to read them in the huge queue at the coffee shop.

> *Sunny Farm is Wales's oldest Alpaca Farm – started in 1993! We breed and raise Huacaya Alpaca and sell on the fibres to yarn manufacturers in the UK exclusively. Did you know that Alpaca fibre, unlike sheep's wool, is without lanolin and so is hypoallergenic? With its naturally soft, durable texture it's the perfect yarn of choice for today's knitter – and it's even warmer than sheep's wool! At Sunny Farm we are so proud of our lovely ladies that we want you to come and meet them, at our B&B and guesthouse, open year-round for short breaks and school visits. See our website for more details: www.visitsunnyfarm.co.uk*

As my panini order is cooking, I put a new task in my iPhone app: *Possible link-up with Alpaca Farm? We could get JP there for a blog post and cross-promotion?*

He has always said he wants to have a go at spinning fibres into yarns and God knows we could all do with a break with everything that's been going on. A country retreat with some extra PR boosting could be just the ticket. I add to my To Do list: *Also contact Extreme Knitting lady, dog knits company and fabric company for possible visits/cross-promos.* Specialist companies like these may have small, dedicated audiences, but put them together and they amplify into one big, big community. So if we could get JP's audience to look at Extreme Knitting and vice versa through some good-quality blog content, everyone's a winner. To paraphrase Mark Zuckerberg, the communities are out there. You don't create them, you just give them a space to meet. And if it made him gazillions, it can't be wrong.

Christ! Communities – meeting. The big reveal! I look at my watch – how is it ten to three already? I'd better leg it with my bulk load of brie-and-cranberry panini and muscle my way into a front-row spot. JP will kill me if I miss the big moment.

But the stand is already ten bodies deep by the time I get there. It'll have to be a back-door job. I push my way along and reach the little back room, using my elbows to wade through the really keen craft nerds who are gazing at our stall in near-hysterical wonder. The back room will give me the perfect view *and* a really good angle for 'behind the scenes' blog photos. Just in time – JP is clearing his voice and taking a sip of water, care of Patti holding up a glass with a straw. But what is he wearing? That's not the shirt he was in this morning…

'OK, people!' His voice calls out confidently over the heads of the predominantly female crowd. It suddenly hits me that it's bonkers how JP can happily talk to a whole hoard of women at once and stay on topic, but put him one on one with a lady he fancies and he's a bit of a bumbling idiot. And I say that with love.

The crowd giggle here and there but then obediently hush.

'Thanks for coming! Thanks for answering my call. No, don't worry, I'm not starting a yarn cult where we all live in the woods and only eat what we can hunt and wear what we can knit.' Someone lets out a throaty, bosom-heaving sigh from the back. 'But I am starting a collective of sorts. You see, my crafty passions bring me real happiness, a real feeling of calm in a bat-shit crazy world. But most of the time, I'm just doing it for myself, to satisfy my needs.' Someone laughs, and I wonder if those two mum mates from the hat class are back. '*Now*, I know there are people who could seriously benefit from my favourite thing in the world, in a very practical way. So I want you guys to know, too. Ahem.' He clears his throat and Ben makes a drum-roll noise by slapping his hands in a blur on the desk. Patti steps forward and pulls off the dark blue shirt JP has been wearing. I swear this morning I helped him into a checked flannel one.

The crowd gasps as one, and I am taken along by it. What the Dickens?!

Under his shirt, JP has a really clingy white vest, stretched so tight you can pretty much see his nipples. And written on the vest in thick black marker is:

WOOLLY HATS FOR ALL!
COULD YOU KNIT FOR
A PREMATURE BABY?

Written along his casts in the same chunky scrawl is *#AboutaKnit #165aday*, a hashtag for each wrist.

Good grief. Flashes of camera phones twinkle around the stall like the Christmas lights being switched on at Oxford Street.

'A good friend of mine had a little boy, born four weeks early. And in all that stress and worry, she was struggling to find clothes just the right size. What can we do, people? We can make clothes in any goddamn size we want, with our hands, while we watch telly. So I'm asking you, could you knit for a premature baby?'

163

A few hands go up.

'Could you?!' He raises his voice to more of a bellow and the crowd twig and shout back, 'Yes! Yes!'

JP beams into his audience. 'That's what I thought! But I don't want you to knit one hat. I want you to knit 10. Or 20! There are 165 premature babies born every day in this country alone. That's crazy. So I want us to take care of just one birthday. 165 hats. We can do this! I want you to knit like you've never knitted before – the patterns on my site, as are yarn guidelines. These little beanies need to be machine washable at high temperatures, that's important. You'll also find lots of video how-tos with our new friend Beginner Ben. Say hello, Beginner Ben!' Ben waves, the crowd go ahhhhhh as one, and he smiles rigidly at JP with 'I'm going to kill you' eyes. 'You'll recognize Beginner Ben as my new recruit on my vlog and he's popping his knitting cherry with us, one step at a time.' A wolf whistle sends the crowd into a buzz of giggles. 'In fact, I had a word with one of my friends here at CraftCon, who just so happens to have a spare demo slot this afternoon,' Ben's smile drops and his face goes white, 'and Beginner Ben and I will be doing a *Manly Knits 101* in an hour's time on the main stage!'

The audience whoop and clap but Ben remains absolutely static.

'Anyway, back to the real deal. We're going to distribute these hats to babies in the South-East, though local health visitors. If you can knit the hats, we can get them to the mums who need them. They'll feel good and you'll feel good, what's not to like? Take pics as you go, spread the word with the hashtags and to all your stitch-and-bitch groups. If anyone wants to yarn bomb in the name of our cause I can't stop you.' JP gives a butter-wouldn't-melt wink. 'In two weeks, I'm going to host a knitathon, a whole day dedicated to mini hat-knitting so we can reach that target. Or better – smash it! I need you to tune in while your own needles are clicking and make this the biggest viral thing since… since a cat played the piano. Let's make sure everyone in our crafty world knows what an important issue this is!' A whoop goes up from the crowd.

'So that's my news, guys. If you want to get a head start, I have some lovely cotton-mix double knits that would be a good fit, right here for a fiver for two. You could probably do at least six hats with that! Imagine!'

There's a surge towards the fruit baskets and I hear a worrying crack of wicker.

'Plenty to go around, ladies!' Maggie uses her 'please be sensible' voice on the whipped-up crowd, the one she used on us when we had silly putty in the summer of '96. But this bunch of knitters have seen male flesh and they are feeling wild. Money and yarns pass back and forth like a ping-pong match and after a few minutes, Patti clambers into the back room with me. 'Isn't it great? We're going to have to replenish!' She dashes out again, a big plastic bag of skeins under each delicate arm. I can't deny the sight of readies getting tucked into an already-jammed cash box is brilliant, but at the same time that fleshy display is not what I'd call great. Not at all. And it's definitely not what I'd call on-message either.

After 20 minutes the fever burns out and the crowd disperses, finally giving up hope that JP will remove another layer of clothing to reveal maybe just crocheted nipple tassels. The guys finally get to tuck into the panini I brought back, although they're now cold and unpleasantly congealing.

'Doeshn't matter, shish,' JP says with his mouth full, as Patti holds up his sandwich for him to take another bite, 'I'm shtarvin'!'

'Yes, all that stripping is bound to take it out of you.' I have my arms crossed and my foot is tapping out an uneven rhythm. I know it's all the classic signs of anger and irritation – I know that all too well from my training on reading body language in others – but I can't help it.

JP awkwardly swallows a big mouthful. 'What?'

'Have you got time for a quick chat?'

'Nope, me and Ben have to get over to the main stage in fifteen minutes. What's on your mind?' He lowers his eyebrows.

'Ah.' Ben looks from me to JP and from JP back to me again. He's had the same training. He can read from JP's facial cues and body language that JP is readying himself to meet my anger with some of his own. 'Why don't we… get me a drink of water, wet my whistle before my big stage debut?' He points his thumb off the stall and far away. Patti seems to clock his meaning and heads towards the cafe. But Mags is slower to catch on.

'But what about——?' Patti takes Mags gently but firmly by the sleeve and pulls her away.

'Come on then,' JP says when we're alone. 'What's got your FiloFax in a flap?'

I try to pick my words carefully. 'That whole stunt… thing. Where did that come from? I only ask because it kind of took me by surprise.'

JP's eyes skim over the exhibit centre, taking in the throng of fellow crafters. It might be nearly half past three, but they are still going strong: shopping, chatting, comparing projects in progress at the little break-out areas.

'Yes, that was the plan – catch everyone off guard, with the last thing they'd think of. Make a splash.'

'But me? Why did it have to catch me off guard? I wasn't ready for that, JP. I could have... helped.'

'You would have told me not to do it, you mean.'

'No!' I fiddle with my cuticles. 'Not exactly. I might have said *refine* it a little. It was a bit,' I pause and drop my voice slightly, 'bold.'

'Exactly! It was bold and attention grabbing and everyone will be tweeting it and spreading the message about the knitathon.'

I fold my arms across my chest again. 'But what message, JP? That you wear skin-tight vests? That you strip in public? Because I think that's what's going to stick in their minds, not the image of cute little baby hats. And where did you even *get* a vest like that?' I've slightly lost my cool now. My business skill of controlling my language to lead people down the conversational paths I need them to go has deserted me and instead I'm in a maze of frustration and annoyance, getting properly lost.

JP rolls his eyes. 'OK, so it was a last-minute thing, while you were walking around. I was a bit stressed about how I was going to make the announcement live up to the hype – my vlog had about 200 views and I'd had hundreds of retweets. So I was chatting with Ben and Patti and we thought – go big or go home, right? So... it was her vest and some Sharpies.'

'Yes. Well.' I bite the inside of my cheek. 'It was big, all right. *Full Monty* big.'

JP lets out an exasperated sigh. 'Come off it, sis! I got my message out, I started people talking. *I* did that. You don't control everything round her.'

'Oi!'

'I'm not...' He stops for a minute, breathes and nods before carrying on in a slower voice. 'I'm not saying I'm not grateful for *everything* you've done for me and everything you are doing for me now. But you've done quite a lot of... steering recently. I know you want us to talk to these QVC guys.'

'MCJ.'

'Yeah, them. And maybe that will be good in the long term but I don't want to forget who I am in all of this. OK, so maybe the reveal was extreme, a bit odd. But that's me sometimes. And that's what makes me stand apart from everyone else. I'm doing it my way. And you've got to let me.'

I hold up my hands. 'But I'm refining your brand identity, I'm looking for partner—'

'You're looking at your brand identity right here. And it is what it is. I'm my shop and my shop is me. It might not make me as rich as that guy who owns Amazon – what's his name, Jeff Beavers?'

'Bezos.'

'Him. But that's not my deal. Just... you're amazing, but I'm not a project, OK? I'm not here to be managed. We're in this together. Partners?'

I look at my brother. Not the tallest. Not the brightest. Not the cleanest, sometimes. But the best brother. Perhaps I have projected too much of my unused energy on him. Rule number one: listen to the client's needs. But I was too busy singing my own theme tune to listen on this one.

I clear my throat. 'Partners. And I get it, I'll take it down a gear. But you know your nips were visible in that vest, right? And Mum might see that. And send it to all her mates.'

JP visibly blanches at the thought. 'OK, so next time you get wardrobe clearance. But that's it.'

'I'd say shake on it, but how about a hug instead?' I squeeze him round the middle.

'That's better,' he grumbles into my ponytail.

I step back and appraise him once again. The dark blue shirt is back on, which I realize must be one of Ben's. 'You stand by the whole performance, yeah? You're happy with delivering your message that way? Sure?'

He nods quickly. 'Yes. I said. Why?'

'Because there are 300 people sitting in front of the main stage, who maybe didn't catch it first time round!'

Chapter 15

An overturned wicker basket has never felt so inviting or luxurious. With my back against the wall and my feet up on the desk, I am done. My feet are sore, my legs ache, my throat is raspy from saying for the 100th time, 'Check out the vlog! Yes, it's two for £5! No, he's my brother but yes, he is single!' The cold beer in my hand is the most amazing life-giving liquid anyone has ever drunk, ever. You will have to prise it from my dead, blue fingers if you want a sip. CraftCon has defeated me.

From the numb silence woven around our party I'd say the sentiment is shared by us all. Patti has her head on Mags's shoulder, JP is sitting in our only real chair (broken-bone privileges), Ben has just got back from the last run to the van with Stan and is now slumped against the wall to my right. Stan didn't come back with him, saying he needed to check the engine oil, but I wouldn't blame him if he's having a quick siesta in the back before the two hours' drive home.

It's been a knackering day, but a great day. Ben was a bit of a legend on that main stage. Whether he really was as clueless as he made out, the fool to JP's straight man, or whether he was playing up for audience engagement, it worked. When JP touched on sock knitting and double-pointed needles, Ben asked, 'But how do you know which end is the right end?' And the whole room hooted. They talked through the basic skills needed to complete a baby hat, with Ben as the newbie guinea pig – if it's not me, I'm over the moon. Hopefully, all those ladies in the audience going gooey over not one but two cute knitting guys will join the movement and send us their hats. At this rate we're going to have seriously good numbers to pass on to the health visitors to go well beyond our neck of the woods, and maybe – just maybe – cover the whole South-East, like JP vowed. I'm also chuffed to bits at how much stock we've sold today – it's pretty much all gone.

The tannoy bing-bongs over our heads. 'It is seven p.m. CraftCon is now closed. Exhibitors, please vacate the hall within 20 minutes.'

'Time to head home, chaps.' Maggie slowly stands up, gently moving Patti into an upright position. 'What a day! My first CraftCon. I will come again.' She smiles the same twinkly smile I have known nearly all my life – and then it hits me: I was planning to throw her together with Stan more today but I didn't get round to it! I had my walkabout, then the stall went bonkers for JP's striptease, then we went over to the main stage and then we finished selling our socks off and it just slipped my mind. Stan took up residence in an armchair in one of the break-out areas for most of the day, a paperback thriller in his hands. It would have been so easy to send Mags over to him with an invented errand: Had he seen the scissors? Would he like to share a HobNob? But I totally forgot. What a wasted opportunity. As soon as I have enough energy in my fingers again to use my phone, that's also going on my task list: get Mags's love life rebooted.

We all stumble on weary feet and trundle off to the car park. The knackered silence follows us into our seats, out of the multistorey and onto the motorway.

I must have nodded off soon after because the next thing I know, we're lurching to a stop and I'm aware that I've left a small patch of drool on Ben's shoulder.

'Sorry,' I mumble, my cheeks flaring red.

'Not to wo—'

'Oh, shit balls!'

'Huh?' I hear Mags wake with a snort in the passenger seat.

'Bloody tyre's gone! And I used my spare just the other week… Oh, flaming arses!'

Everyone is now awake and blinking miserably at the realization that we aren't home. Far from it.

Usually I'd leap into action in a situation like this: think of practical solutions, a positive spin on the whole thing to stop it spiralling into an argument, and get things sorted. But I'm so tired. So very tired. And JP's words about me taking too much of a lead recently are still stinging in the back of my mind.

'Right.' Ben's face is lit from beneath by the glow of his phone screen. 'Luckily we're already on an A road. And it looks like there's a pub just ten minutes from here. Delilah, why don't you, JP, Mags and Patti go and line us up some drinks while Stan and I wait for the AA? And some dry-roasted peanuts too for me.' He's smiling but I can see from the lines under his eyes that he's also too exhausted to really be that chipper. 'We'll join you in a bit.'

—

The walk to the pub felt more like a trek to the summit of Everest. We trudged along a scrubby path that ran along the main road, waving our phones around for light and drooling over the idea of a crisp G & T or a full-bodied Guinness or even just a sodding lime and soda as long as it was wet, cold and in our mouths pretty damn soon. Ben might not get so much as a sniff of a peanut as I planned to hoover them all up, without exception.

When we do make it to the King and Crown by nine p.m. I could ugly-cry with relief. 'Please, please tell me you haven't stopped doing food?'

The barman looks along the row of our pale, dusty faces. 'Sorry, kitchen's closed. But only just. Let me see what I can do.'

And he comes back with the Holy Grail. A huge mixing bowl filled to the brim with chips. They aren't the warmest or the freshest and maybe they've been reheated more than is ideal but they are salty and fatty and they are *ours*. We snuffle and shove and gobble them down, Patti and I taking turns to ram a handful into JP's mouth. What Stan and Ben don't know can't hurt them.

When the last little deep-fried scrap is hoicked out by Patti on one neat finger, we raise our glasses over the small pub table and let out a sort of grunt of a 'cheers', before sinking our drinks. By the time Stan and Ben reach us it's half ten and we've sunk a fair few other drinks too, out of exhaustion, out of boredom and to numb the worry that at this rate we might be sleeping on the ripped leather banquettes at the back of the pub.

'Here they are! The returning heroes!' Mags's cheeks are bright pink and her hair is unravelling from its loopy bun. The look is a little too 'bag lady' for my plans for her romantic life, but that's for me to sort another day. When the dartboard isn't spinning on the wall. Oops.

Ben and Stan both collapse heavily onto little stools.

'I'll get you drinks,' JP lisps a little.

Patti prods him on the thigh. 'Nope. No thumbs, 'member?' She laughs a big, messy, honking laugh that you can't imagine would come from such an elfin creature and then that sets the rest of us off.

'I'll go,' Ben mutters and I have just about enough sense left in my gin-soaked head to realize he could probably do with a hand, with all he's been through.

'Sucks.' I lean against the bar as he orders, half to seem nonchalant and half for actual bodily support. 'Long wait for you guys.'

'Yes.' Ben very carefully studies his pint being pulled, as if he's going to lamp the barman for even spilling one drop of precious beer. When it's handed over he takes three consecutive gulps with his eyes closed, shakes his head a little and opens his eyes, to find me staring at him. God, I am pissed though.

'I've never seen you fully drunk, Blackthorn.' He lowers one eyebrow at me. 'It's fun.'

'I am not drunk!' Even to my own woozy ears, it doesn't sound convincing. The half-stumble backwards doesn't help. Ben grabs my forearm just in time. I feel the grip of his fingers on my arm like he's connected to a car battery.

'Thank God I ordered two drinks, so I can at least try and catch up before last orders. What's everyone else having?'

—

Ben carries a crowded tray of drinks, crisps and nuts back to the table, where the group has fallen into mini huddles: Patti is expansively describing the art museum in Bilbao to JP, flinging her arms far and wide to get across the scale of the place, while JP just moonily gazes at her sweet but angular face. Stan is soberly talking to Mags about the responsibilities of his job and she's nodding fervently – I suppose in lots of ways it's similar to how she looks after Extra Granny most of the time. But I must remember to steer her away from job talk with Stan in the future. It can't be that fun for him, or her. Disabled parking and medication schedules aren't the best candlelit dinner chat.

So that leaves Ben and me with a pint and a double G & T, and each other.

'I can't face a twiddly little stool, Blackthorn – come and sit at a booth thing with me.'

So I walk after him, trying to keep to a roughly straight line.

'Looks like your brother is in heaven.' Ben tilts his head in their direction.

'Ahh, yeah. Bless him.'

'It's been… interesting, seeing you guys together. Seeing more about you. Who you are, outside of work.'

'You too!' I sip my drink. 'Actually, I realized the other day – I don't know *anything* about you. Apart from the fact that you are *not* posh.' I wave my hands decisively. 'And you got my client list. And that's it. Tell me…' My eyes look round the room, struggling to bring things into focus here and there, but settling on the jukebox. 'What's your favourite song?'

'"Tiny Dancer",' Ben replies without missing a beat.

'Whoa, you had that one ready to go. So, why? Why Elton – or Dwight Yorke, as he was christened.'

Ben presses his lips together, as if he's about to laugh or something. 'Great knowledge. That famous musician-slash-centre-forward. Um, it reminds me of being a kid. Used to sing along to it in the car with Mum, when we'd

175

go and see my grandparents in Cornwall. For a while we had just this one cassette, so we played it over and over and yelled it out as loud as we could. "Tiny Dancer" is great for yelling. How about you, what's your favourite song?'

I am really stumped, and I don't think it's just the alcohol destroying my memory cells. I get out my phone to check iTunes, see if my recently played list will nudge me. But there's only one Clean Bandit song on there that I downloaded in the gym because it spurred me on during Spin class. I'm not sure it counts as a favourite on those grounds. God, when was the last time I just listened to some music?

Maybe the conscious silence between us catches the others' attention, or maybe they're just being plain nosey.

'I know what Dee used to love to listen to,' Mags chimes in from across the room.

'Oh! Aha! Ha ha ha ha!' JP's eyes are lit up with a sudden memory and he laughs so hard he nearly falls off his stool.

'What?' Ben asks, his smile widening into a full-blown grin.

'No idea what they're on about.' I wave my hand in front of my face but a memory is stirring. A memory of loose plaid shirts and baggy red trousers. Of two cheeky faces...

'She was still in primary school, just 7 or 8, I think. And they put on a talent show and she and her little friend Amber—'

'Noooo!' The shriek that blasts out of my mouth is louder and shriller than I even knew I could make.

'Yesssss!' JP is laughing so hard that he can hardly breathe. 'The... backwards... baseball caps!'

Mags continues regardless, the red wine marks on her lips visible as she talks. 'She played that song over and over in her room to get it right. Drove her parents bonkers. Even brought it on a Walkman to my house! What were they called? Those ones who do that jungle TV show and the talent one. Peter and Declan?'

Patti put her hand in the air, like it's a capitals-of-the-world quiz. 'Ant and Dec! Oh, didn't they used to be in a band? PJ and Duncan?!'

Mags nods. 'That'll be it! The girls didn't actually sing it per se, but Dee and Amber mouthed it as they did their dance routine. Which was a good job too, it was so energetic. I think her mum still has the VHS somewhere. Oh, I remember – their arms whirled about...'

I can't hear the rest of Mags's reminiscing as I've got my head on the pub table and my hands blocking my ears. 'Noooooo. Nooooooo. Burn that tape!'

I'll just stay here till they stop. And till the room feels solid again, less wibbly. Gah, I haven't been fully drunk in so long. In *years*, now I think about it. I limit myself to two wines at work dos, to be sensible. But nothing about that fifth G & T was sensible. But instead of feeling things get quieter and the world becoming still, there's a blast of noise.

When I dare to lift my head off the sticky wood veneer, my eyes can't really register the blur of activity in front of me. Can gin impair your optic nerves? Can it cause mini strokes?

Patti has undone one of the straps of her dungarees and is flushed with exertion, standing near the dartboard. Ben's cheeks are just as rosy as he wheezes out a breath. 'We nearly had it,' he says, looking at Patti. 'My arms went a bit wrong. One more go? Ready?'

'Hang on!' Stan chips in merrily. 'I've found it on that there iTunes. Downloading now. Aha. Here you go.'

JP lets out a big whoop and Patti and Ben leap into action as the tinny music comes through Stan's phone speakers.

Oh my God.

Ben's arms fling out in time to Patti's, as their legs kick out in unison though not entirely in corresponding angles, making them drunken little human Catherine wheels. They execute the PJ and Duncan dance move pretty niftily, all things considered, turning on the spot and moving straight into an arm roll. Before I realize it my feet are hopping about under the table and I'm mouthing the lyrics.

Patti staggers forward and I catch her just in time. 'Surely you are too young and cool to know that!'

She laughs. 'Did a "Lost in the Nineties" party at uni, sorry. I'm not that young – 24 isn't that far off… what are you, 30? Anyway, those lyrics are timeless! Any lyric that rhymes "stores" and "pores" is good by me.' She attempts a body roll as she sings but it looks a bit more like she's got an itch she can't scratch. 'But you're the master, I hear. Come on!'

She's pulling hard but I've got my trainers fully dug into the swirly carpet.

'Literally over my dead body. Literally. You'd have to attach string to the limbs of my corpse and even then I'm sure the rigor thingy would stop you. Nope!'

I fold my arms over my front. That's the end of that.

But Mags is lifting her eyebrows hopefully, and Ben has a lopsided smile as he shakes his head slowly. No, though. No, no. No. There's no way.

Chapter 16

When JP advised me that CraftCon can take a three-day sofa-fest to recover from, I hadn't really factored in that we couldn't both do that and still run a functioning shop on Sunday morning. We are almost the only shop in Fenwild open on a Sunday (bar the trusty corner shop) but any extra revenue is worth it in my eyes. Who'll man the till when we're both complete wrecks? My gin hangover has me feeling sicker than a parrot on the stormy seas with a case of appendicitis and IBS. Despite slapping on the last remaining bit of my MAC concealer, there's a definite green tinge to my skin in JP's tiny bathroom mirror. My muscles ache like I've been through some hellish half-marathon but I've got none of the feel-good benefits, cancelled out by all the booze toxins still sloshing about in my system. I think you could flambé me. I just hope I can work out change correctly like this.

I carry my third cup of tea of the day, so far, through from the kitchen to the shop, grabbing the keys en route to open up. It's 10.30. I bet I won't see a soul till 12.30, it being a sunny September Sunday – even the most ardent knitters must have a park to doze in or a riverbank to picnic on, to soak up what is probably the last bit of good weather of the year. I'll have time to get some focus back in my vision and sweat out a bit more gin, and if I'm really struggling by two p.m, I can drag JP in. That's a lie-in of

179

love, right there. He doesn't deserve a sister as good as me. I might even cheekily whack Netflix on the iPad just out of sight behind the sales desk; have me a little *Good Wife* fix.

I'm in a bit of a courtroom daydream as I undo the bottom lock, imagining myself making witty remarks on top of killer legal moves as Devon is in the witness box and I see him crumble like yesterday's shortbread. Take him away, officer! I find you in contempt! You've ruined a perfectly brilliant career! And you smell of too much fancy aftershave!

But my enjoyable mind-rant disappears as I lock eyes with four teenage girls, waving through the shop window. Huh? Maybe they're lost?

'Morning... can I help you?' The fresh air is like a very welcome cold flannel on my face.

'This is *About a (Knitting) Boy*'s place, right? His shop? We saw the video last night, sooooo funny and we've always said we want to check this place out. So, can we come in?' A chirpy redhead stands at the front of the group, peering over my shoulder at the craft cave beyond. It takes my knackered brain a few seconds to realize I am actually *blocking* perfectly good customers from entering the shop.

'Yes! Yes! Of course, come in. Are you guys knitters?'

The redhead starts talking at full speed and I catch words and phrases like 'Intermediate' and 'Sock Phobia' and 'Snood', and it really still feels way too early. So I decide to point them towards the yarns and hope they'll suit themselves.

'All our yarns are over there. The ones JP mentioned during his... moment are right at the end. Perfect if you want to knit a hat for our community project.'

'We've done four.' A tall girl with a full-on afro giving her another five inches of height nods coolly.

'Amazing! Thanks a million. Another four for our total. Did you bring them with you?'

'Not four in total, four *each*. For starters, anyway.' The tall girl digs a paper bag out of her rose-gold satchel and passes it over.

I hold the bag tightly to my chest, until it starts to make a crinkly noise. People are amazing. Oh God, here come the gin emotions...

The chatty redhead scratches idly at her curls and dips her head towards me. 'I don't suppose,' she catches the eyes of her friends and smiles, 'Beginner Ben is here, is he?'

'No!' I say, maybe a little too loudly, the memory of last night's nostalgic brand of shame shivering down from my head and along my spine. I did not want Ben to know that I once cross-dressed as Ant McPartlin. I did not need the barman or the cleaning lady or the manager who eventually got us to leave to know that about me. If only you could choose the brain cells that you wanted binge drinking to kill. I would choose to forget telling Ben he had 'awesome moves' when we dropped him at the station for the last train back to London. Oh God, I think I winked as I said it. What came over me?!

Though maybe I wouldn't want to wipe it all out. JP actually asked out Patti, for starters – and she said yes! I don't think he thought we could hear as the engine idled outside the frame shop. Every random part of the evening was fun. The kind of pure, silly, thoughtless fun I haven't had since... since maybe my university days. Since that time my housemate dared me I wouldn't sign up for the Cocktail Society, mainly because it went by the name Cock Soc. I did join, and it was so inescapably joyful to throw house parties and mix neon cocktails and pontificate about the best bourbons for an Old-Fashioned that I became the vice president the next year and sat with a beaming smile in the Fresher's Fair as a second year, yelling, 'Cock Soc! Come and be a Cock Soc-er!' It was a laugh, it was a bit stupid; it was the kind of thing now that I'd advise a student not to do or put on their CV, because it looks a bit ridiculous. But sometimes ridiculous has its place. And drinking and chatting and nodding along to the jukebox last night felt like more of a tonic than a bucket of the G & T kind – it left me feeling lighter, somehow, like someone had just taken a huge suitcase out of my hands and stowed it away safely out of sight. I wasn't in charge, I wasn't steering, I was just part of the flow. I might be starting to sound like Piglet playing a game of Pooh Sticks, but it was pretty jolly just to let the flow lead the way. I need that in my life. I didn't realize this until all my tasks and actions and sense of purpose were whipped out from under me, but now I know: I should be having more fun.

So today I'm going to let my hangover be the current that carries me – towards bacon sandwiches or digestive biscuits or even a cheesy telly marathon, if it comes to that. These girls seem clued up enough to buy what they need without getting a sales job from me.

'Um, sorry. Beginner Ben is not here today. But watch out for the next vlog, I'm sure he'll make an appearance!' He's going to have to, now I've promised it. After all, he said he wasn't sticking around just for the favour anymore – he's enjoying himself. 'I'm just going to be out the back. Shout if you need me!'

I'm having a nice little sit in the kitchen, safely out of sight, wondering if I can commando-crawl into the living room to grab my magazine without attracting attention, when the shop doorbell jangles.

Ah, they've gone. The old Dee is gutted to lose revenue for the balance sheet and the MCJ stats, but the new Dee of booze and fun is secretly relieved. It'll be nice and quiet now.

Instead the noise level grows – there's *more* chat than before. And then the bell goes again. I stomp out to the stool by the till. The shop is… almost full!

There are more teens now, gabbing away, but also a woman with a very cool asymmetrical fringe who's perusing the fancy hand-carved buttons. When she spots me, she smiles and says with a soft Scottish burr, 'I don't suppose you do coffee, do you?' The way she draws out the 'oo' of 'you' is so hypnotizing I really wish I could say yes.

'No, sorry. But that's not a bad idea.' I whip out my phone and add it to my To Do list, rousing the practical part of my brain again. I'm sure Cheeky's would forgive me in time. I could kick myself for not thinking of it first – hot drinks are not just a great mark-up but a brilliant way to get customers to hang around for longer, stare at the merchandise that bit more, let the caffeine give them the last boost they need to make a big self-purchase. We probably don't have the space but it's something to consider, anyway. And God, I'd kill for a macchiato and an almond croissant now. Maybe with these eye bags today I could trick one of the teens into believing I'm a poor elderly lady who needs a youth to fetch her treats. The calcium is for weak bones, of course.

I plonk myself down on the stool as the first group of teens bounce over with their chosen skeins. Their energy makes me want to wince. It hurts my head just to watch in motion.

'We'll come back again,' says the redhead, obviously the self-appointed spokesperson of the gaggle. 'With more hats! You know, it would be cool if the Boy could list his working hours in the shop. And when Beginner Ben is coming. Just in case anyone is interested...' She digs a friend in the ribs and the little mite goes flamingo pink.

'Another good idea, thank you.' I ring up her balls of lime-green wool. Just get through these sales, my inner cheerleader manages limply, then you can collapse in front of the TV with a hot-water bottle and a stack of toast that reaches the ceiling.

Except I never get the sofa or the toast. More customers come – lots of trendy knitters in their teens but also cool thirty-somethings, mums with toddlers or would-be mums with bumps, grans and even Marcus, our local poster boy for lunges and lambswool.

He leans on the counter as I put his purchases through. 'Man, it kicked off on Twitter for this place last night, right?'

With all the exhaustion and A-road trekking and necking of drinks I actually didn't login to see what the social media impact was. 'It did?'

'Well, put it this way, if stripping off on camera gets you a thousand retweets, I might just think about doing the same for my personal training services.' The little old lady in the queue behind him starts to fan herself frantically with her ribbed vest pattern.

I'm too shocked and still too hazy to know what to say, I just shove his change into his hands.

'Not that you need a trainer, clearly.' His eyes flick from my stomach to my arms. Eww. Something in my stomach shifts. It's either the booze or his totally inappropriate comment. Or both.

'Uh... OK.'

'You know,' he leans forward on the counter, 'if you ever want to train *together*, really put each other through our paces, I'm on Tinder.'

'I bet you are. But I'm not. And I'm good for training buddies, thanks, and I'm pretty busy with the shop so... No.' I'm shaking my head very definitely. It's worth the jangling feeling in my skull, in order to communicate how very not into this I am.

Marcus frowns. Maybe this is the first time someone hasn't fallen at his handsome feet? Whatever. I have a social media moment to capitalize on. I lunge for my iPad. 'JPeeeeeeeeee!' I shout, even though it's only 1.15 p.m. and it's not great shop etiquette.

'Sorry,' I apologize to the startled OAP in the queue.

After ten minutes of grunting and bashing about upstairs, JP stumbles into the shop, still in yesterday's clothes and definitely carrying an air of yesterday's beer with him. Luckily Marcus took the hints that I so subtly gave and has gone. 'What? Oh God, who are all these *people*?' He takes a few steps back and hides in the kitchen.

'Apparently we're blowing up. Look!' I shove the iPad at him. 'Look at all those retweets. And your YouTube subscribers have gone up by 400 overnight. Christ on a bike, this is brilliant!'

Smiling still feels dangerous in my toxic state, as though moving so many facial muscles might break something important in my head, but I don't care. This is just what the business needs – a huge surge of popularity and tonnes of buzz, driving people to JP's website and lots of lovely purchases. This is going to make for some excellent stats for my MCJ presentation! I'm going to add 'social media burlesque' to my knowledge bank of business expansion tools. Maybe JP could do seminars on it…

The shop door opens slowly and Becks steps in backwards, pulling Chester's pram behind her. Before I can heft myself off my stool to go and help, one of our shoppers beats me to it. Crafters really are a polite bunch. Becky leaves the pram parked over by the rainbow of zips and waves at me. Her faces goes from a grin to a grimace and then quickly back to a plastered-on grin again: the expression of a true friend who is clocking how very awful you look, but then is adamant not to let you know.

'Hey, guys,' she cranes her head round the door to the living room as she spots one of JP's casts in the kitchen. 'So, how was it? You look like… you worked hard.'

Ideas are whirring ten to the dozen in my head, shaking off the gin straightjacket that had me feeling so sludgy all morning. My stomach gurgles, not wanting to get left behind.

'Actually, Becks, do you fancy a walk and a coffee? I'm starving. And, JP, it's your turn on the till. Don't give me that look. I know the casts slow you down, but you can still hit a button or two. Your audience awaits!'

As they spot JP from across the shop, two clusters of teens start advancing on the cash desk. Definitely time to make my getaway.

With each of us clasping a perfectly greasy and salty sausage roll, Becky and I start walking around the park.

The fresh air is doing great things for my hangover as I take deep lungfuls in-between bites of my porky heaven, and I think it must be hitting the spot for Becks too as she closes her eyes a few times and inhales slowly.

'I might not have eight hours' of sleep behind me,' she says softly, 'but in moments like this, looking at this beautiful park…' she waves her sausage roll towards the oak trees that line the playing field, sending pastry flakes scattering over the pram's hood. 'And being here with Chester, fit and well, and with a good mate to talk to, life is something pretty awesome.' She nods and bites into her steaming snack.

I bump my roll against hers. 'Amen.' I take in another big breath. Islington might have great sushi at three a.m. and somewhere to buy a handmade cashmere throw and matching dog coat, but it doesn't have air like this. Or friends like Becks.

'So how are you? How's this guy treating you?'

She shakes her head. 'Nope. No. We're not doing baby chat. I talk about this kid non-stop. I mean, because *I love him* and he'd totally be my *Mastermind* subject. But I do all that with Mum and the baby group ladies and all the health visitors. With you, I want Real World chat, please. Tell me about the convention thing, and how the site transformation is going. And Ben.'

'What about Ben?'

'Um,' she bites her bottom lip, 'well, just that he's gone from being big old enemy number one to "Oh, Ben has been helping us with a vlog" and "Ben had a great idea the other day". And he came with you to CraftCon, so…'

'Only because he owes me a favour. He got all my clients when I was booted, so I'm making the most of his guilt for my own ends.'

Her eyes go wide and her mouth falls open.

'Business ends!' I add quickly.

'Hmm. To be continued,' she mutters, as she navigates the big chunky wheels over some tree roots. 'Can you just slow down, Blackthorn? You're charging round like this is some kind of 100-metre dash. First rule of maternity leave, don't walk fast. You'll only get extra knackered and the aim of the game here is to fill up a very long, boring day. Chill. We are not at Buggy Fit now, you keen-o.'

My brow gets sweaty as I remember my weird conversation with Marcus back at the shop. 'Speaking of which, the instructor came to the shop again. I think he's a right perv – he asked me out!'

'Um, why does that make him a perv? You're not 14 or related to him.'

'Well, hitting on your clients is tacky. Bet he does it to all the ladies there.'

Becky shakes her head. 'Nope. If you remember, they are all new mums so either in a relationship or very much put off sex for the foreseeable. Could it be,' she clutches at her collarbone in mock horror, 'that someone... *fancies you*?!'

'Pssht.' I bat the idea away. 'He's cocky. Too many muscles, hair too fancy. Probably super-high maintenance. I don't have time for that.'

Becky narrows her eyes in my direction. 'You have time for craft conventions and speed walking around a park with me. Speaking of which, can you just not rush, Blackthorn?!'

'But rushing is my chilling – it burns up my energy, brings me down to a healthy medium. And besides, I've got all these ideas right now for how we capitalize on the momentum of yesterday. Long story short – JP stripped on camera and now he's going viral.'

Becky laughs. 'My brother stripped in a Magaluf nightclub once and he got something viral that week, too.' She clamps her hand over her mouth. 'Oh my God, I just made a joke! My mum told me, while Ches was in hospital and I was feeling really blue, that one day I would laugh again, and I would crack a joke. And it's happened!' She holds up her hand for a high five and I oblige. Really I want to hug her but I think that would trip us all up, mid-pram-push. 'But, OK, you're going to have to show me the clip at some point.'

'I think you can handle it. Just about. But now that stunt has brought all this mega traffic to the site and his social media, so we really have to work to keep that engagement. People click though for something funny but then you need great content to keep them coming back for more. I'm thinking… a *daily* vlog from JP, and more from Ben.' Becky raises an eyebrow but I push on. 'People seem to love his take on being a newbie male knitter. Maybe a cross-promotion with another company from CraftCon – there were some amazing people at that show, all sorts. Some competitions, maybe, to win knitting kits. JP could put those together. More classes at the shop, to keep the footfall up and money coming through the tills.'

'Wow,' Becky breathes, 'it's like talking to a really clever Del Boy in a nice cardigan. Hey,' she pulls the pram to a gentle stop, 'I could do a blog post for you! I wouldn't appear on camera unless you guaranteed Michelle Obama's wardrobe and a personal trainer for a month, but I could write something about the hats and Chester and us. Unless you think that's mad? I don't sleep for more than three hours at a stretch, so I have literally

189

no idea what's mad and what's sensible. I'm still putting my shoes on the wrong feet and not noticing until I'm at Bounce and Rhyme.'

I grab Becky by her arms to break the crazy rush of words. 'That sounds *great*, thank you. Something from your point of view about what the knitted hats mean to you would be a fantastic human-interest piece. And it would reach out to loads of other people going through the same thing, as well as motivating our yarn army to knit some more!'

Becks leans down to softly stroke Chester's cheek as he snuffles happily. 'And this boy is such a beaut he could sell anything – ice to Eskimos, the lot. I'll put in a few nice photos to go with it.'

'Perfect! This whole thing started with him, it's only right he should be our poster baby. Mags was just saying the other day that Chester is the most beautiful baby she's ever seen. And you know she's too pure-hearted to ever lie.'

'Ahh, lovely Mags. What would you guys do without her, eh?'

We start our slow meandering walk up again, passing the old bench and village noticeboard. My brain clocks it as somewhere we should get our schedule of classes posted, to make sure every local knows what we're up to.

I tune back into Becks as she's saying, '… and your poor mum all that way away with JP a bit bashed and you… taking some time out from work.'

'Ha. That's a very nice way to put it. But we've been emailing Mum loads, and facetiming, and Mags keeps her totally filled in. She keeps us in shepherd's pies and scones – we won't expire before Mum gets back. But we would be so lost without Mags. She gives so much to everyone else, I just worry she doesn't put herself first enough.'

'How do you mean?' Becky indicates to me to take my turn at pram-pushing, so we swap places. I'm more than happy to get the bird's-eye view of this little munchkin.

'Well, she's all about family, but she's not been on a date in decades. I think she's hit it off with Stan, JP's OT? But she might need a little chivvying in the right direction – she's been off the market so long, I think she's even forgotten the basics of flirting and chatting someone up.'

'Yes,' Becky turns to me, her hands pressed together. 'Sometimes people can be a bit oblivious, can't they? They need a gentle prod.'

'Exactly. So I might try and help her out there, lovely old Mags.'

Becky's eyes squint as she looks at me. 'Yes, some people are just clueless.'

–

With Becky walked back to her front door, amazing smells of roast chicken wafting out of the windows, I swing by the corner shop to pick up a hangover-busting Sunday lunch for my brother and I. Irn-Bru and Pot Noodles. Maybe not roasted, but chicken flavour at least.

And now my trainers are pounding at the pavement in a steady speed walk, making up for the slow mooch with the pram earlier, the blue plastic bag hitting my leg as I go. There really is so much to compute about this weekend, especially as my brain comes fully back online. With my ability to handle more than one number at a time waking up from its gin bath, I work out that our shop takings are up 300 per cent today. Just today! And I haven't even seen what the online sales might be, with the after-effects of all that social media attention. JP's business has never looked so bright-eyed and bushy-tailed, which is ironic when its owners have never felt so much like roadkill. But with this kind of profile in measurable stats, now is the time to send off my presentation to MCJ. Just in case interest does dip or flatten in the next weeks, I want them to bask in the glory of this amazing spike. Strike while the hashtag's hot! Just as soon as some hot water and a spoon has transformed my lunch into something roughly edible.

–

I get a bit waylaid from my tasks when I do get home – JP needs help for the last hour on the shop floor, batting the teens away from getting that bit too close to his torso, and sending them instead towards our newest colour-changing yarns, which as you knit them form a rainbow on your scarf or hat. Yarn cakes, they're called, and I have to admit they're really cute. Then he needs me to lend a hand (but keep my eyes mostly shut) as he gets washed and changed, and goes over to see Patti at her uncle's house. I keep my lip buttoned, though I really want to ask if this is a date or a 'just friends' thing. He'll tell me when he's ready. And when I finally think I'm going to get some quality time with my iPad, Mags turns up with a moussaka and some garlic bread. Which I demolish as she stands and watches me carefully.

'I promised your mum I'd make sure JP was eating something green, so don't tell him, but there's puréed spinach in the pasta bake for tomorrow.'

After we've done the washing-up together and had a good natter about old holidays and school plays (Mags still ascertains that JP had a choirboy's voice and could have been the next Aled Jones if only he hadn't blown raspberries all the way through 'Little Donkey' in year three), Mags goes home to relieve the day shift of carers looking after Extra Granny. And so at nine p.m., I do a few stretches in front of the kitchen table and sit down to polish this presentation like it's the Crown Jewels and I'm the Queen with a few secret debts to pay. I am ready to pitch this baby with lots of lovely chunky new stats to work in. If I'm going to do JP justice, I'd better bring my A game.

I'm making a few notes in my fancy leather-bound *Masterplan* notebook that Mum bought me as a joke a few years ago, when my phone rattles against the wood and makes me jump half out of my skin. I didn't realize I'd been sitting in total silence, just my mutters and grunts of concentration as a backing track to tonight's mission.

> **Ben**
> I still feel half dead.

I blink at the screen. Maybe he meant to send this to someone else? There's no question or anything.

> **Delilah**
> Well, pull it together, sunshine. Beginner
> Ben is going to be very busy next week…

> **Ben**
> What?!

> **Ben**
> So what's in it for me?

> **Delilah**
> Balances out all that nasty guilt of yours.
> JP will love you for ever.

> **Ben**
> JP is clearly the one I'm doing it all for.

There's a wriggle in the pit of my stomach. Is he being sarcastic? Is he... flirting with me? I chase the wriggles away with sensible thoughts. No. No. He likes JP as a mate and he's being literal. That's all. The gin is making me temporarily dramatic. All the same, I smile at my phone screen. You can't help but like people who like your siblings. It's excellent that JP has found a new ally in life and also someone else to come on board with *About a (Knitting) Boy* and lend a hand. And lend a fresh face to the vlogs.

This lift of good feeling behind my ribs sends my fingers flying again, tweaking here, expanding there, maximizing all the sales points and stats that I know will knock MCJ's socks off. It's only about an hour later that my phone buzzes again and I realize I didn't message Ben back.

> **Ben**
> Goodnight then, Blackthorn.

I really will reply tomorrow, at a more decent hour, but right now – before I lose my nerve – I'm sending this email to Lorraine. Not only am I flying the flag for Blackthorn Haberdashery and *About a (Knitting) Boy*, but I've also invited them to come and see the shop for themselves, so they can take in the retail space while I explain the more back-end stuff too. Over cake. Cake makes any meeting work.

And while this happy buzz fills me, I search out the flyers I picked up from the Sunny Alpaca Farm at CraftCon and whisk off an email to the contact given, asking if they'd be open to linking up sometime in the future. We could come and visit them, make a lovely post about it and in return they could offer a weekend break at their B and B as a competition prize on our site. That way, both sites would get more attention and click-throughs. They'd get a chance to say why people should choose Alpaca yarns for their next project and we'd get to show JP in his element but also in a fresh environment, mix things up a bit.

I'm just about to log off when I see a new email hit my inbox.

From: contactus@sunnyfarm.co.uk

To: Delilah Blackthorn

Dear Delilah,

Thanks for the email! My name is Ruby and I run the office side of the farm – generally, anything not livestock related! So, the B and B management, PR, bill paying. Jack of all trades, you might say… I only get to my emails late in the day, after my family and everything at the B and B is squared away for the night. So I'm glad I'm not the only midnight emailer out there!

We'd love to talk about working with About A (Knitting) Boy. Our MD Jean heard all about his big moment while she was at CraftCon! Sadly, she didn't get a front row seat. Maybe next time?!

We have just had a voicemail from the people who'd booked to come to the B and B next weekend saying there's a family illness and they can't make it. I know it's short notice, but I don't suppose you fancy coming out to see us in a few days' time? The weather's supposed to be lovely so you'll really be able to see our ladies at their best!

Let me know what you think,

Ruby x

Chapter 17

Who knew that the Reading services were such a buzzing place on a Friday night?

I've just filled up Stan's van with a lot of expensive petrol and while I'm in the M&S garage I might as well pick up some snack supplies for our road trip tomorrow. This time, though, I'm going to be the one doing the driving. Not only does this make me feel a little bit nervous because I'll be piloting Stan's beloved and temperamental camper van all the way to Wales, being careful not to crash it on the motorway or dent it in a three-point turn, but I've also felt the major dent to my debit card as I paid for the weekend's insurance over the phone, and there's been a definite crash in my credit rating as yet more money runs out of my account, without so much as a drop going back in.

With each bag of Hula Hoops and wine gums I throw into my basket, I feel more cash draining from me. Car insurance for a vintage vehicle, a tank full of petrol, enough crisps to feed two male bottomless pits, three rooms for JP, Ben and myself at a B and B, albeit cut-price ones... Thank goodness Patti had to work or I would have had to upgrade JP's room to a double. Well, I'm assuming I would, seeing as he's still cagey about what's going on between them. There have been all sorts of little, unexpected costs in the last few weeks and I'm not sure how much longer I can absorb them, with no new job on the horizon. My appointment with Douglas is there in the distance, but as time goes on, I'm starting to panic that one consultation is hardly able to undo a lot of mean gossip-mongering.

As I join the queue, I look at a message my mum sent me earlier: *How are you, love?*

Fine, I replied. *Everything's really hotting up with the shop. JP's doing well – not long till he has a complete set of working limbs again!*

Quick as a flash she replied: *But how ARE you?* And then she'd put in a funny emoji of a woman dancing, which I sort of assumed was her hitting the wrong key.

I've been dithering about this for an hour or so now. It's the reason I decided to get ready for the journey to Sunny Farm instead, and so I took a cab over to Stan's to pick up the van. As it grumbled underneath my feet on the way to the services, maybe sensing it was about to get a good prodding and tinkering with under its hood in my quest to check the oil, I thought to myself: How *am* I?

The feelings of anger and rejection at being let go from my job have started to fade away and I can already imagine that at some point in the future, I'll tell the story of how I got fired and then ran home to learn how to knit. And I will find it as funny as it sounds, eventually. It's been so brilliant to take up an active role in JP's business, and maybe to start with that was all about distraction and therapy – almost. But now I'm just as passionate as he is about bringing more people to the shop. Maybe I've more of an eye on the balance sheet still but in hardly any time at all, I've seen what genuine pleasure and a feeling of calm being in this crafty world can bring. And I haven't had so much ridiculous fun in a very, very long time, it's true. Well, I'm still not any sort of knitter but I have to admit I found myself handing over my debit card to the woman who ran GiganKnit at CraftCon, and I bought one of her jumbo knitting kits. I'm only two rows in, as I'm only doing it when JP's out. He's been spending more and more time with Patti, in fact pretty much every night, but I'm still the world's slowest knitter.

I have an idea I'll give it to JP as a surprise gift, a sort of 'Ha ha, I *can* knit!' joke, and though I don't know if I'll ever finish the kit – it's for a cream cushion cover that's super chunky and thick – I like seeing even just the beginnings come together. And maybe that's what I'm feeling about being involved so much with the haberdashery at the moment. Yes, it's been going for a few years now but it seems like it's finally coming together, really growing into something wonderful and useful and inspiring. So much of that is from JP's heart, and if I can give him a helping hand along the way then anything is worth it. But now it's bigger than the two of us, too: it's Becky, Chester, Maggie, Patti, even Ben and Stan. It's a real team. And all the people out there knitting and all the mums that can gently pull a tiny hat over their newborn's head: we're all united, we're... well, we're knitted together.

Ben has made himself so useful that I couldn't not invite him on this weekend adventure. And since he was saying that all this extra client workload he's picked up means he's having to work weekends too, I thought he could use a bit of a break. The clients can wait just this one weekend without an instant response to every single little problem. Besides, the Beginner Ben posts keep the views rolling in – so put him and JP in a lush green field with some cute, gambolling fluffy animals and you're talking a hit count through the roof. Besides, much as I love my brother, we are kind of constantly in each other's pockets and mixing up the dynamic for a few days in an open space is just pretty darn sensible. And while Ben, JP and I are spending the night at the farm's B and B, we might as well thrash out the plans for all the new content in lots of detail, make a schedule for how it will be posted, in fact, and have a sort of unofficial AGM to look at anything else we could be doing to capitalise on this buzz. I'm keen to make the most of Ben while he's still around and that means both in front of the camera and behind a spreadsheet – he is pretty much as good as me at looking for a company's faults and opportunities, and when I replayed the last vlog post I had to admit that Ben is good on camera too. It seems like he enjoyed it; I find myself watching his smile while he's knitting. Who knows when this will finally all get too weird and tedious and he'll make up some weak excuse not to catch the train to Fenwild? So I'm going to work him like a carthorse until that point. The business needs all the help it can get, so I hope it won't happen just yet.

–

The drive to Sunny Farm is certainly more scenic than when we were last in Stan's van and on our way home from Milton Keynes. About an hour from Fenwild, the landscape really unfolds into a gorgeous, inviting scene: like a green linen bed that someone has lazily made, lumps and bumps of hills, wrinkles and folds where tiny lanes bisect fields and sheep are dotted around pastures like biscuit crumbs on the sheets.

JP happily burbles the whole way about how his followers have really picked up on the campaign and more and more hats are arriving every day – we had 124 at last count! So our target is totally achievable. He chats non-stop to Ben; even when we stop for a loo break I see him go in explaining the virtue of the better acrylic-mix yarns and come out reminiscing about his first Aran sweater. All the while Ben laughs and nods and chips in with a point of his own. He really must have hit it off with JP to do all this for him, I think, as I grab us some orange juices for the next leg of the journey.

After another 45 minutes and so many lovely pastoral scenes that I'm starting to crave just a little graffiti for balance, we arrive. The farm sits at the end of a long, bumpy dirt track, lined with bushes and the odd rusting wheelbarrow. A woman with dark cropped hair is feeding some chickens just inside the farm gates and waves at us. Seeing as it's the only property for a few miles, she can safely guess we're here for her and the alpacas.

We all unfold ourselves from the van, slyly do a quick stretch and then go to shake hands.

'You must be Ruby?' I ask.

'Guilty!' she laughs. 'You caught me doing one of my non-office jobs, but I love these girls so much and they're the secret to my best bakes – fresh eggs.' She taps her nose. She looks to be in her 50s, with somewhat weather-beaten but radiant skin. 'Right, enough blather. Let me show you to your rooms, then we'll get on with the tour while the light's still good. Do you Go Pro?'

There's a beat as we all adjust our expectations from Alpaca Farmer to Unexpected Techie.

Ruby rolls her eyes good-naturedly. 'I run a website and some social media myself, my dears. I do happen to know the power of video!' she calls over her shoulder as she starts walking us towards what must originally have been a farmhouse, but now has a wooden alpaca-shaped sign hanging from the mailbox, spelling out Sunny Farm B & B.

True to her word, Ruby has us out by the animal enclosures just 20 minutes later.

'Hey,' Ben calls from a corner fence post, one leg up on the rung of the fence so that he's three foot taller than usual, 'if I stand like this, I can get a little bit of 3G. I could do a Facebook Live of JP meeting the animals?'

'Great idea!' JP nods.

'But a better idea,' I yank Ben down by the back pocket of his jeans, 'is that I film it and Beginner Ben gets in on it. Two crafty heart-throbs for the price of one!'

Ben frowns down at me, but I think he knows better than to try and disagree.

Ruby hands over two buckets of feed. 'Now you're going to want to be slow and steady. They are clever but shy, and they don't like being startled all that much. But after 10 minutes they'll warm right up. And they hardly ever kick these days!'

'Sorry, what?' Ben tries to ask but Ruby is shoving him into the pen.

'Three, two, one, action!' I yell, enjoying my mini Spielberg moment.

'Hey, guys!' JP beams up at me, the sun making his eyes even brighter. 'Beginner Ben and I are on the road! We've come to Wales, to see the amazing people at Sunny Farm and how they make some of the UK's best alpaca yarn. But, it's not really the people we've come to see, to be accurate, it's the amazing alpacas themselves. They're pretty cool. So we thought we'd show you on this live stream. Hello, fella,' he turns to a sable-grey animal a few metres away, 'do you want to be on Facebook, yeah?'

Either this animal is really not keen on social media or more likely, JP's casts swinging as he walks slowly towards it gives it a weird vibe because all of a sudden—

'Ugh!'

It has spat right in JP's face.

'Ha, ha, ha! Did you GET THAT?!' Ben laughs, only to be barged by a chestnut creature sidling up behind him, so that he stumbles into JP and they both go head first into the turned-up mud. Luckily it's relatively dry, but not really what you want caked into your jeans on a Saturday afternoon. Because maybe not all of it was *mud* mud, if you get my drift.

'Oh! No!' Ruby squawks and rushes in to retrieve them. 'They're usually so much calmer than this, but then they hardly see any men. Maybe it's because you're so big and manly?'

I can barely hit the stop button on the camera for laughing.

–

JP puts dibs on the first shower after dinner, now we're back at the B and B. Stan has taught us well by now: I wrap his casts up in cling film and he's good to go in soaping himself down, no assistance needed and no nightmares for me.

We've done as much filming as the setting sun will allow, after which we retreated to Ruby's small office, tucked away behind her kitchen in the B and B building, where we made some plans for a competition in the next month and planned out how both sides will push it through their social media channels. It's been great to have a heart-to-heart with someone else also running a small business in the craft industry. Ruby just gets that it's all about finding that passionate craft community and then giving them something worthwhile to stick around for, with so much else competing for their attention.

'Most of our B and B customers are knitters or crochet fans who want to come and see the animals for themselves. And let me tell you, you couldn't want for better guests! Never had so much as a broken teacup or a soiled pillowcase with those lovely, clean crafters.'

'Speaking of which, we should get settled in!' My stomach is rumbling and I don't really fancy Ruby digging up any gross-out stories of guests who did indeed go bad.

'Bathroom's up on the second floor and if you leave your clothes outside your door I can,' she flicks her eyes up and down JP's ruined jeans and Ben's brown cords respectively, 'do something with them by tomorrow morning. And feel free to make yourself some dinner in the kitchen there. There's milk and butter, plus a few other bits and pieces in the fridge. And of course my girls' fresh eggs, have as many as you can manage!'

'Thank you,' the men chime as one. It's not just the mud giving them a matching look: the bromance really is in full swing. I weirdly feel left out, but somehow I don't think my black jeans would have thanked me for a mud bath.

As JP climbs the narrow stairwell, I peer inside the fridge. 'So… toast?'

'Delilah, really.' Ben takes my hand from the open door and twirls me away, so he stands in my place. 'Toast. For dinner. Come on now.' He leans his head right into the ancient old fridge. 'Aha! Ham, peppers, cheese. If we can find an onion and start cracking those eggs, we can have a half-decent frittata on the table in 20 minutes.'

I must look a bit sceptical, or maybe even a bit afraid, because Ben asks me, 'Do you know how to make a frittata?'

'Umm…'

'Good grief. Well, it's like an omelette but—'

'That's not going to help me, sorry.'

He scratches the back of his head. 'OK, so scrambled eggs then—'

'Umm…'

'Blackthorn! How have you survived as an adult this long?! How did you make it through uni, for God's sake?'

I shrug. 'Toast.'

Ben pushes up the sleeves of his long grey T-shirt and I'm surprised to see a very small, dark tattoo starting just by his elbow – it must go up his bicep. 'Then here is something I can teach you for once. *Eggs 101*. Wash your hands.'

Without really thinking, I do it. And then I obediently crack open six eggs into a bowl. After which I carefully scoop up the swimming bits of shell that shouldn't be there. I add salt and pepper, mix it up with a fork, and then Ben gets me doing the chopping – ham and onions and pepper into matching thin strips. All the while he just leans on the counter beside me, watching and advising, correcting how I hold the knife a few times to 'save your thumbs and my sanity, while you're at it'. He's a pretty good teacher, it has to be said. When the onions start to make my eyes sting and I feel like I just want to clamp them shut for ever, he quickly takes the knife from my hand and presses a tea towel up to my eyes. 'Breathe in through your mouth,' he says right into my ear, 'that's the trick. It'll soon pass.'

With the whole world black and Ben's voice so close, for a second it feels like it's just me and him in the whole world. I'm suddenly very aware that he's just millimetres away from me.

And then I hear the familiar heavy footfall of my brother making his way downstairs. I twist away from the tea towel and wipe under my eyes with the backs of my hands.

'What's all this?!' JP yelps. 'Who let her *cook*?'

Ben takes over the actual cooking of the frittata but I still stand by my knife skills – each piece of pepper is so finely sliced I think they would answer to the name Julienne from a mile away.

JP is once again mud free and bouncing with energy. 'I've just had the most amazing email. Mind-blowing!'

'If it's from a Nigerian prince I think I can save you a lot of heartache there,' Ben chips in.

JP doesn't even pause to give an eye roll. 'There's this charity – Early Days. They work with premature babies and their families. They saw the CraftCon video go viral and they want to get involved! They can help promote the campaign, help distribute the hats to take the strain off the health visitors. And they've even suggested setting up a JustGiving page so that people who can't knit can get behind us and sponsor. Like, a sponsored swim kind of thing. They can then use that money to provide families with hotel rooms near hospitals for extended stays, and buy new medical equipment. Isn't that just… I mean, why didn't we think of that?' He bats me on the shoulder as if it's personally my fault. But it is a great idea.

'That is spot on. Let's do it. Do you want me to get in touch with them? Be the point of contact?' I suggest.

'Nope. I've got it. Thanks.' JP takes a seat at the scrubbed pine table. 'So this has just got a whole load of other ideas whirling.' He rolls his casts around in the air. 'We've got to go big. Make this more of a PR spectacle. Get the hats and the cash. Be like Bob Geldof, but swear a bit less. I was watching back the live footage from today and it got the most amazing engagement – 167 shares, 540 likes and just in a few hours! So I was thinking about that, and my CraftCon moment,' JP studiously avoids my eyes at its mention, wary of me going on another rant, I imagine, 'and about sponsored swims and getting the cash and everything we could do for this charity. Our viral video and today's live stream – what do they have in common?'

'You looking like a tit?' I suggest.

'My rugged good looks?' Ben attempts a smoulder over the frying pan as he takes it off the heat.

JP just shakes his head and keeps on. 'They were unpredictable moments of film – live events that the viewers felt part of. And they were crazy popular. So that's it. That's what's going to take this to the next level and get the message heard!'

'What is?' I spin my phone round and round on the shiny tabletop.

Ben places a plate with a steaming slice of fluffy egg heaven in front of me. 'No phones at the table, Delilah,' he says in a mock-posh voice.

'A big event. A one-day spectacular.' JP's eyes go wide. 'One that people can come and be part of, in the flesh, or watch at home as it unfolds. Like inviting everyone and their auntie to CraftCon, except that you don't have to buy a ticket. All the mad spontaneity of Ben falling on his arse in the mud, but with less laundry.'

'I'm all for that.' Ben sits at the chair opposite and picks up his knife and fork. 'Tuck in then, sous-chef. So JP, what would you do at this event? Where are you going to hold it?'

Exactly what I would have asked if I hadn't had a melting mouthful of cheese and caramelized peppers. Mmm. I pick up a forkful and offer it to my brother but he shakes his head, eager to be free to talk ten to the dozen still.

'A one-day knitathon. A knit to the death. We want 165 hats, right, for one day of premature babies born? Well, let's knit another 165 hats in one single day. People at the event and people at home, on their webcams. We'll orchestrate it all under one roof. Our roof! The event, but also the social media hub. I'll get my most trusty, most crafty followers to come along, the ones I know can knit like the devil, plus put out the call for new recruits. We can live-stream the whole thing – from the setting up, through to the needles doing their magic, the money rolling in, then to the after party.'

'After party?' I feel my bank balance shiver at the idea of loading bottle after bottle of cider into a shopping trolley.

JP gives me his schoolboy smile. 'BYOB, don't worry, sis. I'll make sure everyone knows. But what do you think?'

'Well...' I'm running it through in my mind. What are the drawbacks? The potential pitfalls? Could it impact negatively on the business? Would it be too much for JP himself to handle? 'It sounds great.' I slap him on the knee. 'Brilliant to have a big moment to promote on social but also to get loads more bodies through the door. I'm going to have to speed up on getting that coffee machine now. But I like it!' And I really do. It's an idea backed by real knowledge and insight, and it totally matches JP's brand values while still doing great works for a cause we love. I only wish I'd thought of it myself.

'Seconded.' Ben raises his glass of beer in JP's direction. 'Love it, mate. So when are you thinking of doing it?'

'Two weeks' time.'

'Whoa.'

'Yeah, but I should be cast-free by then and maybe not exactly knitting at top speed, but at least able to help someone with a dropped stitch or just make a cup of sodding tea.' He looks down at his fixed fingers with a scowl. He really has been so patient and Zen about the broken-wrists conundrum, being a chilled-out type, but even he's craving just to be able to brush his own teeth smoothly now. 'Plus, I'm thinking of all the teen knitters and knitting mums we have – I want them to be able to come along while the half-term holidays are on then.'

'Nothing like a scary deadline to speed things up.' I put another huge mouthful of delicious frittata in my mouth. If this is the only dish I could attempt in a real kitchen, I think I could happily live off it for ever.

'So we're agreed? A major live event?' JP looks between us, a twitch of doubt at his lips, pulling them down.

'It's your baby, little brother. Well, it's your baby hats, I should say. Go for it.'

–

The next morning, JP kicks Ben and me out of the break-fast room the minute that our plates are cleared of the last baked bean. 'I want time to talk to Ruby about how we can link up for the knitathon and have some time to plan all my ideas out, while I'm in the zone.' Before I can offer my help with typing or taking notes, he continues, 'I can press the home button and talk into Siri if I'm struggling, no problems, OK? You guys go and get some nice landscape shots and alpaca pics for the edit.' He's not really asking, so we pull on the communal wellies left by the huge oak front door, and trudge out onto the gravel path.

There are so many layers of bright colours coming to life as the thin mist rises over the valley. Green, orange, yellow, the odd smudges of grey or brown where a stone wall interrupts the fields. And of course the odd little fluff balls that are the alpacas, like polka dots studding the land. In a place like this you could believe yourself to be in any century, or even any other dimension. You could be living in a hand-built hut, hundreds of years ago, or in a world where you have to fight orcs off your vegetable patch. It's timeless and magical all at once. I've been snapping for ten minutes before I realize neither of us has said a word, we've just been breathing it all in. Ben has his hands in his pockets, turning slowly in a circle to take in the full vista. Occasionally he'll wordlessly point to a lovely shot and I'll follow his finger with the lens.

'Comfortable silences, right?' he says eventually.

'Sorry?'

'Nothing. Do you think you could be happy living in a place like this?' It's not mean-spirited, the question, more thoughtful. Like asking: Would you rather have three legs or two heads? 'You've got everything you need – your work, your passion, a home, family, Sky TV, don't forget the fresh eggs,' he makes a quick bow to two chickens across the yard from us. 'You could go into a town when you needed or wanted to, but you wouldn't be a slave to routine. Or to anyone else, for that matter.'

I slip the camera into my pocket. 'It sounds good when you say it like that, but there's always a line to toe, on some level. You might run your own business, but the bank manager calls the shots. You're still a slave to him, in a way. Or her. And the animals you've got to feed and wash and muck out. Though otherwise, it does sound pretty great. I just worry...'

'What?'

'Well, there are so many unpredictable elements to a business like this – the weather turning bad, the trends in fashion or craft for this particular kind of yarn, your animals could be struck down with... alpaca plague.'

'Alpaca plague?' I can hear the smile in his voice without even having to look at him.

'You know what I mean. Too many things potentially affecting your output and therefore the money you can make.'

Ben takes up a very Devon-like pose – all big gestures and flapping hands. 'Be careful, Blackthorn, you're sounding risk averse here. Where's the blue-sky thinking? Where's my chai latte?'

Part of me wants to laugh. 'My mum and dad had to fold their small business when we were little. For a while we had nothing at all. That kind of thing stays with you.'

Ben straightens up and takes a step towards me. 'I'm so sorry. And of course it would.'

After a less than comfortable silence that stretches into three minutes he says quietly, 'I guess you feel about small businesses the way I feel about credit cards. My mum had to use one when I was little, just for a handful of stuff like shoes for me, new tyres for her car. But the interest when she couldn't pay it back… I don't think she really cleared it till I was through uni and I vowed that my student loans were the only ones I'd ever take out. Full stop. I mean, I didn't mind not having stuff back then, that didn't matter, but I really did hate the debt following us around. That heavy feeling of owing something that feels so much bigger than you can ever afford.'

'God, I'm the same. If I earn it, I save it. That's been me from day one on my first paper round. I suppose that's what's made me nervous about these places – you can do something you really love and that gives you this unique freedom. But what if there's no money at all in the thing you love? No stability? That's why I get so involved with JP's business, I suppose. I want him to be secure. And that's also why I've been pursuing this investment with MCJ – to give him some protection for the future.'

Ben pushes his hands into his pockets. 'Your brother is one of the most level-headed, grounded people I know. He's secure. Whatever he does, he'll be secure.'

'But you don't know what happened, when he was a lawy—'

'He told me over a few beers. He's very open about it. It's incredibly admirable. I wish I had the guts' He looks me directly in the eye and clears his throat. But after a blink he looks away again. 'Your brother will be fine, investment or no investment. Whether he makes a million or just a few new mates. He knows happiness. And maybe part of that is from the childhood you guys shared. He knows to make the most of something small. Just like I did when I opened my Blackburn Rovers socks on Christmas morning, when I was 11. I knew that was all Mum could afford just then, so that meant the world. Even if it was the away strip. And I will swear that I love them in a court of law. In fact, I still wear them on match days.' He flashes a deep smile at me and I take the olive branch to get us out of this conversation that's pulling us into some deep, gloomy quicksand.

'But when you hear about my S Club 7 pencil case, complete with dent on one side, you will die of jealousy. I was the talk of the playground.'

Ben looks gravely serious as he stares at the floor. 'My heart has shattered. I've just discovered my mum didn't love me after all. Not if I couldn't look at Bradley and Tina's faces during maths.'

I punch him on the arm.

'Is there a cheesy '90s band you don't love? S Club 7, PJ and Duncan… Next you'll be telling me you can do the Steps' greatest hits in your sleep, complete with dance moves. Though their hand waving isn't really that hard, compared to the PJ and Duncan leg and arm thingy. I mean, you certainly found it hard, that night in the pub.'

A dizzy memory pops up of me being finally forced to get up and dance that night on the way back from Milton Keynes. On my second go round I totally lost my footing, maybe the plot, and twirled down onto the pub floor. I was a mess of tangled limbs and double gins. I blush at a hazy recollection of Ben having to grab me round the waist to lift me off the floor. Then the rest of the night goes fuzzy again.

'Oh God, I'd completely blocked that out! No one filmed it, did they?! And I thought owning S Club 7 memorabilia was embarrassing enough. Blimey. You know, I never told anyone this, not even JP because I desperately didn't want my parents to know, but what I'd been hoping for was a glitter pen art set. In fact, I don't want anyone to know *that*, either.'

Ben's scrutinizing me and I feel self-conscious all of a sudden. He steps towards me and says quietly, 'You know, Blackthorn—'

'Guys!' JP yells from the front steps, choosing this moment not to be secure and centred but to be loud and obnoxious and send the alpaca skittering away. 'We need to be on the road in 20 minutes! Loads to do!' He's rotating his hands in a sort of hurry-up motion but with just his fingers moving it's pretty weird.

'Now there's our true slave master,' Ben mutters darkly as we head back to the house.

Chapter 18

I'm getting worryingly familiar with the layout of Costco now. I could gather a 52-pack of loo rolls, 375 teabags in a box and a whole herd of Toilet Ducks with my eyes closed. But when you've got a lot of people to feed on a budget, it doesn't get better.

'These cakes!' Mags's eyes twinkle in the baked goods department. 'The size of them! And so cheap! Should we get one today, just to try it, do you think?'

Her hands are already sliding around a Red Velvet that looks like it could crush in a man's skull it's so huge and heavy. 'Why not? Like you say, good to test one before we have to come back and load up again ahead of the knitathon.' Today's shopping trip is all about preparing for the extended timetable of daytime and evening classes we've put on in a hurry while our stocks are high. Becky messaged me to say her blog post's coming together, but it's slow going seeing as she usually only has 20 minutes to herself every day and sometimes she has to use part of that for brushing her teeth.

But she followed up with a PS: *What about some kids' classes during the day?* The autumn half term is coming up and the limited offerings Fenwild has for entertaining children means parents quickly run out of ideas, cash and sanity in their efforts to entertain their little darlings. Anything to keep kids occupied is bound to be popular, if the play parks crammed full of glassy-eyed 40-somethings are anything to go by. So JP has plotted out a very basic knitting course to make a teddy's scarf and we're running that in the afternoons this week, with our usual course for grown-ups at a later hour. We're going to get through a lot of cake. 'Actually, why not get four?'

The hulking great cakes fill the trolley like sugary sentinels, keeping watch over our shop supplies. But they also remind me that before long, I'll hopefully be offering slices to the people from MCJ, as well as the chance to invest in Blackthorn Haberdashery. I started to feel nervous the minute I emailed over the pitch. I sneakily suggested a meeting time when I knew JP would be out with Stan, having one of his last OT sessions. It was written in biro on his naked knitting ladies calendar.

It's not that I feel worried about the meeting, it's just that with the whirlwind of the knitathon keeping JP's head in a right old spin, I don't want to overload him with this. And if the company do come armed with a very big cheque, he's going to need a calm moment to take it all in and process it. In truth, I've been so impressed with how he went from zero to a hundred miles an hour on this idea – on the drive back from Sunny Farm, he recorded a bumpy but authentic *On the Road* vlog to tell his subscribers what and where and when this knitathon would be, then he made a date with Patti to put together some graphics to help promote it, then he put in a call to his favourite yarn suppliers to see if they could donate any wools towards the cause, and they had a good slagging session over this mega American firm – Wow – and their horrible colour charts and textures. He's juggling so much, and so calmly. The big sister in me can exhale a tiny bit. But the business consultant in me is also excited to see his passion and energy and his know-how: it means that investment has come at just the right time. If he gets a big wallop of cash, it could really help him expand at a time when *About a (Knitting) Boy* is on every cool crafter's favourites list.

I think I'm going to need a wedge of refined sugar at the meeting as much as anyone. It's been a while since I was in any kind of formal meeting situation and that hardly ended well for me… The weird thing is, I've stopped missing it. I've stopped craving the adrenalin, I've stopped wondering how my old clients are getting on without me. I've started enjoying eight hours' sleep a night, I've started slowing down and just chatting to Mags about her garden or scrolling through Patti's Instagram that shows off all her paintings and sketches. I've started having time to just muck about – like at CraftCon and at Sunny Farm. I was always shooting from one thing to the next, back at work, always flogging myself to make someone else's business look great or make tonnes of money. And, yes, my bank account was getting nicely padded too, but I hadn't made any great memories or great friends. I barely had time to see old ones or even my family all that much.

But I need to remember all my old meeting techniques to do a good job with MCJ on JP's behalf. I want the very best deal for him. I want him to be safe in the job he loves for a very long time indeed.

And what job would I love in the future? If it's not my old role, what do I do? Have I forgotten who am I amongst this happy-go-lucky craft world? Am I losing the plot?

'Crackers!' Mags points one finger in the air decisively. 'I need crackers for cheese. I think they're this way.'

'Aisle 7,' I reply without thinking.

We head that way, the giant cakes making the trolley even more unwieldy to push.

'I'm cooking dinner for Stan, you see, and I thought it might be nice to finish with a cheese course.' She says this as she's carefully examining a box of water biscuits the size of a plasma TV, but a little spot of pink blush appears at her cheeks.

Well, hello, Mags. Good on you. 'That sounds *lovely*. How did that come about?'

'We were talking about my favourite recipe for coq au vin and he said he'd love to try it. So I invited him over. Nothing flashy, just good home cooking. He's a very interesting man. Lots of travelling, which I haven't done in my life.'

'Yet,' I add.

Mags looks at me thoughtfully. 'Well, quite.'

This is a turn-up for the books. I've been planning on getting these two alone together and they've done it without me! What a happy coincidence. And just like I want to capitalize on JP's flush of extra popularity through his site and the shop, I really want to help Mags make the most of this moment too. She deserves some extra love: she certainly shares hers out with the people in her life.

'Oh, I've just remembered I'm supposed to get my hair cut tomorrow!'

'Ahuh.' Mags loads a crate of wholemeal crackers on top of our trolley. Costco doesn't do subtle and neither do I.

'But the problem is I've got to be in to sign for a big stock delivery. You don't want to take the appointment, do you, Mags? They get so sniffy with you when you cancel at the last minute.'

She pulls at the end of her long, loose plait. 'Why don't I wait for the delivery instead?'

Good point, well made. 'Um, no. I need to… check it really thoroughly. Last time they sent the wrong dye lot. Wrong shade of… puce. Really upset some loyal customers. But you go to Benito's. You'll love him!'

'OK, dear. I will. You're very thoughtful.'

A new do could give Mags an excellent pre-date boost of confidence. She's so gorgeous, she just needs reminding of it. Out of the corner of my eye, a pop of sky blue catches my attention. There's a small rack of pure cashmere wraps just by the fleeces and jogging bottoms. Not the usual Costco item, and although they're slightly cheaper than you'd find in a high-end London boutique, they're not a mega bargain. But that blue would really complement Mags's eyes beautifully. Before she can clock the real price, I grab two and exclaim, 'Can you believe these pashmina thingies are two for a tenner?! I'm getting them for us.'

Mags runs a hand over the wrap I pass her. 'Gosh, that's soft! So clever what they can do with cheaper synthetic materials now, isn't it? You'd think that was cashmere!'

Here's hoping she doesn't bung it in the washing machine before the big date… And my bank account will just have to put up with the non-essential purchases, just this once. Well, twice.

After a short wait in the queue, our smiley sales clerk starts running through our bulky bargains. This always takes a while, given that the boxes and bags need so much grappling to manoeuvre them, so I might as well check my messages. The employed Dee couldn't have gone ten minutes without refreshing her inbox but these days, without realizing it, it can be hours before I remember I have the whole world connected to the device in my back pocket.

My screen is bursting with notifications. I've had to sign out of the *About A (Knitting) Boy* social channels from my phone – I couldn't handle all the updates of new follows and retweets and comments. It was headache forming after a while, even though it was always exciting to see. But these are all happy texts and emails and WhatsApps from the people pulling together for the knitathon.

WhatsApp group: KNITATHON!

Patti
I have an art school bud who does video installations and he can lend us his kit to capture the event from different angles. What do you think?

Ben
Sounds awesome! I've started the JustGiving page for people to sponsor the knitters per hour, but have we settled with a name for the event? Or just knitathon?

Dee
Got to keep working JP's brand – About a Knitathon? And let's just hope Nick Hornby doesn't sue...

Poor JP. He really can't wait to get those casts off in two weeks. He is quite literally itching to be able to text and email and knit and butter toast smoothly again. Not to mention he is itching from the irritation of sweat and plaster of Paris mixed together.

When I tap on to my email app, there's just one to be read. A few months ago this fact would, conversely, have made the super-busy Delilah's heart leap into her ears: Am I out of the loop? Am I old news?! But right now this email only makes my heart do the good kind of somersaults – it's from MCJ.

From: Lorraine

To: Delilah

Subject: Re: Blackthorn Haberdashery and About a (Knitting) Boy investment opportunity

Dear Delilah,

Thank you so much for the email. What can I say? We were blown away! Usually we can find a million reasons not to take things further on the first page of a business plan but with yours we were hook, line and sinker. We would love to talk to you more about this, and would especially love to visit the store itself. How's tomorrow for you? We've just had a day of training postponed so

221

my calendar is – unusually for me – wide open. Let me
know if that suits.

L

My head swims with a feeling of triumph that I haven't felt
since my last bonus cheque, back when I was employed.
That was when I was all about the money, but now I'm
happy because this is all about JP and securing his future.
Some things are worth so much more than money. I do a
shoulder shimmy as I wait for the till to spit out our total
and Mags gives me a bemused look. I can fill her in on
the whole shebang back in the car, but for now I'm just
savouring the satisfaction.

They're in! If they want to meet this soon they really
are hooked. I quickly tap out an enthusiastic but mature
response, even if what I'm really thinking is, Yesssssssss,
you are putty in my hands. My fingers tap out the message
in a rushed blur, then I open a new message to Ben: *MCJ
are IN!* With a million thumbs-up emojis after. Before my
eyes leave the screen he sends back a response: the emoji
ladies dancing in a long conga line and those party blowers
and balloons. He knows that feeling of landing a deal, after
all – it's like a birthday and Christmas and Easter rolled into
one.

Seeing as the knitathon is mostly coming together
without any input from me beyond a few details here and
there, it seems sensible for me to invest my time in this
side of the business for now. This time next year, with an
oomph of cash flow, JP could be doing a nationwide tour
of knitting events, not just one. Think of all the exposure
– and baby hats – that could bring! He's going to blow a
gasket with excitement. And speaking of which, I'd better
fill him in on the whole picture tonight if the investors

are coming tomorrow. They'll want to meet the face of the business at some point, seeing as he's the core of the branding. That's how I'd be thinking anyway. Time to bag up this shopping and get home. I'm on a mission!

–

But mission is sadly the only word for it. As I open the side door to the flat, I'm hit by a truly foul smell. Now, I've lived with a next-door bedroom to a teenage brother back in the day, but even JP couldn't create this kind of stomach-churning stench just with his body odour and fermenting cornflake milk.

'Oh, gracious, what's that?' Mags, her arms full of loo rolls, stops short behind me.

'I don't know, but it's not good.' Something's gone hideously wrong. I switch on the lights to help track down the source, but they don't respond. The power's gone. Oh, brilliant.

'JP? JPeeeeeee!' But with no grunt in reply, we must be alone.

Mags wafts her hand in front of her face in what is a futile gesture. 'Maybe he's with the lovely frame girl?'

I ping a message to Patti: *Is JP with you?*

She replies: *Yeah. Why, you OK? X*

It's not worth panicking my brother at this stage, not until I sort it all out. I can fill him in later. If he's with Patti that either means they're pretty much seeing each other every day, or he stayed at hers last night. I'm going to come back to that thought when this place doesn't smell like a rotten fish rolled in Stinking Bishop cheese. I crawl into the dusty space under the stairs, as Mags illuminates me with my phone torch. The circuit-board switches are all flipped and when I try to right them they stubbornly flip back again. So something is tripping them out. Right. I unfold myself from the cupboard to find my auntie wringing her hands, my phone clutched between them.

'I hate to do this, but Mum's carers are finishing their shift – I have to get back in 10 minutes!' She winces like she can feel my pain – or, rather, she can most likely still smell it.

I dig up a confident smile. 'Don't worry a jot, Mags. It's just a tripped switch. I'll find whatever it is that's overloaded things. Happens all the time. Not a big deal.'

'Really?'

'Really.' I give a double thumbs-up for good measure.

With Mags speeding off on her way home, I'm frantically unplugging all the kitchen appliances when the smell gets stronger. To unplug the crappy little fridge freezer, you have to wiggle it from its under-the-counter space next to the sink and when I manage to do that and jerk it out, the smell hits me like a parking fine. Unwanted, with lingering dread and a feeling that this is really going to cost me. So maybe a *bit* of a big deal, then.

There's a black sooty circle around the grill at the back of the appliance and a matching one around the socket itself. I would say 'Bingo' as I creak open the fridge door, except the smell inside makes me want to gag. So it's the fridge freezer that's blown out, tripping the circuit board and leaving the once-frozen chicken breasts and already-too-old takeaway cartons inside to really work up a honk. JP's been a fixture at Patti's solidly over the last few days and I've had my nose to the grindstone and been lazily eating fish and chips for dinner, so it's possible neither of us has noticed this for 48 hours. I don't think this is the kind of thing to share in my weekly email to Mum or she'll ring social services and ask for the Hopeless Adult Offspring rescue team. I might have to bribe Mags to keep quiet about it too.

As I step back to get even a little distance from the pong, I realize my shoes have trouble pulling away from the lino. Shit. There's been a little leak of sticky defrosting juice. This smell is not going to vanish with the fridge to the nearest tip, not if it's got into the floor. Or the stock! I sprint to the shop floor, only releasing my breath when I can see the floorboards in the heart of the shop are still bone dry. And a little dusty, if I'm honest. But even if the stock is bone dry, the smell is definitely putting the kibosh on MCJ rocking up tomorrow. If selling a stake in your business is anything like selling a home, they say it's best to have an aroma of fresh rolls in the air, not rotting cabbage.

Seeing as the offending troublemaker is now unplugged, I try to set the circuit board back to its rightful ways. But the switch just keeps flipping back. I don't get it. I google *Why the fuck won't my circuit breakers switch back?!* But the jargon quickly swims before my eyes. I'm out of my depth. I need help.

I snatch up my keys and leg it out the back door and four shops down to Sylvia's Hardware. Sylvia's has been here for ever, as long as Mags can remember at least, and it's the kind of warren of a shop where you could find spare plugs, cake tins, light bulbs or lawnmower blades, as long as you have the keen eyesight and endless patience to wander the little aisle and have the owner, Keith, poke around in cardboard boxes for you. But Keith is like an encyclopaedia of DIY – he's exactly the expert I need right now.

With a wheeze I pour out the story of what's happened back at the shop and he nods towards the door and starts trundling out onto the street, flipping his shop sign to *Closed* as he goes. Keith, all muscles and fat, is the kind of guy who looks sturdy and dense enough to prop up a roof or jack up a car, but only if you want your roof about five off the ground – he only comes up to my shoulders. But despite his less than long legs, he picks up quite a pace and soon we're both staring at the circuit board as it fails all over again to flick back to life when he tries all the switches one by one. Keith then has a good look at the back of the fridge. His gasp of breath couldn't be sharper if I'd stabbed him with a bamboo knitting needle.

'Cripes, love. You need this seen to.'

'The fridge? No, I'm just going to chuck it. It's so old and obviously knackered now so—'

'No, no,' he waves his thick hands in front of me. 'The wiring! I don't like the way that socket's burned – see, there? I don't know what kind of survey you might have had when you bought this place, but some of these old shops still have the paper casing around their wiring.'

I blink. 'Sorry, I thought you said paper.'

He nods and tucks his hands in his jeans pockets. 'Sadly, I did. It's a very old thing but sometimes it goes unnoticed for a long time. They used to use rubber around the wires, with a paper layer in between. The rubber perishes over time and the paper goes dry and brittle, leaving the electrical wires exposed.'

Paper. Electrical. Exposed. None of these words feel good as they hit my ears. 'But... how... *why* would anyone think paper around wire was a good idea?! It's bloody flammable!' My voice cracks on the last word, a sob barely caught in my throat.

Keith shrugs a little sheepishly, maybe embarrassed on behalf of all DIY practitioners everywhere. 'Add to the list with asbestos and lead piping, my dear. Look, I'm not saying the house is going to burn down in the middle of the night,' I grip the kitchen counter behind me with white knuckles. 'Or anyone is going to be electrocuted as they browse for girdles or whatever, but I don't like the look of it. I won't rest easy till you've had these double-checked.'

He won't rest easy?! What about our livelihoods? Shit, what about our lives?!

I'm worried that if I don't swallow down something I'll be sick all over Keith's tan work boots. But I can't switch on the kettle. I can't even drown myself in tea while I puzzle this out. So an old Nutella glass full of water it is.

Keith watches me gulp down the water and then thump the glass on the draining board. He scratches the back of his neck. 'Look, I've got the number of a guy – electrical engineer. Best you're going to get. I'll ask him to rush out here, as a favour. But in the meantime, I'll switch your mains supply off. As a precaution.' I think he adds that last bit because my eyes have gone as big and white as side plates. Keith lets himself out, probably glad to have escaped an emotional disaster zone as well as a potential bonfire of a house.

I don't know how long I stand at the sink, rooted to the spot, before my brain switches back into gear. Just as I'm thinking, *Let's get that number. Let's call that guy. We need a plan, Dee. Now more than ever we need a plan,* my foot kicks a paper bag by the washing machine, a heavy bag whose bottom is now ready to tear at the merest nudge since it's now soaking wet. And as I pull back my foot, about a dozen baby hats spill on to the floor. The stinky, sticky kitchen floor. And then it hits me, as it should have done right away: if the shop is a potential death trap, not only will we have to close to customers but we probably can't have the event here. JP is going to be utterly heartbroken. One of the tips I remember Mum and Dad giving us when we first set up the shop was that if anything goes wrong, don't touch it before the insurance man does. If we need to rewire and then replaster and repaint walls and therefore claim on our policy, they'll need to come and assess it all first. And God knows how long that might take.

So there's no way we can open the shop to either knitters or investors. We're screwed.

–

I've emailed MCJ to let them know – with no hint of my panic – that the shop is 'just too madly busy to put on pause tomorrow, after all!' One useful thing the world of work has taught me is how to glide up top while your straggly legs and webbed feet are pedalling for all their worth under the water.

I keep refreshing for their response, twitchy with the worry that I've now blown it and lost my moment with them. What if they've been doing background checks on me? What if they've called my last employer to check me out? If I was warming up my big-cheque-writing pen, I'd want to know the people I was giving money to were sound and stable. What if Devon's nasty little rumours have reached them too?

After another refresh, I pull my Marigolds back on and start on my next round of rinsing, gentle rub through suds and then more rinsing as the baby hats get a thorough sanitizing. The thought of icky fridge juice getting anywhere near a delicate little premmie baby's head is so, so, so very wrong, and without electricity the washing machine is just a useless white box. Luckily our cooker is gas, so I have one very slow source of hot water; I've got a gentle hand-washing detergent for woollens that JP stocks in the shop, I've got a washing-up bowl of tepid suds and I've got rubber gloves: I'm going old school. At the back of my mind is the warning JP gave me when he handed over my first ever hand-knitted gift: an unbelievably soft beanie hat that was all the colours of the peacock spectrum: green, blue, orange, gold and purple, one stripe effortlessly merging into the next in an ombré style. 'You *don't* hot-wash pure wool!' he'd said in his best bossy voice, which I knew was only a half-arsed impression of my own. 'Not unless you want thick, scratchy felt.' I know JP stipulated that the baby hats should be knitted in machine-washable yarns of the synthetic variety, but I just can't take any more chances with this precious cargo. Not only will each of these little hats make all the difference to a new person's first months in the world; they mean so much to JP. They're the start of a whole new dream of his. A dream which looks like it's souring into a nightmare at this rate. And I'm not going to accidentally felt his dreams.

So each hat gets an oh-so-subtle wash and then several rinses, a careful wringing and then a quick pat dry before I transfer it to my indoor washing line. OK, so JP doesn't have a washing line. He's a bloke: he puts wet pants on the radiator, even in the height of summer. But I've improvised: I found the offending bunting that had caused his spectacular fall and I string it up around the living room, Sellotaping it to the tops of doorways and picture frames like a Christmas garland. The hats just so happen to fit perfectly between each triangle of the bunting and at least all these blooming, cheery colours side by side are doing a little something to alleviate my mood.

Despair is not really a Delilah emotion. I see problems and I make opportunities from them. Usually. But now without the MCJ pitch and without the big knitathon on the horizon, I feel rudderless. I don't even know what I'm aiming for anymore. There just seem like too many problems to pick apart: I got sacked, JP broke his wrists, the investment isn't yet in the bag, and the charity plans may now be stalled indefinitely. Our shop might well shock me the next time I brush past a light switch. And all our hats smell like sour cream and onions. It all feels like too much. And I don't feel like me.

All these thoughts swash about in my head like the foamy water in the sink. I can't remember the last time I didn't have a plan. Washing these hats is at least making me feel like I'm doing something, but it's more a relief to put off the bigger issues than really fixing anything.

'You are a picture.'

I nearly hit my head on the light fitting, I jump so high. Becks is leaning against the doorway from the shop into the living room, watching me peg the hats onto the washing line.

I drop a wet, sky-blue bonnet onto my foot. 'Blimey! You scared me!'

'So you *had* forgotten the shop door was open?'

'Um, yes. Sorry. I had it propped open earlier, airing out... bit of a smell in here, sorry.'

Becky wrinkles her nose to one side. 'I can pick up a faint whiff of something minging. But right now I smell of baby poo and throw-up 24/7 so I'm hardly one to talk. What's happened?'

I flop down onto the sofa behind me and tell the story of the combusting fridge, the paper wiring and Rudderless Dee.

-

It doesn't take much for Becky to get me out of the shop – we aren't going to make any sales with that smell hanging around and the thought of the unsafe wiring hiding above my head, about to jump out at us in a ball of fire at any point, is hardly conducive to a nice, relaxing cup of tea at home.

So, without me really noticing, we've come to the library.

'It's not *that* weird,' Becky rolls her eyes at me as I hold the door open for her and the buggy, clearly doing a bad job of hiding my confusion. 'It's nice and quiet, there are colourful things for Ches to look at. And it's not my house. That's key. Every day I try and see a room that doesn't live in my house. And going to a coffee shop is costing me thousands in lattes and gingerbread men.'

She wheels over to the children's area, marked out with bright – if conspicuously stained – carpets and big wooden boxes full of picture books.

I feel pretty daft sitting my adult frame down on a toadstool-painted seat clearly made for a toddler's bum, but hey – it's not going to electrocute me. So that's something.

'Here,' Becks shoves a book my way. 'Read this one to Chester. It's his favourite, because of all the dogs. He loves dogs and cats!' Becky chucks him under his chin, bringing away a strand of drool as she does so. 'Oops. Well, this is what muslins are for!' She coos at him. His little feet kick out in different directions. There's nothing to say it isn't his favourite book, of course, but I think maybe, just maybe, Becky could be reading too much into Chester's gurns and arm waves at just ten weeks of age. I'm no Supernanny, but it's probably more likely that it's gas than genuine literary affection.

'*Hairy Maclary from Donaldson's Dairy*,' I start to read out loud, from the cover. 'Sure. Why not. It's not like I have a share report to read, or a balance sheet. Or even the Bloomberg Twitter feed. Might as well be a kids' book. That seems right for me, just about now.'

Becky drops the now-soggy muslin into her laps and folds her arms. 'OK. This won't do.'

'Sorry?'

She shakes her head. 'I can't do mopey. Not on three hours' of sleep at a time. Not with beach-ball boobs straining at the most God-awful bra you've ever seen. If I wanted self-pity I'd… I'd… I'd stay in and let myself wallow in it! But that's not what this is, Blackthorn. You'll read that book in a lovely, happy, cheery voice so my son appreciates the fun of books and then we'll have a chat and get all this sorted out.' With a decisive nod towards the shiny book I'm holding, she seems to make her ruling.

It's pretty hard to do a sing-song voice reading aloud about small dogs and tall dogs and thin dogs and spotty dogs while you feel like you're about to be called into the headmaster's office, like a naughty teacher about to be bollocked for stealing pens again. Though with that appalling pay, fair play to any teacher who hocks biros on the sly to make ends meet.

'… straight back home to bed,' I finish and Chester seems to show his appreciation with a wet 'Gurrrr' sound and a flap of his hands.

'See!' Becky puts her *CBeebies* presenter voice back on. 'Books are fun! Books are fun!' she chants into his pram. 'Have a chew of your giraffe, baby boy.' She puts a long-necked rubbery giraffe into one of his tiny hands, and he promptly whacks it into his own face.

'You. What's up?' She swivels to look at me. *CBeebies* has gone and now the channel's turned to *Question Time*.

'Well… the shop is completely out of action, I told you. We can't open to customers, we can't have the knitathon there now. JP is going to be gutted. And I – I don't know where to go next. How to fix this. I…' I bite down on my bottom lip, unsure whether I should share my plans with MCJ to her. But it just sounds like another embarrassing story of limp failure and after being canned I can do without one more of those in my repertoire. 'I don't know where to go next. I need to get my career back on track, but where is it even headed now? Do I want to go back to the City? I've never *not* had a five-year plan that didn't work out perfectly. And now, not only did my current plan go spectacularly wrong when my boss fired me, but I can't even think of a new one to get me back in action. I don't know what I want. What kind of job, what kind of future. What to aim for.'

Becky blows out a long breath, sending the wisps of hair around her face, the strands that have escaped her loose bun, up on a puff of air. 'Blimey, chill out, Dee!'

Not exactly the listening ear I'd been hoping for, if I'm honest.

I get up and slot the book back into its box. 'Yeah, no. I will. I'll go for a run or something, clear my head…'

'No, no,' Becky pulls me back down onto the stool beside her. 'I didn't mean it like that. Sleep deprivation makes me a bit brutally blunt, these days. I literally mean

– go easier on yourself, chill out, take a breath. *Who* has a five-year plan they stick to?! Who even makes one before it sends them mad? If you'd asked me five years ago what I'd want by now, I probably would have said to be married with a kid. But I wouldn't have said that I wanted to spend three weeks in hospital on a knife edge of panic, or then feel like some frumpy milk machine day and night when I did get home. I couldn't have planned the way Chester came into this world, not if I had all the baby books on Amazon. And even the part of the "plan" that did come good – having a baby, a bloke, a family at home – hasn't exactly been everything I might have planned for.' She winces as she goes on. 'The non-stop washing, the lonely days, the bleak nights, when you snap at your other half because they won't follow the sterilizing instructions properly…' Her hands grip into fists in her lap for a second. 'But that's how things are. And there are a million great things in my life. Some of them by plan, most by accident. And in these last months I've realized all you can ever truly control is just deciding to enjoy the little things.' She looks around the library and smiles.

'What do you mean?'

'Um,' she casts her eyes about for inspiration. 'The shiny foil on that book, see? Like a disco ball. Or when Chester and I go walking and we see a squirrel do some mad act of acrobatics from one tree to the next. A chat with you,' she nudges me in the ribs. 'The smell of Mum's Victoria sponge as I sit on her sofa and get an hour off from my own mum duty. Even when we were still on the ward, things like the pattern of shade the leaves made through the hospital window. Someone bringing you a cup of hot, sweet tea. Sounds mad and hippy-dippy, but when you have no say in the big things, you can at least choose to notice the small things and enjoy them right there and then. Like hand-knitted baby hats. Small things can mean a lot.'

'Right. I see.' I fiddle with a small square book on the table beside me. It's got touchy-feely animals on the front and one battered fluffy chick in particular looks like he's been nearly completely plucked of his yellow fur by over-enthusiastic little readers. Worn down. I know how he feels.

'No, you don't, do you? Maybe when you've been used to crazy big bonus cheques and business-class flights, marvelling at a squirrel and a cup of tea does sound a bit sad.' I open my mouth to disagree – that isn't what I think at all – but she holds up a hand to keep me quiet and continues, 'But you just need a fresh take on things. Reset your expectations. Tell me, what are your happiest recent memories, from, like, the last year? Be totally honest.'

I run my index finger over the baldy little chick. 'Um, well...'

'Be totally honest. Don't overthink. Just, happy. When?'

'Getting drunk in the pub that night, after CraftCon. Looking out at the lush countryside around Sunny Farm. Eating Jaffa Cakes on the sofa with JP, like we were kids again. Holding Chester for the first time, when you got home. Actually, just hearing you'd got home was a high point.'

'Ohhh!' She clamps her hands over her mouth as her eyes go twinkly with tears. 'But ignore me – go on.'

'I suppose, I've been happy to be here, to be home more.'

She nods. 'And from that list you just gave, how many moments were from the time you still had your job?'

She's got me there. And for a weird moment I see how lucky I am, strangely, to have this time here: to be a part of Chester's life from the start, to see JP's goals get bigger and brighter (and even to see him find a new major crush), being able to cheer Mags on as she re-enters the dating world, to realize that Ben isn't the B-movie villain I assumed but actually a really good friend. If I'd carried on with the status quo, these are things that I might only have known from texts or Facebook updates between meetings or waiting in departure lounges. I wouldn't have been part of the here and now, only the distant after. My career might have been a few months further down the line, and my bank balance would have looked a damn sight healthier, but my life would have passed me by. But enjoying life doesn't pay mortgages.

I let out a long, slow breath and rub one of Chester's perfect but tiny feet through his sleepsuit, printed all over with green stars. 'OK. So my old job wasn't making me happy. I don't want to go back there, I know that, but I have to do *something*, Becks. I can't not earn money. I know enough about myself that I need stability, I need to know the roof is staying firmly over my head. That it's not going to be cardboard boxes on the pavement.'

She frowns. 'But it's never going to get that bad – you have the shop, your parents have a spare room, there's even lovely Mags. And us! People love you – no one's going to let it get that bad.'

'But it can happen. We lost *everything* when my parents' business had to fold and they… they were so sad, for so long. For months Dad hardly got out of bed. We don't talk about it now but I just remember thinking, I won't let this happen again. And then when JP had his breakdown,

I realized it's not just enough to have my own back-up plan, but I need to keep my eye on him too.'

'So that's what this whole shop makeover thing has been about?'

I shrug. 'It makes me happy to know he's OK for the long term. I can relax then. And without a job, I kind of need the shop to make money for my finances, as well. But now I'm just really glad I've been here to see everything going on, to lend a hand.'

She lets out a soft, short laugh. 'You lend a hand to something the way a conductor lends a hand to an orchestra – with a baton in it. You've made a mega difference. There's this whole extra boost of energy to the place, and to JP now. I think he's a lot more confident with you around.'

'Really?'

'Absolutely. That, and his cool new squeeze. Oh God, listen to me – "squeeze"! I sound like someone's mum!'

Now it's my turn to laugh. 'You are someone's mum!'

She pokes my leg, hard. 'Yes, but I don't want to *sound* like it. I wanted to be twenty-three for ever, naturally. Though with so little sleep and only eating digestives in the five minutes I get for lunch, I feel more like a hundred and three. Oh, I've nearly finished my blog post, by the way. Writing it, like, fifty words at a time and then rereading them to find they're nonsense or a bit of my shopping list has crept in, but I will get there.'

'Can't wait to read it. Thanks.'

'Well, it's just me wittering on about premature babies, happiness and breast pumps and—'

I wave my hands quickly to cut short that worrying sentence. 'Not just the blog, but for listening. And being so wise. I'm just going to focus on the little, good things for now.'

And hope that I can figure out a new future while I'm eating Jaffa Cakes and washing baby hats.

Chapter 19

It's not an official thing, but I think JP has moved in with Patti. I assumed he'd come with me and temporarily move in at Mum and Dad's when I told him about the situation with the wiring. I even went so far as to offer to pack his shower gel, some socks and pants, and the latest issue of *Modern Knitting*, to put in the boot of Mags's car, along with my laundry bag of bits and pieces.

He was eerily quiet on the phone as I went through what happened with the fridge and Keith's warning about the wiring. The electrician he recommended is coming next week – fully booked until then – so that means the shop is shut indefinitely for now. All I heard in response was the long, slow release of a sigh and then JP say, 'Hang on,' followed by a muffled sound like he was putting his hand over the microphone. When he came back a few minutes later, his voice was level. 'I'm cool here, actually. I need to have a bit of a think, Dee. About what to do next. Call you later, yeah?'

And then he hung up. And I was instantly strung up with panic.

I'm pacing Mum and Dad's living room, staring at my phone in my hands like I can Jedi mind-trick it into buzzing with a call from JP. I need to know he's OK. I need to know this hasn't tripped him up, not again. That was a long time ago, granted, and he's so much happier now but a big sister never stops worrying. It starts with scraped knees and it goes right through to their almost-30s with heartbreak, misery and depression, it seems. But bombarding him with missed calls and messages isn't the way to go right now, even if I can feel my heart thrumming in my ears with worry: he's made it clear these past weeks that I can't overstep, and if I did it would just make him push me away. I have to wait for him to call me. And it's bloody hard.

But the force is not with me and all I'm doing with my emotions is creating a sweat-dampened phone and a sore hand from such a tight grip. It dawns on me there's someone else JP has opened up to lately – Ben. JP might have confided in him today about the whole debacle, he might have the inside track through their bromance. I could sneak some reassuring intel that way.

It's 4.15 p.m. now. I could be in London by the close of play.

> **Delilah**
> Hey, Ben. Fancy a drink tonight?

> **Ben**
> Yes. Absolutely. I could be in Fenwildby
> 7.30.

> **Delilah**
> I'll come to you. Would love a chat...

Picking an old post-work bar just below the office was a bit of a rookie move on my part – I'm now constantly twitching and looking over my shoulder, checking for former colleagues breezing through the doors. I'm too highly strung right now to answer questions about what I'm doing and dodge the gossip-fishing they'll surely do. But it's only 5.35 and most of my old workmates will still be hard at it till at least 6.30 or 7.00.

To look busy and not at all sad, desperate and unemployed to any passer-by, I tap out a message to Ben.

> **Delilah**
> Here a bit early! I'll get us some chips.
> Bottle of red?

I'm just putting my purse back in my bag a few minutes later, when Ben pushes through the heavy chrome doors and walks my way, quickly and effortlessly climbing up onto the high stool next to me.

'Oh, hey! I didn't think you'd be out so early. I've only just ordered. Slow day, was it?'

Ben shrugs and flips a beer mat. 'You know.'

'Well, I *used* to...'

His eyes flick to mine. 'Shit, sorry, I didn't mean—'

'I'm kidding! It's fine. Least of my worries right now. Just surprised you're able to sneak away on time from all those juicy clients of mine.' I give him some mock-evils and he smiles.

'Ah, yes. No, it's fine. I'm on it. So – what are all these worries you've got?'

I start to plough into everything that's happened in just a handful of hours since I messaged him about landing MCJ – having a potential powder keg for a premises and what that means for the shop's performance and the planned knitathon.

'So I can hardly invite MCJ to come and see our very fabulous, very flammable retail space and having a big looming insurance payout on the horizon won't get them very excited, either. But I don't think, in good faith, I can cover it up. That's not how I do things.'

A bottle of red is put onto the bar in front of us and two glasses clink together as they follow suit.

Ben starts pouring. 'Agreed. But change the story, Dee. Go to *them*. Lying about the situation – no. Smoke and mirrors? Always. A "major rejuvenation project", maybe? Then once they're fully immersed and bought in, you can subtly reveal the details.'

The wine feels very good as it goes down – warm and almost fiery. I need this. I need a splash of alcohol and someone who really knows us – and the business – to thrash it all out with.

'But I'm worried, most of all, about JP. The investment I can knuckle down and get it on track again, somehow. But I'm worried about how JP will take it. He must be so, so disappointed.'

Ben frowns. 'But I thought he didn't know about how far you'd got with this just yet?'

'He doesn't know. But it's the knitathon, having to cancel it. It's just the sort of thing that could trigger a dark time for him. And as he's hanging out with Patti, I haven't seen him – I don't know how bad the cancellation has hit him.'

'He's not cancelling.'

'What?'

'We were texting about it this afternoon. He's going a hundred miles an hour to find a new location, and maybe even a pop-up shop space for the next fortnight, to keep the tills warm. He didn't say?'

I rub at my forehead. 'No. He didn't say.'

Ben looks down at his shoes for a moment. 'Maybe he just got carried away in all the momentum. It sounds like he and Patti have set up a sort of crisis HQ in her bedsit and they're cracking on. I wouldn't worry,' he leans forward and covers my restless hands on the countertop with one of his own. 'It actually sounds like he's thriving off it.'

His hand feels weird on mine. I mean, the hand *itself* isn't weird – it's not like it's scaly or covered in slime. But this moment of physical connection, feeling the very real weight and warmth of his fingers over mine, completely throws me and I forget what we're talking about. It's not like I haven't known Ben has hands and the ability to move them around of his own free will, but I suppose I haven't ever really entertained the idea of them moving in my direction. But he is a guy. I'm a girl. I just don't think I've ever thought of him as a 'guy' guy before now.

'So what's your move going to be?' He studies my face closely.

'Um, sorry?' I have to shake my head a few times to dislodge the words *Ben's hands, Ben's hands* playing on a loop in my brain.

He pulls back and puts his hands – Ben's hands, Ben's hands – into his suit trouser pockets. 'If the knitathon isn't cancelled and if you could *spin* the situation with the shop premises, what's to stop you pushing on with the investment? Funnily enough, it sounds like now more than ever the cash injection could really work wonders.'

'Oh. Yes. I hadn't thought of that angle.' I take a big glug of wine. 'I must be getting rusty.'

Ben smiles. 'There's no rust on you, Blackthorn. You're the master of the boardroom, the Queen of the closers.'

He's distracted by a buzz in his pocket. As he takes out his phone, his eyebrows shoot up. 'There, see. JP says he's found a new venue already! It's all back on, no worries.'

I put my hand to my bag. No echoing buzz of a message for me, then. JP has just chosen to tell Ben, not me. I feel a little pinch behind my ribcage. Why is he keeping me out of this? Is this the first warning sign of an emotional shut-down? Should I call Mum?

'I... I think I should go.' I grab my jacket and slide off the stool with as much grace as my jangling nerves will allow. 'You're right, I should be pressing on. Get a new meeting booked, get my pitch totally polished.'

'But, hey—' Ben puts his hands – *Ben's hands, Ben's hands* – on my jacket sleeve this time, gently tugging me back down. 'Two heads are better than one, right? I can play devil's advocate, look for any chinks they might want to expose. Let's throw things around. We can role-play!'

The waiter, putting our metal bucket of chips down in front of us, tries not to react as he hears this last part.

'And besides, the chips have only just arrived. Sit down, Blackthorn. This isn't a solo project, remember? This is for JP too.'

He points down and I sit, oddly obedient for perhaps the first time in my life. I have to admit, the fact that Ben likes my brother so much helps me completely bury the old image of him as a privileged, pompous douchebag. *If you've got JP's back, I've got yours – end of.* And it would help to have a fresh pair of eyes on my pitch. Ben's become a real core part of everything we're doing with the campaign, someone I can really talk to. Is 31 too old to be making new friends? Whatever we are now to each other – friends, former enemies turned knitting allies – I'm really glad Ben is around.

He straightens up a little on his stool. 'So I'm MCJ. You walk into the meeting room, sit down confidently at the table.' He clears his throat, getting into character. 'Good morning, Delilah. Thanks for coming in.'

—

'Thanks for having me, Lorraine.' There's no wobble in my voice, no telltale shake to my hands. I am the epitome of a cucumber straight from the fridge. I'm owning this. I have to. 'Shall we get straight to it?'

I open my A4 leather document wallet. My parents bought it for me right after university, to keep my CV looking pristine when I went on my first interviews. Back in my last job, I would have taken my devices to a meeting, with everything I needed on them, but my old iPad doesn't look too flash so I'm hoping to pull off a classic, refined look with the wallet. It's more 'haberdashery' than an iPad, anyhow.

Lorraine nods, her sharp bob of icy blonde hair swishing forward as she does. Her grin is Cheshire Cat-like in its width and glee. 'This is what makes us so excited, Delilah, about working with you. With your background we know we can get down to brass tacks – you get it. You know where we're coming from, after all.' The two suited blokes flanking Lorraine at the shiny boardroom table nod along with her. They have the identikit haircut of a City guy: short at the sides, just a centimetre longer and tousled on top to give the appearance of personality. And their striped blue shirts and navy suits could have been bought off the same rail, except that they're probably handmade. But I'm not here to let my inner reverse-snob run amok. I'm here to land this deal.

I feel a prickle of doubt when Lorraine mentions my background. What has she heard? Who has she spoken to? But she wouldn't have called me in if she'd thought I was too dodgy to work with. Or a few months off motherhood and stinky nappies. She wouldn't want to invest in someone she wasn't 100 per cent sure of. *You're the master of the boardroom. Queen of the closers, remember?*

'Exactly.' I nod just once, making eye contact with the three of them in turn. They might have the advantage over me with numbers but I've got the goods they want – a thriving business with a loyal customer base, combining an event space with an influential social media hub and a charity project garnering plenty of good PR. MCJ are known for their ethical investments – JP's business is as tasty to them as a mountain of fat free Jaffa Cakes would be to me. Well, lick your lips, fellas, and open that cheque book.

I hand over three sheets of our most recent month's turnover, the statistics that outline what a huge surge JP has seen in online followers and how that's given us a 13 per cent bump in online sales too. Tasty.

'As you can see here, Blackthorn Haberdashery has never been more in demand. My co-founder's recent launch of a community initiative to knit hats for premature babies has driven new visitors to the shop, both in bricks and mortar and in e-commerce. *About a (Knitting) Boy* is now one of the best-loved and most trusted knitting YouTube channels. And we all know that kind of authenticity can't be bought or made. It's grown slowly and with dedication. We feel that now is exactly the right moment to consider outside investment to really grow and show what this business is all about. That is genuine connection with the craft community and supplying them with the best materials.' My eyes never leave Lorraine's: I've been rehearsing this in my head, in the shower, while running, doing the washing-up; since the days Ben helped me whittle down the pitch to its core essence. He really knew how to challenge me on my approach, without making me doubt myself. All that 'shadowing' when we were rivals actually turned out to be a good thing – he knew just how I worked.

Lorraine smiles as I talk, and her two flunkies scribble notes furiously. A schoolboy trick of trying to look like you're on top of things in a meeting. But I know who I'm really talking to here – the power in this room comes with an expensive bobbed hair-do and flawless manicure.

I pause to take a quick breath and then carry on, seamlessly. 'In fact, we're running a knitathon in two days, to benefit our charitable project. In just our local area it's generated a huge response and I think it could easily go nationwide with the right capital behind us. We'd be delivering much-needed support to families with premature babies as well as strengthening our brand recognition. It's a strategy that—'

Lorraine waves one finger in my direction, subtly cutting me off. The burgundy polish on her nails flashes with a high shine. 'That's all great, Delilah. In fact, we're well aware of the charity project and how it's been picking up momentum. It's one of the reasons we want to move so quickly on this. It's absolutely great. You know how charity work ticks the boxes for our own brand image – I wouldn't expect anything less than for you to do your homework on us, after all. But I'm going to level with you here. One professional to another, yes?' She lowers a blonde eyebrow in my direction. 'In this case our goals are more profit-related. Directly. We're looking to invest on behalf of Wow Wools, a very large American company who mass-produce a variety of yarns. They are well established in the US craft market but they've struggled to get a toehold in Blighty. What we're looking to do is parcel together a number of small retail companies for Wow Wools to own a majority stake in, and those stores would then exclusively stock their yarns. What's exciting about,' her eyes flick down to the handout I passed her, '*About a (Knitting) Boy* is that Wow would also be getting an influencer in the community, to really push the brand to his audience. As you said yourself, that kind of genuine voice with a loyal following just can't be bought. Well,' she laughs a light, tinkling laugh and her cronies quickly join in, 'in this case we *would* be buying it, but you know what I mean. All in all, you have just what we want to make up one of our parcel of seven stores so far. Wow Wools could become the exclusive supplier for your hat knitting project. Their branding would appear on all your materials and they'd push things through their own social media channels, of course. They'd supply the words for your brother to use in his blog, all that would be carefully managed. Here, we have a mock-up.' She wets her lips with a sip of sparkling water and nods to one of her henchmen. He draws a sheet of paper out from his file and holds it up for me to see. It's one of Becky's pictures of Chester wearing one of the very first donated hats and they've splashed a huge neon-yellow Wow Wools logo along the bottom half of it. I feel a sick twist in my stomach. 'And with the clout of a huge corporation behind you, supplying the product at a great price as well as all your business strategy and a content plan, you'd both be able to step back from the business and feel the benefits of a generous investment, yes?'

Lorraine leans back in her chair, catching the eye of the suit to her left and flicking him a brief smile.

'Let me boil this down,' I rub my hands against my charcoal-grey trousers to absorb some of the moisture I can feel gathering on my palms, 'you're looking to Trojan-horse these Wow Wool products into the UK? Through the charity work we're doing?'

The suit on the right rubs his hand through his uniform hair. 'Don't quote us on that, but yes. This company is looking for the route to market, and as the market has resisted we're looking to own those routes to market for them.'

My fingers curl into fists. 'And has there been any analysis of just why the market resisted, organically?'

Lorraine blinks. Her smile drops. 'We look forward here at MCJ. We solve problems. We don't waste time on the past. We address what our client wants. And then we achieve.' Her shiny nails tap out a rhythm on the table as she speaks. 'It's not something everyone can do.' She looks me up and down and I completely understand her meaning.

I lean forward over the table. 'What a client might want is not necessarily what they *need*. Or did they not cover that on your BTEC in Business Admin?'

The suits gasp as one.

'I might want to marry Chris Hemsworth and live on a charming houseboat, but it's not what I *need*. Your client might want to be a big player in the UK craft market but what they *need* is to understand why no one wants their inferior product. Because it's poorly made without a passionate crafter in mind, and because we have the very best yarns produced right here on home soil. We even have alpaca, for Christ's sake! And it's warmer and far more

breathable than any of your Wow Wools acrylic nonsense.'
I zip up my leather folder in one definitive swipe.

'I came here to find a worthy investment for a credible
business – credible in both its turnover and its ethical drive
to help its community. Not to be a puppet for a... a... yarn
that I wouldn't even knit a dog bed with!'

I'm snatching up my jacket when Lorraine says, just
loud enough to be heard, 'Inappropriate. Unpredictable.
A liability. Just what I heard. And such a shame too.'

I let the slam of the glass door answer for me.

–

My whole body is vibrating with rage. I'm not sure I've
ever felt this angry. Not even when Bella Turnbull in
year five said Ant and Dec couldn't really sing. Not even
when my first-year uni boyfriend dumped me for a girl
two doors down in my halls and I had to watch them
smooch over the toasted sandwich maker for the next
month. Not even when Devon fired me. Because none
of those things felt this personal. None of those things
were trying to push my little brother around, to cash in
on his hard work and expertise with so little respect or
thought. MCJ aren't the investment do-gooders they've
so cleverly painted themselves as – they're just the same
kind of bully-boy idiots so many other big firms are, and
they chose to bully the wrong craft nerd. Because his big
sister won't take that shit.

My anger powers my journey back to Fenwild without
me so much as noticing a platform number or the miles
between London and home speeding by. I'm. Just. So.
Mad.

I don't even properly notice the blue gingham bunting
Bob has carefully Sellotaped around the windows and

ceiling of Cheeky's Greasy Spoon. The foil of the *It's A Boy* banner hanging in the middle briefly catches my eye as I storm in. With everything going on, Beck's baby shower has been pushed to the back of my mind, though I made all the preparations and plans for it weeks ago. Becks extended the invite to the rest of the team behind the knitathon, seeing as we're all a kind of bonkers craft family now, so JP and Patti are sitting at a table with Becks, a lacy tablecloth spread in front of them, a huge sachertorte on a cake stand like a chocolate beacon in the centre. I will switch back to the baby shower, and get a gobful of that cake, just as soon as I get this off my chest…

I stomp over to the counter. 'Tea, three sugars, please,' I bark and then stalk off to join the others. 'God, have I got something to tell you.'

Becks gives a little wave with her one free hand, the other under a muslin draped over her shoulder as she feeds Chester beneath it. 'Hey! Isn't this lovely? Thanks for sorting it all. What's going on? Are you OK?'

'Nope!' I flop down into a spare chair and dump my bag beside me.

Patti and JP exchange brief looks.

'So, long story short – there was an investor interested in backing the business. You remember, JP? And you told me to handle it?'

He nods. 'Um, yeah.'

'So I worked on a pitch for them. I got the shop in good order, sorted out the website, made it all more slick and polished. They couldn't fail but see it as a great prospect – all the hits you've been getting, how the revenues have been going bananas since the premmie hat knitting campaign started, really upping the profile and brand recognition. Making people care about our shop as a craft destination. Then the sodding wiring raised its little dodgy head and I couldn't get them over to see the place itself.'

Bob brings my tea over and I take a scalding glug to ease the scratching in my throat. It doesn't work. I spend two minutes spluttering.

'So it's gone away?' JP is frowning at me.

'No! Well, yes! So, Ben helps me refine the pitch – I'm the Queen of closers and all that. So I go in there and say, "This is a profitable business with a responsible ethos that will get it lots of great PR." But then they say they only want to invest if you'll exclusively promote Wow Wools through the campaign. They even put their logo on a picture of Chessie from the site! And you'd have to talk them up on your vlog.'

'Which I won't do!' spits JP, making Patti flinch. She's probably never seen him anything other than calm, the Zen master of knitting that he is.

'I know! I know! I told them to shove it.' I slump backwards into the chair, the last puff of anger escaping my ears and evaporating into thin air.

'The hats campaign was part of your pitch?' Becks asks in a small voice.

'Yes. It's been great for exposure.'

Her cheeks blanch. '*What did you say?*'

'Well, just that—'

JP leans forward in his chair. 'This campaign was never about exposure. Brand building. Any of that,' I can tell he's biting back a swear word, 'stuff. Dee, it was about a real community, helping real people. Families, babies. Babies like Ches.'

'My baby,' Becks says in barely more than a whisper. 'And he is not a marketing tool. I can't believe… you take my blog post down, and all my photos, OK? Take it all down! And you can forget about your free poster boy from here on in.' In one movement she whips Chester up from under his gauze curtain and lays him in the bright buggy. Torn abruptly from his tea, he lets out a monster shriek of contempt. Becks sorts out her feeding bra and top, then starts wheeling towards the door.

'Becky, hey! No, you don't understand… it wasn't like that. Come back! We haven't even cut the cake. The meeting, it… it just happened and I… made a good opportunity from it.' Even as the words leave my lips I know they are awful and empty.

'And there was me thinking you'd changed, Dee. You went off and got all serious, all fancy on us, forgot all your friends. I thought you being back meant you were different. And you certainly made a good show of it. Coming back here with your tail between your legs, saying that you want to spend time with people, not big piles of cash. Buying me a fancy cake for my "baby shower". But you're just the same, aren't you? You're just about the money. It's all you've been able to talk about from the minute you stepped foot in here. Well, consider yourself one customer down now.'

She backs out of the door before Bob can get there and hold it open for her. I look to my brother. He's holding Patti's hand under the table; I can just about glimpse it.

'Where did that come from?' My voice may not have wobbled back in the MCJ boardroom but it's on a roller-coaster ride now.

JP keeps his eyes on the Formica tabletop. 'Take a moment, Dee. Think about it from Becks's point of view. It sounds like you were cashing in on what she went through, like this whole campaign was about her story helping us – rather than us helping her.' He rubs his hands down his face slowly. 'I've got to say, I'm with her. It makes me feel pretty shitty. I thought getting some investment money would be about doing more of what we do, not... selling out.'

'Yes, exactly – that's why I told them to get lost!'

'But *you* told them. Because *you* went alone. I said I was OK with you following up on the investment people, to check them out. I didn't think you were going to swan into their office and offer them my entire life on a silver platter!'

'That's not what it was. I'm not a bad guy here, JP! I was trying to get you some security, for the future. I was trying to look out for you.'

His eyes finally find mine, but I can't read them. 'I'm not a kid anymore, Dee. And I'm not the guy you found on the sofa, unable to move or talk for the shit in his head. I don't need you to worry about me like this. It's not right.' He turns away again, looking out of the cloudy cafe window. 'I... I think I need a bit of time, sis. Bit of head space, yeah? Just to work out where we all stand.'

Patti bites her bottom lip, smudging the lilac lip tint that offsets the new orange streaks in her hair. How I wish this conversation wasn't happening like this, in front of other people, in a public place. I want to spontaneously combust into nothing, just to get away from the cold, rolling feeling in my stomach. How I wish this conversation wasn't happening, full stop.

Did I really get it so wrong? Why can't they see I've been doing it all for the right reasons?

JP stands up slowly and Patti stands next to him.

'So, everything for the knitathon is pretty much sorted. Supplies, social media, location. So we're set, yeah? You can get back to your job search. Back to where you're at home.' His jaw is clenched and I can tell he's fighting something very angry inside. 'We don't need you at the knitathon if you just want to change us, telling us what we're doing wrong so... just keep away. I'll be in touch, Dee.' He shuffles out from behind the table awkwardly, and then they're gone.

I'm sitting there with only four cold cups of tea for company. I want to go back to this morning – when I was full to the brim with energy and confidence, striding into that meeting and doing what I know best. I don't want to be here: no investment, no job, friends who think I'm a heartless monster and a brother who's basically told me to stay out of his life for now. He doesn't want me at the knitathon.

I've failed.

My hands are jittery with shock and adrenalin, so I pull out my phone for something to do, something to look down at and hide my tear-filled eyes.

> **Ben**
> HOW did it go? The suspense is KILLING me over here! I'm coming to the village for a drink with JP tonight. Will I see you at the pub? Maybe toast your successes?

I throw down a twenty on my saucer, grab my bags and bolt home.

Chapter 20

I'm in my ancient bottle-green joggers, a blanket slung over my shoulder and I'm hunched over Dad's creaking PC in my parents' office, with all the lights off.

JP said I should stay away from the knitathon. But he didn't say I couldn't cyber-stalk it. It's one day until the big event and his words and Becky's from yesterday are still ringing in my ears. They didn't stop clanging away in my brain all night, in fact, like bellringers on too much Red Bull.

He is not a marketing tool.

You're just the same.

Back to where you're home.

Keep away.

I hardly slept, not helped by the fact that I'd raided Mum and Dad's cupboards for some kind of instant snack and all I could find was some stale Rice Krispies and the coffee machine. Sugar, caffeine and misery have never been a winning combination for a restful night of shut-eye.

I went over and over everything: what I've done, what I've said, what could have been different. Eventually I locked my phone in the shed, because manically refreshing it every ten seconds was doing my head in. JP didn't want to hear from me and I respect that. But the curious cat came back and I found myself logging on to the old computer and going straight to *About a (Knitting) Boy*'s Facebook page.

A new vlog. My clammy hand slid the mouse across the screen and clicked. In it, JP wasn't quite at his usual level of energy or bounce, and it strung at my heart to know I'd been the cause. He told his band of crafty followers that they'd soon be switching on to a live-stream feed, so everyone could keep their eye on how the knitathon preparations were going, ahead of the big day.

'You'll be there, right?' JP pointed down the camera, giving a cheeky wink right at the end.

Yes, little brother, I'll be there. Even if you don't realize it.

–

So since first thing this morning, I've been glued to the live stream of JP, Patti, Ben and Becks setting up the school hall: sweeping it, arranging tables and chairs, drawing up big motivational signs and little snack stations with crisps and nuts ready to be opened tomorrow. Becks has taken breaks to change Chester and give him a push in the pram to get him off to sleep. I've seen Ben and JP huddled in the corner a few times, Ben putting his arm on JP's shoulder and talking with his eyebrows lowered, creasing his forehead. At least if I can't be there to help out, I know Ben is. And he's kind of like the male me, I suppose. Which is a weird thought. When my eyes take in Ben, I have to admit there are a lot of feelings fighting out behind my ribcage: I'm worried he'll think less of me too now; I'm so lucky he's been part of this whole escapade; and I desperately don't want him to disappear from my life. I think he's… important to me now.

My stomach rumbles. It's 11.32 a.m. How did that happen? Last night's chewy cereals are a distant memory but I certainly couldn't face them again for lunch. I would call for a pizza but my phone barely gets reception at Mum and Dad's. And what I really need now, if I'm honest, is something wholesome and homely, something comforting. Something that Mum would make. Or…

'Cooee! Dee, love, are you here? Ooof, why are all the curtains still closed?'

Mags's head pops round the study door. She takes in my joggers, my lank, unwashed hair and probably gets a whiff of stale air seeing as I haven't left the house in nearly 24 hours. 'My word. What's been going on here, then?'

–

'I have to teach you to cook.' Mags is wagging her finger in my direction, but her smile says otherwise – I think a part of her loves having an excuse to cook one of my childhood faves and 'fix' me a little.

She slides the macaroni and cheese into the oven to allow the breadcrumbs on top to go all deliciously crispy. My heart is lifting and my mouth is watering, all at the same time. And while Mags has been busy grating, chopping and cooking, I've been able to offload the whole sorry tale of the MCJ thing without having to look her directly in the eye. I think I know which way she's going to sit on this.

'Hmm.' She wipes her hands on the back of her flares. 'A right old pickle, my pickle.' She fiddles with the tea towels, hanging them just so on the oven door handle. She comes around the kitchen island and puts her arm around my shoulders. 'I know you meant well. You have such a good heart, Delilah. And such a strong brain. Sometimes, it's hard to juggle the two, I imagine. I wouldn't know!

Cotton wool for brains, here.' She laughs her twinkly laugh.

'Rubbish, you're really smart, Mags. And kind. You're the most giving woman I know. I was trying to do good things but, but maybe I was… going a bit overboard, doing a bit too much?'

The delicate raise of her eyebrows tells me I'm on to something. 'Maybe. I think JP wanted to prove something with organizing his knitathon, you know. That he could do it alone. I think that's why he's been keeping his cards close to his chest, away from you. He has a different way of doing things and just thinks you're…'

'Overbearing? Controlling? Calculating?'

Mags rolls her eyes. 'He's your brother. He loves you. He's never going to think those things. But perhaps now is the time to stand back a bit, let him do his thing. And you can do yours.'

I snort out through my nose like a petulant teen with only an hour of Wi-Fi time left. 'But what *is* my thing, Mags? I thought it was my career, but maybe it's not. Right now I'd happily rip up my CV to use as coasters at the knitathon, if JP would let me.'

'Well, then, that tells you something, doesn't it?' She leans the side of her head against mine.

'What?'

'That you're not all about your career. There's more to you than that. You're a devoted sister and a good friend too. There's that Ben chap, he's nice.' Suddenly my neck starts to feel red hot and prickly. 'And it's so lovely you've rekindled your friendship with Becky. She's a lovely girl. Woman. Well, you're all still girls to me.' She waves her hand and moves away to do more unneeded tidying. 'Oh, must water those plants for your mum.'

But Mags, bringing up Becky, reminds me of something – before she stormed out of the cafe, Becks said to take her blog post down. So she finished it, then. And JP must have uploaded it, typing one finger at a time, as he does these days. I slouch back to the grey PC and bring up JP's blog, then start to read.

WHERE IT ALL BEGAN!

Hey guys, my name is Becks and no I'm not a boy and no I don't really knit (well, I'm a beginner!!!) but I'm all behind the big knitathon and I wanted to tell you why.

My gorgeous son Chester was born very early – weeks and weeks before he was supposed to enter the world. He came in a bit of a panicked rush, so much so that I still can't remember most of it. But out he came and now he's ours. I'm putting a picture in at the bottom of this blog. He's gorgeous, right?! I know all parents are biased but I DO ACTUALLY have the most beautiful baby in the world. Fact.

Right, I could go off topic here, talking about his perfect fingers or his lovely pudgy chops or the way he recognizes me and gives me a special hand wave every morning. I say morning, I mean 2 a.m., 4 a.m., 5.30 a.m....

But at the start of his life things didn't feel so rosy. We didn't know what health complications he might have, being born so early. And we couldn't bring him home for ages while we waited for all the tests to be done. My other half and I spent a lot of time on that NICU ward, I can tell you. And even though the nurses and doctors were BRILLIANT (literally brilliant – go, NHS! You rock!), we felt so alone. So scared. This little helpless chap needed us, but we were powerless too. For so long, I couldn't even hold him. Turns out we are among the lucky ones and he's going to be totally fine, but every day I remember how close we came to being unlucky, and how many people are dealing with those circumstances.

But in the midst of all these grey clouds and rainstorms, a little ray of light poked through. I was in a supermarket, on the verge of hysterical tears, and I met an old friend. She's Delilah and she's About a (Knitting) Boy's sister. She doesn't know I'm going to talk about her in this post – so hiya Dee! Surprise! Ha, ha, ha, ha!

Dee bought me a coffee and brought me round and since then she's been an amazing mate. And through her and JP, so many of YOU have been amazing and knitted hats not just for Chester's little bonce but for hundreds of other premmie babies too. It's so important that tiny babies stay warm but more than that, by making something by hand you are showing someone else how much you care. And in dark times that means so much; I can't really find the words. You might be able to tell words aren't really my bag – I am much more of an emoji girl!!!

So ahead of the knitathon I want to say this – THANK YOU AND KEEP KNITTING! You are the sunshine in other people's lives, just like Dee was in mine on that grey day. When you're at your lowest, you need hope. And it comes through other people.

So if you're coming along to our big event, I'll be the one with the goooorgeous baby and I'd love to say hello! So would Chester.

Lots of love,

Becks xxxx

P.S. Sorry if this is bonkers, it's my first ever blog xxxx

The tears are sliding down my face and leaving dark polka dots on my joggers. I log into the blog as an admin, but before I carry out Becks's wishes and delete the post, I copy and paste it into a word doc. It's too beautiful to lose for ever, even if I don't deserve such a heartfelt thank you now.

I have to make it up to them. I have to. Even if JP keeps me out with an electrified fence and guard dogs trained to rip off all my limbs, I have to sort this out. There must be something, there must be...

My eyes catch on the familiar pink tone of a neatly folded *Financial Times* on the desk, on top of the pile of post. Mags must have put it there. I could find a new job, a new avenue. I can make my own money to put back into the haberdashery, to take the knitathon nationwide this time next year. Just give me a spark of an idea, a notepad and a coffee, and I can show JP that I'm using my skills for good, not profit-making evil. I only work because I want us to be safe. But I know that there's more to 'safe' than paid bills and nest eggs. There's happiness, and a joy in what you do. Even if I don't know what might bring me real joy professionally, JP does know so I can vicariously live through his happiness, for now.

There must be something out there for me to put my energies into; I must be able to find the upside in this disaster. Right? Melanie Griffith did it in *Working Girl* – picked up a newspaper and made her own path. And since that film inspired my love of hoop earrings and power dressing, it can't be that far from reality.

Between slurps of sugary, but now, cold tea that shoot bolts of trembling energy into my system, I hurriedly turn the pages. Opportunities. Don't think of your life as a pile of shit. It's a pile of opportunities. But the columns of narrow, dense text start to lose their meaning, one after the other – sentences unravelling like a thick black woolly jumper being pulled apart, row by row. All I can see is jargon and company names and arrows pointing this way, that way, backwards. I might as well be trying to decipher one of JP's expert-level Fair Isle patterns. In Swedish.

But just as I'm about to give up, I see something that does seem familiar. A name.

No, that can't be right. He can't have... surely not?

Clive has been poached by Next Gen Now, my old company's biggest rival. And his new job is incredibly senior. But, he was...

I'm shrugging on a baggy cardi of Dad's from the back of the office chair. Need to call Ben. Ben will know what the frig is going down with this nonsense. When the landline rings, half buried under a wilting pot plant on the windowsill, I think he must have read my mind.

'Ben?'

'Ah, hello? This is Douglas McNaulty. May I speak to Delilah Blackthorn?'

I take the phone away from my ear and stare at it for a second, like it's an enchanted lamp and by picking it up I've awoken the genie of career magic, Douglas. The longed-for, much-anticipated Douglas. And now he's calling me!

'... Hello? Is anyone there?'

'Yes! Yes, yes. I'm here. I mean, Delilah is here. I'm Delilah. You're speaking to her. Me.'

'OK. Great. Look, I know this is last minute and I've already moved your appointment once before, but I've just had someone call, stuck on a broken-down train outside Manchester. I know how keen you are to meet – all those chasing emails you sent certainly left an impact. So I wondered if you wanted to take the appointment?'

'For today?!'

'Well, for *now*, I should say. Could you get here in 45 minutes? I'm in Kingston, not all that close to the station, I'm afraid, but plenty of free parking. If you have access to a car?'

'Yes! I do. And yes! I'll take it.'

I've always been good with adrenalin: exams, sports days, public speaking; I always found the jittery burst of adrenalin would help me race towards my goal and get there that much faster. And I took that from school to university and then to work, too. And though adrenalin helped me quickly and effectively sweet-talk Mags into dropping her car keys into my hand two minutes after I put the phone down, it might not have been totally my best friend today.

Because I'm sitting in traffic just outside Kingston, checking all my mirrors to see if it's safe to cheekily pull into the next lane over, when I see a flash of myself looking back at me. The sleep-crusted eyes, the lank hair flopping over my forehead, the cereal crumbs around my mouth.

Adrenalin sped me up and out the door so quickly in order to make Douglas's deadline, that it trampled all over Reason and Sense who were shouting that I needed to at least take a shower and change out of my joggers first. But, nope, I'm still in my joggers. And I smell pretty bad. Oh, shit. Douglas's advice is probably going to be: Firstly, stop living under a bridge. Secondly, buy some shampoo.

Christ. But what can I do now? My phone map is telling me I'll be there in ten minutes and if I detour to find a life-saving Boots and an M&S I will be slightly more presentable, but late. Why did I say I could be there? Why? Why do I always have to prove I'm an A★ at everything?! Right now I'd only get top marks in smelling like a bin.

I pull up outside number 5, Douglas's house-slash-office. Two minutes to spare. There must be something... something.

—

'Delilah, do come in.'

'Thank you. I'm sorry about my attire – you caught me... just before I was about to start some marathon training.'

Douglas takes in Mags's grey yoga pants, which I found in her gym kit, luckily in the boot of the car. I hope he doesn't have CCTV covering his front garden, or he'll know exactly how awkwardly I changed into them in his bush. Not to mention getting a flash of my arse. Her tie-dye scrunchy and matching billowing top might not be to my taste, but they're keeping the greasy hair off my face and making some sort of a semblance of an 'outfit'. Bless the Crocs she walks in, because she also had a roll-on deodorant in there, which I've rolled on just about every bit of visible flesh I have. It was that or the car air freshener behind the ears.

'Oh, right. Impressive. Which marathon?'

'London.'

'Blimey. You're making an early start.' He raises an eyebrow.

I rub my hands together. 'Well, you know what they say, the early runner catches... the personal best worm!' My chuckle is weak and hollow, bouncing off the floor tiles and tall ceiling of the porch.

'Well, do come through. Can I get you a coffee?'

'Espresso, if you have it.'

He nods. 'Good stuff. We have a little less than an hour in this introductory session. Make yourself at home and I'll be through with the coffees.'

I move into the front room and take in the range of seats: a squashy sofa in brown leather; a chaise longue in grey cord, two neat armchairs in the same grey material and a big wing-backed red velvet chair. I remember reading a business book about how our choice of a chair reflects a lot about our professional selves – do you stay on the outskirts of the room, do you want to blend in? Or do you pick the biggest, boldest spot because you're not afraid to be heard? Adrenalin tells me that this is the kind of stuff Douglas is going to make a note of. I'm going for it.

'Ah.' He stands in the doorway. 'That is actually my chair.'

I fiddle with the metal studs on the end of the scarlet armrest and for the first time notice the little console table next to me, with what is clearly Douglas's phone, notebook and Mount Blanc pen. 'Oh, ha, ha, ha! Yes, sorry. It just looked *so* comfy. I'll er…' I scuttle over to the sofa and sink down about two feet as it absorbs my weight. Not the strategic advantage I was going for, but at least a touch less mental-looking.

He hands me my coffee which I decide to sip very slowly (adrenalin does not need its partner in crime, caffeine, to step in just yet) and then sits down into his huge chair. Maybe he has read the same book about chair power and he just wants people to feel in awe of him. Oh, shit, I'm not paying attention and he's already talking.

266

Seeing as this is going to be the key to my future and cost me the last of my flowing cash, I'd better tune in.

'... so that's the basics of what I do here. And now we start with some questions.' He must see me flinch at this and read the panic in the whites of my wide eyes. 'No preparation necessary. In fact, that's a bonus. If you're here seeing me, then the right answers aren't coming naturally to you. So we need you to think differently. You need to get out of your own head. Yes?'

He doesn't know how right he is.

Douglas clears his throat. 'What I've come to believe, through years in this line of work and reading every business psychology book Amazon have ever stocked,' he allows himself a little laugh, 'is that people only ever do what's in their best interests. It's a throwback to our caveman days – you do what you need to do in order to survive. And by "best interests" I don't mean that all people are selfish. Some are. But some people – most – have it in their best interests to make others happy, so what they do is for their loved ones. In caveman terms, you keep your tribe happy so they in turn keep you amongst their ranks. So being selfless is, in a weird way, a little selfish. But when we confuse what we want with what others want, that's when things get muddied. We're here to find what Delilah Blackthorn wants.'

I exhale. So far, so painless. I really think this is going to do wonders for me. I really think this is where I start to look onwards and upwards.

'So Delilah, why do you think you got fired?'

'I'm sorry?'

'I've had time to read your CV, to do a little research about you. This is a 360 process, so I've spoken to a range of your former employers. Why do you think you were fired?'

'Um… I don't… it all happened so quickly.'

'Were there warning signs?'

'Not that I saw.'

'Your work was up to scratch? Your working relationships were healthy?'

'Yes. Yes. Well…'

'So perhaps "no"?'

A flare of anger spreads up through my chest and into my neck. I didn't come here to have rumours thrown back at me. I came here to change them.

'Absolutely not. I worked hard, and smart. I had a full roster of very happy clients whose businesses were in growth. My colleagues all liked me. But somehow, rumours started. Rumours that were way off base.'

Douglas rubs his chin and writes something on his notepad. 'So do you feel the termination was justified?'

The anger bubbles a little bit further up my neck, getting dangerously close to barking through my mouth in a stream of language that Mags definitely wouldn't approve of. 'No. Not at all.'

'And yet you accepted it?'

'Huh?'

'You didn't think to appeal it? Go to a tribunal? From what I've read and heard, Delilah Blackthorn doesn't give up without a fight. One colleague said you once worked for twelve hours straight on a big presentation, then slept for two hours in the conference room before taking a video call with Japan.' Douglas flips back a few pages into his notebook. 'Ben Cooper? He speaks very highly of you.'

The hot feeling in my chest turns down a few hundred degrees but keeps glowing.

'Could it be that a part of you was glad to walk away?'

I blink and look down to study my knees. There's a hole in Mags's yoga pants and a patch of my hairy leg is winking at me through it. I couldn't have appealed or gone to a tribunal, not with the waiver I signed when I joined. But it's true I didn't fight on any other levels. I could have doorstepped Devon, tried to talk him round and to see sense. But I didn't do that. Did I want to walk away?

Douglas wrinkles his nose in thought. 'Let's circle back to that strand. There's something there, I think. Every report I had on you was radiant with praise. And yet things went wrong and your employer saw fit to end your contract. Something went wrong along the way and I do think it would be beneficial to work out just what it was. For your future happiness, for starters. And speaking of that, here's a question most of my clients enjoy, to get them warmed up. Forget work for a second. Delilah, what makes you happy?'

My mouth hangs open and I'm suddenly aware that I didn't brush my teeth this morning, so I clamp it shut again.

Douglas is looking at me, a subtle head tilt conveying trust and sympathy; that much I have also read in business psychology books. It's not that I don't trust him: I know he's got all the right credentials and he's certainly put in the time to get a full picture of me and what makes me tick. But I'm worried now that he's got more of a clue about that ticking than I have; I'm listening to the clock inside me and there's nothing. No tick, no tock. I don't

269

know what makes me happy. I was kind of hoping he'd tell me...

'Don't overthink it.' Douglas has steepled his fingers and is resting his chin on them. 'I'll ask again and you just say the first thing that comes to mind. I know it sounds a bit woo-woo, but when it comes to job happiness, we're looking at an all-round picture. Knowing what makes you happy in the rest of your life is an incredible insight. So, Delilah, what makes you happy?'

I shut my eyes. I try and let the vision come to me. A sofa. Two arms in plaster. Fish-and-chip wrappers. The sound of laughter.

'Home.'

Douglas makes another quick note. 'Good, good. So now you can put Home at the centre of everything you do, and work can surround it. Work supports your home, but it doesn't supplant it. Does that sound about right?'

No. It shouldn't. Not to the old Delilah. But then Home to the old Delilah was a silent flat in Islington that she saw briefly before work and after gym sessions. Somewhere she didn't even bother putting up a Christmas tree. Somewhere she'd never hosted a drinks night or a poker game. It was a shell. But the Home I'd been thinking of just then was Fenwild, not Islington. Home is the haberdashery, even if I'm not a dyed-in-the-wool crafter. And that's where I'm happy.

I nod dumbly.

'That's a really important realization. It seems to me the work you have been doing has dominated your life, but a huge part of you wants to get back home. Professional work is hugely rewarding before you even get to the financial side, but there must be a balance with our emotional life and social life, too. Do you feel you've got that balance at the moment?'

No. I don't. Not the old Delilah, anyway. She was always working, working, working. She was pretty much always alone but because she worked so hard, she hardly noticed. But in the last few weeks I've laughed and mucked about and drunk and played. I've found old friends and new. I've been around the people I love.

'Yes. Yes, I think so.'

Douglas grins. 'Then you are already ten steps ahead of most of my clients, if I may say so. When you can clearly see what's important to you, your happiness, you can find a clear path to it. I want to talk a little about what you've been doing these past weeks – with your family business. The skills you've used there. But first, let's come back to the tabled point about your dismissal. Thinking about the fact that everybody is motivated by their own interests, what motivated your boss to fire you, do you think? I'm sorry to go over this but I think you need to draw a line under it.'

I knock back the espresso, the lukewarm bitterness not all that pleasant against the back of my throat. 'Honestly? I don't know. I can't see it. Getting rid of me meant instability for clients, damage to the company's reputation, depleting an already overstretched workforce. He must have felt, I suppose...'

'Yes?'

'That keeping me was a more dangerous proposition. Which I just don't get.'

Douglas's pencil is poised over his pad. He nods to get me to go on.

'Something made him think I was a danger to his success – his best interest is his bonus, at the end of the

271

day. He'll do whatever he can to protect that. Devon must have been *convinced* that I was going to sabotage our targets in some way... But my work was good, I'll stand by that till the day I die. And you say all my colleagues and clients gave me good references?'

Douglas raises his eyebrows. 'Beyond good. Rave reviews. Well, everyone I could get hold of. One chap didn't reply to my email and when I called I was told he'd just moved to a new job. Uh,' he turns back a few pages again, 'Clive. Your former assistant, I believe? Would he have any reason not to support you in this new stage in your life?'

Clive.

The headline in the paper comes back to me – about Clive taking up this new crazy-senior position for his age at Next Gen Now. What was in his best interests? Me getting fired and him stepping into my shoes. Ah huh.

Clive.

Well, well.

Chapter 21

I'm not sure which unnerves Clive more: seeing me in the yoga kit of a 60-something hippy or the huge Joker-like smile plastered on my chops as he walks through the security gate of Next Gen Now. I told the receptionist I was a recruiter who didn't want to leave a name – with a wink to show she was in on something hush-hush. And little careerist that he clearly is, Clive tripped straight on down to the ground floor to find me now leaning against a huge potted cactus. Beware: spiky as hell.

'Clive!' I yelled happily, so he can't turn and leg it, pretending he doesn't know me. 'We've got some talking to do!' I take huge strides in his direction and angle my arm around his neck. The deodorant has worn off by now, little competition for the two-day BO stink from my armpits. And to be honest I'm delighted to be rubbing it on the posh navy suit he's sporting. Because that's just the first step of this epic karma correction. 'Why don't I buy you a coffee, for old times' sake?' I boom right into his ear, frogmarching him out of the building.

I've never clocked before that Clive has really steely grey eyes. He was always so upbeat, so cheerful, bouncing from one task to another. But with a face like thunder right now, his eyes absolutely match. I stop my march by the weird water sculptures that make a courtyard for four skyscrapers right by Tower Bridge – you can just see the bridge closing its mighty arms through the gap between two of them. From a distance, the water is so flat it looks like a bench to sit on. But that bench would give you a severely wet arse. If I was any less mature I might be tempted to dunk his lying head right in. But there are too many witnesses. And I haven't come here for an ASBO. I'm looking for karmic justice.

'I wouldn't want your new employers to think you were *shirking* your duties so I'll keep this short. I know it was you, Clive. The meetings I "missed" with Devon? You never put them in my calendar. The emails going astray? You deleted them. That last presentation you had printed and bound for me, the one Devon felt was so rubbish. You were in a position to tamper with it before he saw it, yes? You convinced Devon I was failing and a danger to the company. That I was involved with a client romantically? Then you spread the rumours, right?'

He narrows his eyes and rolls his bottom lip out in a sneer.

'Cut the *Mean Girls* bullshit. You're no Lindsay Lohan. Just a yes or no will do. I really don't want to spend longer than necessary talking to you.'

'Fine. Yes.'

'What really gets me, on top of all that, is how you texted and emailed after I left. I thought it was genuine concern but you were just checking I hadn't rumbled you. Right?'

He smirks just a fraction. 'Yes.'

'So you got me the boot, stepped into my place. And then used all that CV-padding to land you a swanky new job? Great. Good for you. Well, I was just recording that on my phone.' I lift it out of my pocket. 'So now it's in evidence, let's discuss how you're going to help put things right. Back where they should be, OK? You totally screwed my career and now you're going to fix that. Starting right now.'

Clive folds his arms. 'I did what I had to do to get ahead. *I learned from the best.*' He narrows those grey eyes at me.

Man, that water is looking temptingly cold right now. 'Firstly, it's not what you do to get ahead. You work hard. You work smart. That's what I did. Secondly, you clearly weren't paying attention to me. Because I'm classy as hell.'

And with that, I can't help it, I step towards him in a way you could – if you like – interpret as threatening. Although legally no body contact was made. And Clive instinctively takes a step back and plants his bum against the water feature. Aha, ha, ha, ha.

'Christ! Are you mental?!'

'Why don't you test me a bit more and find out?' If he thinks he's got the copyright on steely, he's got another thing coming. I give him the ballsiest glare of my life. Like someone is stealing the last Jaffa Cake to the power of ten. And then some. 'Pay attention. I need you to action the following instructions *today* and if you don't it will take me about 0.3 seconds to google the direct line of your new boss. *Capisce?*'

With a sulk, Clive nods, one hand covering his unsightly wetness.

–

Ten minutes later, he's walking away with his head full of tasks and I feel a fizz of energy in my fingertips. I have time. There's just about time. I'm putting things right – back to where they should be. But where to start? If

I'm going to pull this off I need all the timings to sync perfectly.

But first things first: I take a picture of Clive's retreating damp arse. That's one for the family album. And I *will* be calling his new boss about this, of course. Whether they keep him on in light of his past misdemeanours is their business. But I won't make that call today. I've got some bigger fish to fry.

—

Mags doesn't hide her nerves very well. She tends to chew on the end of her long plait when she's worried about something. To be fair, I'm back in my parents' study, glued to the PC again. Although now I am fully washed and dressed, I have eight hours of sleep behind me and some colour in my cheeks.

'You're certain you won't come? Stan is picking me up and there's plenty of room in his camper. I just… I know JP wants to stand on his own two feet but I also know how much he'd *love* to have you there. If you would just extend the olive branch?' That plait is going to be a pixie crop soon.

I gently remove it from her mouth. 'I'm certain. And it's fine. So Stan's giving you a lift to the knitathon? That's *cosy*.' I nudge her with my shoulder. 'And that pashmina looks nice, Mags, I wouldn't have thought of wearing it tied up like a sarong like that, but it's really pretty.'

She smooths down the brilliant blue fabric against the navy linen trousers she has on underneath. 'Oh, thanks! Actually, Stan said he really liked it like this so I thought I could wear it again. Unless that's a bit obvious?'

I put down my tea and plant my hands on my hips. 'Hold up. When was this? Don't tell me you had your dinner with him and you didn't even inform me?! And did you even get your hair cut beforehand?!'

Mags purses her lips like she's caught me with my hand in the biscuit packet before dinner. 'Delilah Blackthorn, I am not an idiot. I know how to socialize with a man. I've been dating since before you were in big girl pants. It was bleeding obvious what you were up to with that haircut, but I let you at it because it seemed to make you happy. If someone would only look at me twice after a,' she flaps her hands in the air, 'makeover or some such, then he isn't the man for me!' She blows out her cheeks and ties her sarong that bit tighter.

'Whoa. Sorry, Mags. I was playing matchmaker when I should have just left you to it. Clearly it's meant to be. Are you going out again?'

She nods calmly, but a spot of cherry-coloured blush on her cheekbones gives her away. 'We're going to a Lebanese place he likes when the knitathon finishes. Though your brother is adamant it's going to go on to the small hours.' She rolls her eyes indulgently.

'I know. I've been reading the blog this morning. And watching them set up on the live feed. Looks like it's coming together really well.'

Mags pulls me in for a hug. 'I hate leaving you like this. Please come?'

I shake my head. 'I have to respect JP's decision, that much I've learned. At some point he'll come round. Maybe soon.' I smile and wiggle my eyebrows.

Mags laughs as she pulls away. 'What do you have planned, my girl?'

'Wait and see!'

She bats me on the arm, gently. 'By the way, I did have that haircut, and Benito did me a lovely trim. He said my natural grey was sensational and I shouldn't change it for all the world. He also said he's worried about you.'

I run a finger down my parting. Maybe my roots have been a bit neglected. 'Is it that obvious?'

'Not your hair. Your love life!' Mags throws her arms in the air before grabbing her bag and keys. 'We both agreed that if you put half as much work into finding a decent bloke as you put into your business thingies, it would be a very different picture.'

'Just 'cause you're all loved up and smug!' I cheekily push Mags towards the front door. 'I'll be watching on the cameras – no snogging behind the bike sheds!' She blushes furiously as she leaves.

–

I am sticking to my resolution that I should respect JP and stay away from the knitathon but my heart still aches to be there. I have tea, I have Jaffa Cakes; I have the live stream playing as the knitathon gears up to start. This is as close as I can legitimately be right now. All I can do is watch it unfold.

Patti has orchestrated the makeover of the school hall from an empty space that probably smelt of overcooked peas and rubber soles, to a zingy, energized space of colour and motion. JP's bone-breaking bunting has been strung from the wooden climbing frames against the walls and she's kept some of the wool hats pegged on to it. I'm flattered! First time any of my visual ideas have been successful enough to borrow. She's also unwound some of the bolts of our cheap and cheerful tulle fabrics to billow like sails from the top of one climbing frame to another, creating the feel of a rainbow teepee. This morning, she's carefully arranging wicker baskets full of spare yarns and needles by each chair. Most of the chairs are of the plastic stacking variety; there's only so much set dressing can do. However, she's putting knitted and plaid blankets over the backs of them to make it feel as cosy and welcoming as can be, and then at around 8.30 a.m. Ben comes wheeling in a big armchair on a little mover's trolley and follows Patti's instructions on just where to put it.

Watching all of this motion without sound makes you focus in on the body language and I can see Patti is working hard, really concentrating with her eyebrows drawn, but there's also a sense of calm in her expressions and actions – she's just feeling it and going with it. I wonder if she could teach that to me? I could pay her in hugs.

I'm also focusing quite unashamedly on Ben's arms as he heaves a chair off the trolley and wriggles it to where Patti is pointing. Ben's arms. Blimey. That's something else I have to admit is becoming important to me: perving on Ben from afar.

He then starts to pin up a sign Patti has passed over, in a giant roll. As he stretches, his T-shirt rides up to show his back just above his jeans. I bite another Jaffa Cake in half. The sign says, *Come and Meet Our Chester!* And has the baby-face emoji printed all over it in Andy Warhol-style colour combos.

Patti arranges some bright cushions on the chair. Oh, so this is where Becks can recline, feed Chester when she needs to and otherwise arrange for him to meet his legion of fans. That's really cute.

Ben then busies himself setting up the tables, hauling each one from a supply cupboard at the back. And I busy myself watching closely. JP wanders back and forth, checking in with Patti and Ben and consulting the To Do list pinned to the doors. He scratches his chin and points out that one of the *Knit for your life!* signs is a bit wonky, I think, and it takes me a minute to realize – he's out of his casts! I suppose it has been six weeks or thereabouts. He had told me, back when he first started having sessions with Stan, that you can't exactly leap back into weightlifting after being static for so long, but here's hoping he'll be able to get his needles clacking again today. It's only fitting.

He's opening bags of crisps and pretzels and tipping them into bowls – some bowls I recognize from his kitchen, some from Mags's. There's a real patchwork feel to the event and that's just how it should be. Not flashy, not catered – as I might have been tempted to suggest – but real and all done with people power. That's what today is all about. There's a big A1 flip chart on a stand and Patti is now writing, in her funky old-tattoo lettering, *Tell us your knit-count! Or how much you've been sponsored…* A sort of on-the-hop totalizer for today's efforts.

Ben's arms are working their magic again as he lugs a giant tea urn onto one of the tables. And although he comes so close to the live-stream camera that I could count the hairs on his rippling forearm, he blocks the shot!

I whip out my phone and tap out a quick message.

Delilah
Shift that urn. I can't see!

After two beats the urn moves a few inches to the left and suddenly I can see Ben's face and a very wry smile. He then looks down to his phone.

> **Ben**
> Stalker.

> **Delilah**
> Shut up. Just monitoring my assets.

> **Ben**
> My assets more like.

He winks down the lens and goes off to tackle more tasks, with quite an annoying swagger to his step which nevertheless makes me laugh.

—

It's just after nine a.m. and the hall is primed and ready to welcome the first wave of knitters at 10 a.m. Mags and Stan have arrived, bringing with them bacon rolls and pastries for the team to fuel up. I expect *About a (Knitting) Boy*'s most ardent fans are already forming a hysterical queue outside the school gates, but for now it's just Ben, JP and Patti on a low, long bench, knees almost to their chins as they chomp away. It reminds me of that poster of 1920s' construction workers eating their lunch on a steel girder overlooking New York. These guys have grafted and the day is only just beginning. But they couldn't look happier.

JP breaks off from demolishing his bap to wave excitedly in the direction of the doors. Becks is making her way in slowly, Chester's legs dangling from the baby carrier at her front. It must be a shock for her to see JP with both arms free again, too, as she's soon prodding and poking his limbs to test if they're genuine. She also jumps up and down on the spot when she sees Chester's corner, making his legs flop in a very cute motion as she bounces on the balls of her feet. She sits back into the armchair and Mags bustles off to make her a cup of tea. In coming closer to the video, I can see again the bright spark to Mags's eyes, the flush to her skin. No mind that I didn't have anything to do with her and Stan finding a romantic connection, it's just brilliant that it's happening. And, blimey, who did I think I was, trying to stir up her love life? When mine is deader than a MySpace account. In the background, Patti is flicking pastry crumbs off JP's knees, probably so used, by now, to him being a giant man-baby that she's in the habit of tidying him up. I wonder what will happen when she goes off to art college? It seems they're really starting something. I hope that something can stretch over hundreds of miles…

I check my watch. 9.12. Where's the delivery I was promised? They said delivery for 9.00. My fingers tap out an unsteady rhythm against my phone screen. Another 10 minutes and then I'll start making some calls and knocking some heads. They can't be late. Not today.

The group natter and nibble on, happily excited and unaware that I'm keeping watch, like a crafter's CCTV. My legs are jiggling under the desk. Come on, come on…

Then I see Stan get up and go to the double doors with a puzzled frown. Three men in black polo shirts have pushed their way through, pulling a large, shiny coffee cart behind them. *Grab Your Beans* is painted on the side. Stan is waving his arms in a friendly but firm fashion, until one of the men shows him a clipboard with an A4 printout, pointing at the names. Stan looks back to JP who shrugs and comes to join them. But as they're talking the two other polo-shirted guys are nipping outside again and soon come back with stacked baker's trays. The kind that could have buns or bread rolls lined up neatly within. But the kind that, I know, today has row upon row of sticky iced doughnuts in them.

Now the whole knitathon team are forming a huddle around the cart, all looking at the printout. Save for Ben. He's looking over JP's shoulder, straight down the camera. At me.

So *Grab Your Beans* are here. What about the massage team? Ah, here we go.

Two lithe but strong-looking women in turquoise tunics come in next, footstools tucked under each arm. Now all we're waiting for is the string quartet.

JP's blinking rapidly and shaking his head, pointing at the clipboard from the barista. He looks a little panicked. Oh, no, this isn't what I had in mind. I thought he'd be smiling! Please say I haven't read this all wrong, not again!

But Ben takes JP by the shoulders and turns him so they're face to face. He's talking clearly and calmly, with half a smile. And as he finishes, he points at the live-feed camera. Here we go then.

JP tucks the clipboard under his arm and marches over towards my spy cam. He's chewing the inside of his lip, his face otherwise unreadable. He's searching the coffee table for something and then shouts rapidly to the crowd behind him. One of the massage duo steps forward to hand him a biro. He flips the printout over and scrawls something on the back, holding it up to the camera.

YOU'RE LATE, SIS. GET OVER HERE.

By the time I arrive, having waded through the eager crowd by the gates, the string quartet have pipped me to the post and have set up in one corner, playing jaunty ABBA covers and filling the room with a beautiful harmony. I pop my head round the corner of the gym doors. It's a relief that my contributions towards the knitathon have gone down well but I'm still a bit nervous that the team are going to think I'm buying my way back in. Not that I bought these services, mind you – they were favours from old clients that I called in via the little weasel Clive. I knew he must have taken all my client contacts with him when he left – and he had. Well, if you've had no moral qualms over getting someone fired, why would you mind exporting their contact list? So part of his karma-sorting task list was to call them up, set the record straight about me and ask for a freebie for old times' sake. Plus, great free PR. When I dob him in to his new boss next week, I will mention that he's tried to put things right. But only briefly. I hope he gets canned in a heartbeat.

So now we have all the caffeine, sugar, shoulder rubs and chilling tunes any speed knitter could ask for. I might have made a room full of crafters happy, but is it enough to make JP happy with me?

I swallow what feels like a ball of angora in my throat. If Richard Curtis has taught me anything, it's that a grand gesture can rescue even the biggest of berks. So I fish my GiganKnit project out of my shoulder bag. It's only half finished, but it should serve its purpose.

Holding the huge needle in front of me, the thick cream knitting like my own crafty version of a white flag, I walk into the hall, giving the flag a little wave as I do.

'Stupid sister coming through!' I call, hoping the giant wool will absorb the wobble in my voice.

When I bring it down from in front of my face, I see JP looking back at me, and the backs of all the others awkwardly shuffling off to leave us to it.

'Not technically stupid,' he says, scratching his wrist. 'Man, it feels good to do that.'

'To scratch yourself or to forgive me?' I ask.

He sighs. 'Both. Now, what poor granny did you mug to get this?' He takes the half-knitted cream cushion cover from me and examines the needle as thick as a broom handle.

'I did it,' I say, a puff of pride straightening my shoulders out. 'I was actually trying to finish it for today, for you. I've had a few sleepless nights recently, done a bit of soul-searching...' My voice peters out into a squeak and I take a deep breath in order to carry on. 'Turns out that knitting is pretty perfect for those times when your head is reeling and your hands need something to do other than crazy googling. You were right. I think my stocking stitch isn't half bad.'

JP appraises it and nods.

'And I wanted to say that I get it now. Properly. I get what this whole shebang means to you. It's not just a way to put money in the bank. It's how you live your life, it's your community. It's what makes you happy. And I've realized that if something makes you happy, it makes me happy. So I want to be a real part of it.' JP opens his mouth, a crease appearing above his eyebrows. 'I don't want to change it,' I barrel on, 'I want to preserve it. Like... the National Trust for Brothers.'

He lets out his schoolboy laugh and I feel myself relax properly, for the first time in ages.

Behind me, Mags and Patti are placing their orders with the baristas, but I know they are also massively earwigging.

'Are you telling me you'd be actually, truly, "Chris Hemsworth on a motorbike" happy working at the shop with me, full time?'

I scuff my trainers against the worn parquet floor. 'I was thinking two days a week? And then I'm going to find another part-time role that speaks to the other skills I have. I don't actually know what that looks like right now but I know what I don't want – I don't want to be consumed by my job anymore. I want it to be a part of me, not the whole enchilada. When my old work instincts kicked in with MCJ, I couldn't see the wood for the trees. Now I want to keep what makes me really happy in the middle of everything. Work has to fit around that.'

'Oh! Your mum will be so happy!' Mags bursts out behind me. 'Sorry, I wasn't listening but…'

'It's fine, Mags. I'll give Mum the full story on Skype tonight, promise. If you tell her about Stan,' I whisper this last part.

JP slings his arms around my neck. 'I think the plan sounds cracking. And I've missed you, Dee, if truth be told. It's not nearly as much fun without you. Or as well organized. Sorry for shutting you out.' He leans his head against mine.

'Speaking of organized,' I check my watch. 'We need to open those doors soon! Much as I love this wholesome vibe we've got going here.' I poke him in the ribs. 'If we're going to take the knitathon nationwide next year, we really need to kick some woolly butt today.'

'Nationwide?' JP rubs his chin.

'Well, only if you're happy with that.'

'A nationwide campaign,' he mutters mostly to himself, 'a coast-to-coast charity project…'

Patti sidles up beside me. 'I think he's keen.' She smiles which puts dimples into her pixie cheeks. 'Macchiato, right?'

I take the warm cardboard cup from her. 'Thank you! Ready to knit like the wind?'

'As I'll ever be!'

'Open the doors!' I yell to no one in particular. 'Unleash the crafting hordes!'

Chapter 22

'You've gone a bit wrong on your moss stitch, there.'

Ben's hand suddenly appears in my line of vision and touches on mine, then points to a spot on the cherry-red hat I've been trying to knit all day. Giant knitting is definitely my thing. Tiny, baby knitting is still too fiddly and slow for my fumbling fingers.

'I wasn't even doing moss stitch. Which one is that again?'

Ben rolls his eyes and takes the needles from me firmly. 'You knit one, yarn forward, purl one, yarn back. And so on.' After smoothly completing four stitches he hands the yarn over and then his face drops.

'How do I suddenly *know* this?'

'Ah, Beginner Ben! You're all grown up! You're graduating knit school.'

Ben shoves me over so he can take a spot on the bench where I've been perched. The knitting frenzy has been going on for three solid hours now so most of the craft collective are starting to flag. Mags has gone round advising everyone to take a break, drink some fluids and wait for the pizza delivery currently en route. She's our Florence Nightingale, applying handcream and tea top-ups to anyone with wool blindness. I catch Stan watching her talk to a gaggle of teens who each bought a carrier bag full of completed hats, and there's almost a Ready Brek glow around his profile as he does so.

It's been amazing so far and the buzz is still really strong – bursts of natter followed by comfortable silences as the knitters get busy. Hats being finished and sewn up and pegged to the bunting. Hundreds of pounds being written up on the board. And – just as JP always dreamed – a real community coming together because we put out the call for help, and they answered. Like Ben – going above and beyond to help out.

'If we could drop the Beginner Ben thing, I wouldn't mind.' He studiously avoids eye contact with some teen knitters giggling in his direction by the crash mats.

'But then your fans would have to come up with a whole new group name. You know they call themselves the Benedicts, right? As in Ben-addicts, get it?'

He hides his face in his hands. 'You have a vision of yourself as you approach 32 – together, grounded, established. Being perved on by pre-teens, surrounded by mountains of wool, was not actually in my vision, funnily enough.'

I put down my knitting, very happy to abandon it and its twiddly complications for now, and swig from my water bottle. 'But JP so appreciates it. He really likes you being around and oddly enough you two are a great pair.'

'But what about you?'

'Huh?'

'Do you like me being around?' Ben leans back slightly so he can take me in.

I feel that funny tingle move up my neck again. 'Um, yes. You've really helped with this project. And I've always got on with JP's mates.'

Ben blows out a lungful of air through his mouth. 'Gah, Blackthorn! For someone with the sharpest mind I've ever come across, you can be an almighty tool. You think I'm here for JP? You think I learned to *knit* for JP?!'

My palms go sweaty and I rub them against my jeans. 'Er... well... he did teach you...'

'I'm going to say this very care-ful-ly and slow-ly,' Ben over-exaggerates each vowel, like I'm an OAP who's forgotten which way is up. 'I used to hang around your desk. I used to shadow your work. I came to see you. You. When you got fired and you seemed to hate me, I wanted to put that right. Because I like you. You, Blackthorn. You bloody idiot. I didn't hang around for free pattern books and cups of tea. Or for your brother, though he is really cool. And I'm a bit fed up of being polite about the whole thing. Do you want to go out sometime, or not?'

I don't think anyone has been so angry with me while also asking me out.

I nod, dumbstruck. *Ben's arms*, *Ben's arms*, a voice whispers. So my hands shoot out and they're on his forearms. I just wanted to feel them, see if they were as solid as I've been imagining.

Ben looks down at my hands gripping his arms, and then he leans in and kisses me.

–

I'm not sure how long we kiss for actually, it's one of those world-spinning, colours-blurring moments where it could have been ten seconds or ten years, but a yelp of happiness finally pulls us apart.

'Get in, girl!' Becks calls from her armchair, grinning.

Ben laughs. 'Maybe, ah, another time?' He nods towards three iPhones which are all pointed in our direction by 15-year-olds. One who looks like she might cry, actually.

'Definitely. Definitely another time. Are you, um, free tonight?' I can feel my heart thrumming in my chest.

'Yes,' he replies quickly. 'As long as you mean for something other than knitting. So... yeah. See you later?'

My lips still feel red hot and a little bit delicate. I press them together and nod happily.

-

Becks wastes about three seconds before hurrying over. Ben is now queuing up at the coffee cart, his back to us.

'OK,' she half-whispers. 'Just pretend I've come over to show you the baby or something. But, *oh my God.*' Her eyes go as wide as the doughnut she's clutching in one hand. 'Finally! I would hug you but then he'd know we're talking about him. So?'

I can still feel a tingle around my lips. 'So?'

'Don't play coy with me, Blackthorn. You're not that girl. *Tell me.* I am the mother of a small baby. I need to live vicariously! Did he ask you out? Or did you ask him? When? Where?'

Chester seems oblivious to the coating of icing sugar he's getting as Becks eats and talks at an incredible speed.

I do my best to keep my expression level and not shoot a grin from ear to ear. 'We're going to go out tonight. He sort of asked me, but angrily. It was good, though.'

Becks leans in closer. 'It looked good, from where I was sitting.' Her hiss of swallowed laughter makes Chester flinch a little but he quickly recovers.

I clock all the eyes around the room who are sorry-not-sorry checking me out right now, probably hungry for more gossip about my Phoenix-like love life. JP is thankfully out of the room, I think on a stock run with Patti for more double knitting yarn. Mags and Stan look deep in conversation over a travel guide he's holding: *Cambodia and Vietnam*.

'Please tell me Mags didn't see.'

'I think you're safe for now. And I won't say a word. Mate's honour. Not as long as you keep me fully informed. Any chance you could take that live-feed camera with you on your date?'

'Perv! So… we are mates again, then? I mean, I want to say, I'm so sorry about that whole investor thing, what they tried to do. And for what I said in the cafe. It came out all wrong. I should have thought that it would upset you, someone trying to use him for profit. I promise you I don't see Chester as anything other than the gorgeous miracle he is.' I chuck him under his chin and come away with a small serving of drool.

Becks rubs the sugar off his fuzzy head. 'It's OK. Hormones and zero sleep and a good helping of usual battiness didn't exactly make me the most rational person that day. I blew up without giving you a chance to give your side of things. But with these back rubs and doughnuts I can safely say I know your heart is in the right place! Sucks that you couldn't get some investment for JP, though.'

I shake my head. 'It wasn't the right deal for him. There's better out there. And I can find it, in good time. But right now I'm just focusing on getting myself happy, here at home. I might not have a big nest egg anymore, but at least I've got a nest.'

'So you're staying in Fenwild?' Her eyes light up instantly.

'Yes. I mean, I've got to stick around in case JP breaks anything else or does a public striptease again. And to plan Mags's wedding by the look of it. And I've only just started to act like a proper best mate again. I've still got a lot of rusty friend skills to improve on.'

'You're getting there.' She nudges me in the ribs.

'Phew. Besides, when I do find a new job I can always commute. Can't bear to miss one second of this chap. Can I?'

'Oh, thank God, thought you'd never ask.' Becks gently hands Chester over and he is a lovely, warm weight in my arms. 'Now,' she claps her hands together, 'I've got seriously bad knitting to do!'

Epilogue

About a (Knitting) Boy

Blog post

26 October, 11.57 p.m.

WE DID IT!

Guys, I am too knackered to get on camera tonight, so I'm bashing out this post with my newly flexible fingers! Feels good to be digitally mobile again... And I even managed a gentle knit today. Back in the saddle. Oh, yeah.

So, the knitathon. If you came: we love you. If you watched: we love you. If you donated or sent in hats or shared our message: we love you too. We have now knitted a total of 457 hats for premature babies in the South-East. RIGHT?! Incredible!!! Plus, we raised nearly £800 in sponsorship, which we're sending to a special charity, Early Days. Our Knitting Baby Mamma, Becks, phoned our contact at the charity and she had to repeat the numbers because the lady couldn't quite believe it. We all had a bit of a cry, I'm not too manly to say. This, people, is the power of communities, and craft. Awesome.

If you couldn't make it, keep your eyes peeled for this time next year. We might be coming to a town near you...

And a bit of a downer to share: Beginner Ben wants me to tell you all he's retiring from the vlog life. I think I might be able to sneak him into a few vids but right now he's adamant that if I don't need a knitting stunt double then he's OK to step back. We shall see. He's actually going out with my sister now, so that plus giving up knitting? I think he might need some medication. (Dee: I'm kidding. Mum: sorry if I have spoiled this news for you. Oooops. Ben: better not hurt my sis, ya hear?!)

So now my arms are mine again, I can't wait to get back to proper vlogging and seeing you guys in the shop again. Bring me your lacework nightmares: I'm here to help.

And never hang bunting alone.

JP x

-

From: Guy at TechBank

To: Dee.Blackthorn@yahoo.co.uk

Subject: Re: Charitable partnership opportunity

Dear Delilah,

Thanks so much for the pictures of your charity event and details of its social media reach. Looked like great fun all round! And what a very worthy cause, indeed. You're exactly right that we have been looking to get involved with a UK charity. And to be honest, we've missed your work since you left your former role. It was a complete surprise to us, and we registered our shock and frustration with Devon and the board. Though from his out-of-office bounce-back, I gather he's not currently in the office at this time. Our contract with them is soon to expire and between us, we're looking elsewhere.

We'd love to talk more about sponsoring next year's nationwide charity events and taking them to the next level. Shall we diarize? I'd love to get you in for half a day, because we've actually been in discussions here about expanding our corporate PR team, thinking a little more outside the box. And charitable works is definitely something we could do more of. I expect you're considering a lot of new opportunities currently, but don't forget us! We'd love to work with you again.

Best wishes,

Guy

P.S. Is that really you knitting in one of the pictures? Is there anything you can't do?!

'Oh, you and that screen!' Mags flops some tissue paper down over my iPad, but the glow of what I've just read stays with me, even if the words are now under thin, gold paper layers. Putting a big bank together with charities that desperately need their help would definitely keep my head and my heart happy. The old me would have dropped everything to rush out and call Guy in a heartbeat, but the new me will do it on Monday, because right now I'm with my favourite people doing something amazing.

As Mags turns on the spot to head back into Mum's kitchen, she winces, briefly clutching the top of her arm. In the week since the knitathon, she has taken some bold steps: arranging a month's worth of full-time care for Extra Granny and booking a once-in-a-lifetime tour of Cambodia, Vietnam and Thailand with Stan. It's at odds to her regular, everyday life but it still feels so totally right for her. She's clicked with someone – so why wait? And Mags, maybe more than anyone else on the planet, deserves an escape. This morning she had her jabs and they've left her a bit sore, but she says she'll still come and lend a hand in our mega wrap session. 457 hats aren't going to post themselves. And especially not the way we want them to be sent.

It was Becky's idea, at the end of a very long and happy and productive day in that school hall, as we gazed at the little hills of hats before us, that we should send each one with a message of hope and support to a new mum. We might never meet them in person, but we want a little personal love to go their way, all the same. Since the premmie charity are happy to send a van to come and collect the hats from us the following week, we have a little window to sprinkle in that extra bit of magic.

I was researching bulk-buy bargains of paper and gift tags when Ben came to the rescue. He's been flat out in the office all week, but still finds time to pull a blinder. There were stocks of gold tissue paper in an office supply closet, left over from some champagne gifts given out to clients and so Ben decided to give them a new, worthier home while the rest of the office hopped about in a panic.

I might just have let a gigantic cat out of the bag when I called Clive's new boss on Monday. OK, so it was more like a Siberian tiger. She was so livid that she not only let Clive go (sorry, Clive, cheaters never prosper!) but she also called one of the board at my old company, who just happened to have been her mentor. When she relayed to him that I had been unfairly dismissed because there was the tiniest, thinnest rumour that I was pregnant, not to mention that my gender had been used against me to suggest a romantic relationship and that Devon hadn't even given me half a chance to defend myself before booting me, her mentor called an emergency board meeting to have Devon put on unpaid leave and a full investigation into working practices kicked off. The newest rumour around the water cooler these days is that Devon is going to get not so much a golden handshake as a frosty wave from the window as he carries his cardboard box out onto the street. I would give him another hand gesture altogether, but the end result is just as good. And who knows, with this spotlight on how vulnerable female employees are, they might realize they need to put a woman in Devon's spot and redress the balance. Maybe that's worth another call to my new friend, Estelle, Clive's boss. Ooops, ex-boss.

With Devon now gone, an investigation in the works and clients like TechBank heading for the hills, Ben is doing his best to hold the rest of the team together and do some decent work in the middle of all that chaos. It's not easy and a lesser person might have just shrugged and gone for an indefinite pub lunch, but I know that that's not Ben. He's generous and smart, and these days I don't think that way just because he learned to knit for our campaign or because he's been such an ace friend to my brother. I just think that. Because I fancy him.

I pat my cheeks quickly, trying to shoo away the blush, but Becks catches my eye and smirks. 'Are you sexting on your iPad?' she whispers across the dining-room table, pulling a ribbon bow tight and waggling her eyebrows.

'No!' I hiss, but the blush keeps creeping on me. I wish I could say that was the filthiest thing she's asked about me and Ben, but a quick scroll through her recent WhatsApp messages proves otherwise. During our first date she must have worn her thumbs to the bone, sending message after message, asking what he was wearing, what he said, where did I sit, did I touch his bum? Despite the cyber-stalking, though, it was really fun. We went for a curry in a timeless little place a few villages over, so as not to give Becks/Mags/JP the opportunity to walk past and snoop in on us. Ben and I talked about the things we've done, the things we still want to do, and the time just ran away until they were offering us complimentary brandies and putting chairs on tables. And yes, there was kissing. As soon as I'm done here I'm catching the train into London to meet him for post-work tapas, date number three. And yes, there will be more kissing.

I pull my head away from the memory of the stubble on Ben's jaw or the slightly rough feel of the tips of his fingers and focus back on the task at hand: this is our third session of wrapping and writing messages, and we have two days and 180-ish hats to go. Time to crack the whip and roll out the tape.

'What message of hope have you been writing today?' I try and read Becks's loopy handwriting upside down from where I'm sitting.

She smiles. 'We're with you.'

'That is perfect. I'm nicking it.'

'Oi!'

'Ladies, ladies.' JP gently pulls out a chair and flops down next to us. 'Less fighting, more writing. Seeing as anything I try and scribble looks, well, like a scribble still. But I am ready to tape like a badass. Here,' he swipes the hat I've been wrapping and finishes the edges in a jiff, 'done.'

I pull a gift tag from the big Jiffy bag filled with them. When JP told the charity how we'd like to send the hats on, they supplied little square gift tags with all their contact details printed on the back, so new mums can put it up on the fridge or in their purse and never be far from help. Such a smart move. Maybe something I'll borrow in my new, charitable career direction. I'm definitely going to be asking Douglas's opinions about it at our next session. And I will most definitely be showered for that one.

We pick up our pace and fall into an easy rhythm of snipping ribbon, sticking paper and filling crates with our soft, treasured parcels. JP, Becks and I, with Mags bringing tea and sandwiches every now and again. Patti helped us out at the first two sessions but has shop work to do and a working visa to delay. Turns out, my brother is slightly more appealing that trendy art school and she's going to defer by a term. JP won't go into it in any detail – being a man – but has grunted 'seeing where things go' and 'might learn a bit of German' at me when I've pressed him.

The boxes fill as we work in companionable silence. It would drive us mad to think of a different message for every single hat, so we recycle through *We're with you*, *You can do this*, *Help is here* and *If in doubt, eat cake!* All from Becky's experiences of what she needed to hear when she was a strung-out, depleted, anxious mum in the early weeks. As my hands pass over these little knitted caps, with their fuzzy stripes and cables and bobbles and even some Fair Isle beauties, I feel hopeful. I feel hopeful for all the warmth and security these little hats can bring. And I feel hopeful that we'll make more next year, and more money to go alongside them. Because the hope these knitters have brought together with their crafty efforts has rubbed off on me too. I feel topped up with happiness, I feel part of a brilliant community, I feel…

'Dee, didn't you say you wanted to catch the 4.54 train? You'd better stop fondling that garter stitch and make a run for it.'

I just have time to grab my bag, my keys and punch JP on the arm as I hurry to the door.

A Beginner's Pattern for a Newborn Hat

This hat will be just right for a newborn baby up to 8lb. If you are a total beginner and you're not sure about which yarn to buy, I'd recommend Sirdar Snuggly DK as it's soft against skin and machine washable (which is a MUST for any new parent!). As much as you might want to splurge on a pure wool or cashmere mix yarn – and they do feel like heaven – it's best avoided for this kind of project as you can only cool wash them.

Don't feel you have to stick to traditional pastel colour for a baby – go mad with bright, bold shades or even choose a yarn that has a Fair Isle effect within it so as you knit it magically changes colour! Unique is good when it comes to homemade things: in fact, it's what it's all about.

If you're in doubt that you're choosing the right kind of yarn for this hat, the ball band (the paper wrapped around the yarn) will not only tell you what it's made out of and how it can be washed, but it will also have a symbol that tells you what size needle to use with it. This looks like two crossed needles forming an X and one of the numbers around it will be in millimetres (mm): this is what you want to look out for, and in this case you want it to say 4mm.

For this pattern you'll need a pair of both 4mm and 3.75mm needles. These measurements refer to the diameter of the needles (rather than length!) and the narrower the needle, the smaller the stitch you'll make. You start off with the smaller 3.75mm needles to make the ribbed band of the hat so it has a bit of grip to stay put! When the ribbing is done, the pattern will tell you to switch over to 4mm needles, so keep your eyes peeled...

Check out YouTube tutorials for help with casting on and how to knit two stitches together (K2tog): it really is so much easier to watch someone do it then work it out from written instructions. You might need a few practice sessions in casting on to make sure you get the tension just right. Too tight and you'll struggle to get your needles into your cast on stitches to knit from; too loose and you'll get a holey, uneven first row.

For measuring and making up, you'll need a tape measure and a tapestry needle (this is a needle with a blunt end, which is the best kind for sewing up yarn.) So if you've got these and your yarn, your needles, plus your browser on standby for any problems, let's go!

- Using the thumb method and your 3.75mm needles, cast on 70 stitches.

- The first 6 rows will be knitted in a 2 x 2 rib. This means you knit two stitches, then bring your yarn forward to purl the next two stitches. You take the yarn back again to knit another two. Carry on knitting two, then purling two for the whole row. On your second row, start with two purl stitches and carry on the rib pattern from there.

- When you have 6 rows of rib, change to your 4mm knitting needles. You're now going to knit in stocking stitch. This means one whole row of knitting followed by one whole row of purling, carrying on until your work reaches the desired length of 8cm. When you're measuring how much you've knitted, try not to be tempted to stretch the work too much or it won't be an accurate measurement.

- With 8cm done, it's time to decrease. This means you will start knitting two stitches at once when the pattern indicates to bring down the total number of stitches in a row. That allows the hat to start curving into a point at the top. If you're not sure how to decrease, in this case knitting two stitches together (K2tog), now's the time to watch a few YouTube tutorials and it will all become clear!

- For the 1st decreasing row: knit 7 stitches, then K2tog. Repeat this to the end of the row.

- On the 2nd and alternate rows: purl all the stitch

- 3rd: knit 6 stitches, then K2tog. Repeat this to the end of the row.

- 5th: knit 5 stitches, then K2tog. Repeat this to the end of the row.

- You'll have noticed that the number of stitches you're knitting before you decrease is going down by one. Continue going down by one (and purling on alternate rows) until you have 12 stitches left on your needles and then purl one last row.

- Cut your yarn, leaving a long tail of about 25cm for the sewing up part. Using your tapestry needle, thread it with the cut end of the yarn and then carefully push your tapestry needle through the last stitches on your knitting needle. You can now slide out the knitting needle.

- Make a knot to fasten these last stitches in a circle, and now you can start sewing up the two sides of the hat. Again, search for some video tutorials of how to mattress stitch. You might need to practise a bit first – and keep checking to make sure both sides are coming together evenly. When you get to the end, fasten with a double knot on the wrong side of the knitting.

- Voila! You have knitted a gorgeous hat! Sit back and bask in the pride.

Acknowledgements

First and foremost, thanks to the whole Canelo team who are the BEST in the business bar none: Louise Cullen, Iain Millar, Michael Bhaskar, Nick Barreto, Simon Collinson and Ellie Pilcher. Especially Louise, my editor, who has an endless well of patience, enthusiasm and insight. Which you need to edit me, frankly. Thanks for shaping this novel so beautifully. Also a big fan-girly thumbs up to Emma Graves for this and all my lovely covers.

Thanks to Mike – you've not read one of my books yet. Maybe number five? Sound out the long words as you go. You'll get there.

Thanks JP, for the lend of your name. I left out the twinkling eyes, though. Some things words just can't capture…

Kirsty Greenwood, as ever you're my goddamn rock. Love you.

I genuinely believe in the calming, healing powers of knitting (and any craft, really) and if you read this novel and are tempted to pick up a pair of needles, all I can say is: do it! You won't be sorry. And you'll never be without a woolly hat, ever again.